# A MULTITUDE OF SINS

Also by Virginia Owens

**At Point Blank**
**Congregation**

# A·MULTITUDE·OF·SINS

## Virginia Owens

A LION BOOK

Copyright © 1993 Virginia Owens

The author asserts the moral right
to be identified as the author of this work

First published in the United States by
**Baker Book House Company**
Published in Great Britain by
**Lion Publishing plc**
Sandy Lane West, Oxford, England
ISBN 0 7459 3206 1
**Albatross Books Pty Ltd**
PO Box 320, Sutherland, NSW 2232, Australia
ISBN 0 7324 0869 5

First edition 1993
First UK edition 1994
This paperback edition 1995
10 9 8 7 6 5 4 3 2 1 0

**Acknowledgments**
Scripture references are taken from the King James Version

A catalogue record for this book is available
from the British Library

Printed and bound in Great Britain
by Cox & Wyman Ltd, Reading

*For Dwight Baker and Camille Paglia*

# CHAPTER • ONE

"IGNACIO!"

The boy looked up, a clump of bronze chrysanthemums in full bloom resting on his shovel blade. His nostrils tightened and his eyes flickered in momentary panic. Then he remembered to smile.

Beth Marie took a deep breath. This was a mistake. She should never have hired him. Judging from his English, he might well be—what was the right term?— an illegal alien? Undocumented worker? Sparky Williams, the secondhand car dealer up on the highway had used the old-fashioned term: "Better be careful about hiring them wetbacks, Beth Marie. They don't got a green card, the way the law is now, it's you that'd go to jail."

Ignacio didn't have a green card. Instead he had shown her, his jaw clenching and unclenching, his driver's license and draft card, both of which gave Pharr, Texas, as his home. But then most Mexicans slipping across the border made it their business to get forged documents and several hundred miles north of the Rio Grande as soon as possible. How did she know his were genuine? She'd been too embarrassed to take out her own driver's license and make a comparison right there in front of the boy. But what if the INS showed up?

What would they do to her? What would they do to him?

Beth Marie would never have hired anyone, except that her new job on the *Somerville Courier* meant that she didn't have time to keep up the flowerbeds the way she had promised her mother she would. It was seven years now since Catherine Cartwright had died, and each year Beth Marie felt the bonds that had tied her to that strong, stringent woman loosening. Sometimes the new sense of freedom made her giddy. At thirty, Beth Marie was just beginning to sense possibilities in herself that would never have blossomed under her mother's eye. But at other times she felt disconnected, untethered. Aimless drifting was not a possibility that appealed to her.

Hiring Ignacio would have posed no problem for Catherine Cartwright. He looked strong enough to do the work, and his eyes showed a quick intelligence. She would have scrutinized the proffered documents for thirty seconds, stared sharply at the young man, and handed the cards back gingerly, convinced she'd done her civic duty. "I am not a policeman," she would have answered the hypothetical border patrol agent. "I am an ordinary citizen. I cannot be expected to do your job for you."

Of course, that wouldn't be altogether true. Catherine Cartwright had never, under any circumstances, considered herself ordinary.

Ignacio was still looking at Beth Marie with his fixed smile. The blue bandanna tied around his head was already damp with sweat. He probably hated her.

"No, Ignacio. Not the chrysanthemums. *No es correcto.*" She had no idea what the word for marigold was in Spanish.

He frowned slightly and looked down at the clump of blossoms he had just turned on their sides, then pointed at the hole questioningly.

"Yes. No. I mean, put those back." She propped her briefcase against the porch railing and hurried down the back steps toward him. "Can't you see they're just beginning to bloom?" she muttered to herself.

He frowned and stepped back as she approached, but when she bent down to grasp the spadeful of dirt and roots, he reached out and caught her wrist. "No, *señora*. I comprehend. I put them back." And, stiff with injured dignity, he reinserted the shovel with its offending lump in the hole.

Beth Marie took another deep breath and waited till he had pushed the crumbled clod back in place. When he looked up at her again, holding the shovel handle upright in front of his chest like a crucifer, she said, "The marigolds," and pointed to the border along the walk. The gold blossoms were deepening to brown, many of them already dried and dropping their seeds into the bed. "They're through. They won't bloom any more. It's time for them to come out."

He nodded.

"Take them to the incinerator," she said, pointing to the cinder-block rectangle behind the garage. "I'll burn them later," she added, pointing now to herself. "Me."

He nodded again, his gaze sliding off her face to the side, but not before he let her see the offense there. "Whatever you say, *señora*." He turned away toward the marigolds.

Look, she wanted to say to him, it's not like I'm some kind of oppressive *patron*. I am paying you twice as much as anyone else in this county would. I just don't want you digging up the chrysanthemums when they've only started to bloom. Is that too much to ask?

But she didn't say it. Instead, she marched back to the porch, picked up her briefcase, and got into the Toyota she never parked in the garage, all without saying a word. He just doesn't like women telling him what to do, she thought as she slung her briefcase onto the seat beside her. And he didn't have to call me *señora*; I'm not that old yet.

Unfortunately, she had snapped only one of the catches on the briefcase, and that one hit the emergency brake bar, snapping open and spilling half the contents onto the car floor. It was going to be one of those days. It was already one of those days.

She started the car and backed out the driveway, leaving the spilled pens and paper on the floorboard. She wanted to get away from those dark, reproachful eyes as quickly as possible.

About a mile down the county road, right before it intersected with the highway to Somerville, she pulled over and raked up the mess on the floor, shaking the sand off the yellow legal pad. When she had everything back inside the briefcase, she snapped both locks with exaggerated care.

"There. You satisfied?" She wasn't really talking to the briefcase or even to the disembodied spirit of disorder that often seemed to plague her when she was in a particular hurry. The words were meant for Norton, who had given her the briefcase a couple weeks ago in celebration of her new job at the *Courier*.

"Professional," he'd said. "You want to look professional, Beth Marie. Not that the *Courier* is any hotshot newspaper, but the people there probably think of you as that little hick who's been doing the Point Blank column for years. Whose cow got out last week. Who invited the preacher to Sunday dinner. That kind of thing."

"Norton, I got the job because of the murder, remember? Not because I wrote about cows."

"Well, they let you do that—what did you call it?"

"A first-person account."

"They let you do that because you'd nearly been killed yourself."

"The Houston papers picked it up too."

"Sure. They wanted to sensationalize the whole thing. I'm not saying you're not a good reporter, Beth Marie. Don't get me wrong. All I'm saying is you're going to have to prove yourself over there. I see how those *Courier* people work. They're either little old ladies or kids with a new journalism degree looking for a big break here in Somerville so they can get somebody's attention in Houston or Dallas and move on to better things. I just don't want them pushing you around." They were sitting on the front porch swing, and he pulled her to him in a clumsy hug meant to be reassuring.

Was it because she had been offended by his remarks that she had pushed him away?

"You make it sound like I'm some middle-aged hick who doesn't know how to behave in the outside world." She stood up and went to sit on the front steps.

Behind her Norton sighed but didn't leave the swing. After a moment he started to speak, then swallowed the words and sighed again. There was a long silence. Finally she looked back over her shoulder at him. He had his head in his hands, leaning forward and looking at the toes of his boots. She thought about how she'd noticed the freckles on his arms when she first saw him, how her fingers had wanted to feel the little strawberry blond bristles on the back of his neck. She knew he hadn't meant to make a point of her age, nor did he think she was a country bumpkin. He was just trying to be protective in a clumsy kind of way. He liked football too.

"I'm sorry," she said, turning to face him in the gathering darkness of the late October evening. "I guess I'm nervous about the job."

He lifted his head and looked at her, but the shadows were too deep there on the porch and she couldn't read his face.

"I'm cold too," she said, wrapping her arms around herself, still looking at him.

He got to his feet, straightening to his full height slowly and deliberately. She reached up a hand to him from the steps, and he pulled her up. "Let's go inside," he said.


At the office, actually a partitioned area she shared with Somerville's dowager society editor and the twenty-year-old education editor, she found three pink phone slips waiting for her. One was from their congressman's district office saying he would be in town the following month for an open forum at the university. The second was from the secretary of the local businesswoman's club, inviting her to their next meeting, and on the third was written only "Geoff Granger—*Texas Times*," and a phone number with the "call back" box checked.

Not even waiting to sit down, she dialed the Houston number, unbuttoning her jacket as she listened to the ring on the other end.

"Geoff Granger." The voice sounded simultaneously suspicious and bored.

"This is Beth Cartwright. I'm returning your call."

"Beth . . . who?"

"Cartwright. At the *Somerville Courier*."

"Yeah. Okay. I remember now." A pause as he shifted the receiver. "Say, I'm working on a project there. I saw the piece you did in the *Post*. Great. I wonder if you'd have time to talk to me. Say—" he hesitated as if checking a schedule, "this afternoon around three?"

"For the *Texas Times*?"

"You're familiar with it," he said, inflecting the ending both to make it a question and to imply the impossibility that she wouldn't be.

"Of course." The *Texas Times* was a slick regional monthly magazine that had achieved national attention for its irony and investigative reporting. In its glory days, it had established a reputation for raw nerve, outrageousness, and good writing. In recent years, however, it had gone glitzy and mannered, with a "new South"—or at least a "new Texas"—appeal. Most of it was now made up of arty full-page photographs and expensive advertising for such things as herb-flavored tequila and Italian footwear.

"So how about it? Three o'clock okay?"

Beth Marie paused as if looking at her own calendar. She had it memorized. There were only two items on it for the day. The county commissioners meeting in the morning and an early afternoon interview with the head of the local VFW about the Veterans Day parade.

"Sure," she said. "You know where we're located?"

"Rather not see you there. Some place more . . . anonymous, if you know what I mean."

She wasn't sure what he meant by that but wasn't about to say so. "How about the Holiday Inn? The coffee shop, I mean. It's on the interstate. You can't miss it."

"Sounds pretty anonymous to me," he said. "Three o'clock." The phone clicked.

She put the receiver down and sank into her chair. This was great! Well, maybe. She had no idea what this Geoff Granger wanted yet. What kind of story was he doing? He hadn't said. But if she had to guess, it would be something to do with the prison, Somerville's only claim to fame. Or infamy.

The original state prison—penitentiary, as it was called in 1849—had looked like a fanciful castle, even more ornate than the old Watson County courthouse three blocks away. In sheds behind the castle, prisoners had made cannonballs and uniforms for the Confederacy during the Civil War. Satanta, the last Comanche chief, had thrown himself from an upper story, preferring death to incarceration.

Beth Marie drove past two of the prison complexes on her way to the newspaper office every morning. Three miles before she reached Somerville, she passed the Bromley Unit. The main building was set back from the highway about a hundred yards, surrounded by undulating fields where sleek roan mares grazed with their new foals. The white rail fence along the highway was edged with daylilies and climbing roses. In the early morning, a row of figures dressed in loose white uniforms might be hoeing weeds along the fence, moving in unison like a clumsy chorus line. A mounted guard leaned on his saddle horn and yawned. Later in the day, she often came upon a tractor pulling a flatbed trailer full of white-clad passengers along the grassy space between the road and the fence. She sometimes felt like waving to them the way she would have acknowledged any farmer along the road. The rural setting seemed to soften the realities of crime and punishment. That these men were robbers, rapists, and murderers seemed incomprehensible amid the morning light and smell of hay.

The red brick blockhouse she passed in town was another story. After World War II it had replaced the castle on the same site. The Walls was the most famous of the thirty-five prison units scattered around the state. It was where the state of Texas executed prisoners, originally by hanging, later by electrocution in "Old Sparky," the inmates' name for the electric chair. After a twenty-year ban on the death penalty, executions were now done by injecting pancuronium bromide and potassium chloride into the prisoner's arm.

About the same time executions started up again, the state prison system had come under court order to reform. David Ruiz, an inmate who had been in and out of prison since 1968, finally receiving a life sentence as an habitual criminal, had filed a thirty-page, handwritten petition to a federal court in 1972, claiming that prison conditions were inhumane. The controversy replaced the Cold War debate in Texas. Taxpayers felt the reform measures had taken a bite out of their pocketbooks rather than crime. In the eighties, railing against the reforms and the judge who had imposed them was almost as exhilarating as denouncing Communism in the fifties.

But the reforms had actually turned the prisons into a growth industry for Watson County. Mandates for new buildings and more personnel meant jobs for everyone. The Texas Department of Corrections was now the county's chief employer. Just about every family had someone who worked in one of the seven units inside the county boundaries. The guards' grey uniforms were everywhere—in the grocery stores, at the gas stations, waiting in front of day-care centers. These days, a number of guards were women.

Beth Marie could feel the oppressive weight of The Walls settle on her spirit every time she drove by the massive structure. One never saw the prisoners there, and only occasionally noticed a guard shifting position in the tower overhead. The streets around the prison were lined with sleazy shops advertising clothes for newly released prisoners. The First Baptist Church, made of the same red brick, sat just south of the exercise compound, its regulation white spire asserting itself against the razor wire coiled atop the prison's three-story wall.

In 1974 three inmates at The Walls had taken twelve employees hostage—nine of them women—holding them inside the prison library for eleven days. Briefly, national attention had focused on Somerville. Beth Marie had been a freshman at Somerville High School then, dreaming her way through the haze of adolescence, only vaguely aware of something called Watergate. The hostage-taking at The Walls had been her awakening to public life. One of the twelve employees was a friend of her mother's, a librarian named Norma Thomas. She had been killed, along with the three inmates, in the rescue of the other hostages.

Catherine Cartwright had taken her daughter to Norma Thomas's funeral, even though it was in Holcombe's Funeral Home, an institution she did not approve of, favoring funerals held in churches, preferably Episcopal. Though Beth Marie was willing enough to go, she had been surprised at her mother's resolve. Catherine Cartwright abhorred publicity as if it imparted a moral taint. By the time Beth Marie was twelve, she had memorized her mother's teaching on the subject: *Fools' names, like fools' faces, are often found in public places.*

"Look straight ahead," her mother had whispered fiercely as they marched up the steps of Holcombe's pseudo-colonial mansion while television cameras pressed upon the crowd. Afterward, she went home and had a sick headache.

"Why did you go if it was such an ordeal, Mother?" Beth Marie had asked as she brought her aspirin and weak tea.

Her mother had lifted the camphorated handkerchief from her forehead and opened her eyes at the ceiling. "People can imagine all kinds of things, Beth Marie. They might speculate, make innuendos. Mrs. Thomas deserves better than that. She was a brave woman. She was my friend. I owed it to her." And that was all she ever said about it.

Now Beth Marie sat tapping her number-two pencil on the legal pad in front of her. After her conversation with Geoff Granger, it was hard to focus on the feature she was writing about the local AARP president. She had drifted off in mid-sentence again when the phone startled her. It was Mindy Hill, the receptionist for the local dermatologist. Beth Marie had met her at St. Barnabas before it burned down last year. Mindy and her husband, Ted, had been quite active since then, to judge from announcements in the weekly newsletter. Beth Marie herself hadn't much liked attending services in the old hardware store on the square, the church's temporary quarters. Besides, Norton wasn't Episcopalian.

"I don't know if you're interested or not," Mindy said, "but our new interim priest, Father Kamowski, has started a Kairos group at the prison and we're looking for people to help out."

"Kairos?"

"It's Greek. He says it means something like time. Only God's time. Something like that. I don't know what that has to do with inmates—well, I guess maybe it does. I mean they're doing time, aren't they? Anyway, they have these special teams that do weekend retreats in the prisons. Ted—you remember my husband—he's on a team. You have to be trained and all. And no women allowed, of course. Not in the men's prisons anyway. But at the end of the retreat, on Sunday afternoon, they have what they call a closing. They try to get as many regular people to come to that as possible."

"Regular people?"

"Well. You know. Normal people. Not prisoners. Church members. And women can come to that." There was a pause. "We're not having much success getting women to sign up for the one next week. A lot of husbands don't want their wives doing it."

So you're falling back on the old maids, Beth Marie thought to herself. "It sounds interesting," she said noncommittally.

"I'm going," Mindy said, as though to encourage her. "Ted says there's not any danger. I mean, there's plenty of guards and all. And it's held in the chapel. This one's in the Bromley Unit. Don't you live out that way?"

Beth Marie thought of the phone call from Geoff Granger. What if it turned out he was indeed doing a piece on the prison system? Something like this could provide a way for them to work together. The *Texas Times* was a big step up from the *Somerville Courier*.

"Okay. When did you say this was?"

"Sunday afternoon," Mindy answered, relief evident in her voice. "Four o'clock. All Father Kamowski needs is your driver's license number. The prison officials have to run a check on everyone who'll be there. No felons allowed," she laughed. "I guess you shouldn't have any outstanding traffic tickets either."

Beth Marie dialed the priest's number reluctantly. The voice that answered muttered the church's name in slurred syllables.

"Is this Father Kamowski?" She spoke with calculated crispness.

"What can I do for you?" The voice sounded guarded rather than eager.

"This is Beth Marie Cartwright. Mindy Hill just called me about the—uh—Kairos service—"

"The closing," he interrupted. "You wanna go? I need your driver's license number."

After she'd repeated it twice, he added more civilly, "Have I seen you around, Miss Cartwright? You a member at St. Barnabas?"

"Yes. But I work odd hours sometimes. I'm a reporter."

There was a momentary pause. "Oh, yeah. You're the girl works for the paper. Jack Tatum told me about you. Well, maybe we better talk this over. If you're planning to do a story, that is."

Fifteen minutes later she hung up the phone, vaguely irritated. She hadn't learned much more about the retreat than Milly had already told her. Nevertheless she'd promised to meet the group at the Bromley Unit on Sunday afternoon. And, she admitted, her motivation had little to do with the Sermon on the Mount.

Before she left for the Holiday Inn that afternoon, she went in the employee restroom to check her makeup. She frowned at her image in the mirror, then smiled, trying to show both rows of teeth, the way she had noticed beauty pageant contestants did. But raising her upper lip made her look like she was snarling.

The haircut was good though. Even if Norton hadn't liked it. He said it made her look like an Eastern European dissident, the kind that wore leather jackets. She didn't think that would be a problem for Geoff Granger.

# CHAPTER • TWO

IGNACIO FINISHED DIGGING UP THE marigolds before he returned the shovel to its hook in the garage. Then he felt along the wall just inside the door until he found the key. She had told him about the key herself the first day he came to work for her. She said he might need to use the bathroom. None of the other people he worked for had done that. This had worried him at first. Did she have another reason for telling him about the key? Did she expect something else from him? That had happened to him before. He had been coming to do Señora Cartwright's yard work for a week now, but she never seemed to want anything other than for him to dig up the flowerbeds and replant them.

Ignacio tried not to think too much about the woman. He only wanted to know the things about her that were necessary to his purpose. He had rehearsed her advantages many times. Her parents were dead. She had no brothers or sisters. She lived alone. She had no close neighbors. She was small and not suspicious. She worked for the newspaper in town. They would make sure it was well-publicized. On the other hand, he tried not to notice how her hands flew around when she was hurried. Nor how her dark eyebrows rose in the middle when she asked him a question. He had chosen her only because she would be easier to overpower. Also because she would seem vulnerable and helpless to the public.

When he reached that place in his thinking, Ignacio's hands began to tremble, at first from anger. *No one ever thought how helpless and vulnerable you were, Mama. No one worried about you. You were an easy victim. You suffered. Just like the Virgin, Mama. With a sword through your heart. They dragged your good name through the mud. All of them deserted you. But no more, Mama. I swear to you.* And then the anger would become fear.

At that point, he began to speak to himself. *What if it doesn't work? What if something goes wrong?* And another voice answered him, *What can go wrong? If the woman is hurt, or even if she is killed, then the debt is paid. A life for a life. But if they do what you ask, you will have cleared your mother's good name. You will restore both her honor and your own. Is not your life worth that? You will have made your life a tribute to the truth. Many men live for less.*

Ignacio unlocked the back door and went into the woman's kitchen, frowning at the empty countertops and white porcelain sink. It seemed an empty, sterile place. He had never observed the woman cooking here. In his grandmother's kitchen there was always something to smell—frijoles, menudo, roasting chilies. A dusting of flour on the counter where she slapped tortillas back and forth between her palms. A bucket by the sink where she dumped the peelings and bones. Smells wrapped around you there and held you. Here, in this kitchen with its slick, hard surfaces, things shrank from him. Nothing reached out to his senses.

He passed through the kitchen to the bottom of the dark staircase and began climbing cautiously. He could climb them now without making a sound. That would be necessary. Even though she was small, it would be best to surprise the woman while she slept. He didn't want to have to strike her. There was always the chance she might die.

At the top of the stairs he turned to the room on the right. Her room. Unlike the kitchen, it was full of softnesses he knew he must steel himself against. The thin, white curtains moved slightly as the autumn air stirred. The mounded bedclothes were still in disarray, just as she had thrown them back that morning. A pale blue slip edged in ivory lace lay carelessly tossed on a rocking chair in the corner.

Rosa should have had a room like this, he thought. An even better one. They could have seen to that, the Hidalgos. She could have been the homecoming queen in Pharr. She would have gone to the university. If she had grown up. She would have been a lawyer by now. He smiled grimly to himself. She could have defended her brother.

The smile stiffened. No one had defended Mama. Not even her own parents. They had cast her off, turned their backs on her.

He ran his finger along the glass shelf under the mirror on the wall. A thin coat of talcum covered the surface. He put his fingers to his nose and smelled the off-center sweetness of the powder. This woman saved her scents for her own body, he thought, not for her kitchen, not for food. Women her age should nourish children around their tables, not pamper their bodies with scents. She was the one they should call the names they had called his mother. She was not a virtuous woman. He had seen the car parked in front of her house at night. His mother had never brought strange men into their house. She had kept Rosa and him by her side until they took her away. A woman of virtue, yet they had punished her.

He crossed the room to the desk by the window. He had been checking daily the little book with a calendar the woman kept open there. In it she wrote what she would do each day. The seventeenth was still blank. A Friday. She would be home. That would be the night.

At three in the afternoon, the Holiday Inn was pretty dead. No one pulled off the interstate that ran between Dallas and Houston that early. The civic clubs that met there for lunch were gone, and local workers took coffee breaks at the Texas Cafe on the square. The coffee shop was empty except for a woman running a carpet sweeper over the crumbs the Lions Club had left at lunch. Beth Marie took a chair facing the entrance and pulled a compact from her purse for one last check.

She had just snapped it shut when a tall, thin man wearing a jeans jacket appeared in the doorway. She raised her hand in a tentative greeting. He nodded once and sauntered toward her, keeping the tips of his fingers in his jeans pockets.

"Beth Marie Cartwright?" he said, sliding into the chair facing her. "Geoff Granger."

She had leaned forward, ready to shake his hand, but he never moved his hands from his pockets. "Yes. Glad to meet you."

He smiled. "Don't be too sure. You don't know what I want yet."

The woman with the carpet sweeper came over to the table, and they ordered coffee. After the waitress left, he looked around the room and, finally pulling his fingertips from his pockets, laid his hands carefully on the tabletop. Beth Marie noticed a large turquoise ring on his right hand, but nothing on the left. Under the jacket he wore a black T-shirt and a silver chain. His hair, pulled back in a ponytail, was thinning on top. The lines on his face were deep and vertical. He must be at least forty, she thought.

"So," he said. "You've lived in Somerville a long time?"

"Almost all my life."

"Almost?"

"I was born in Houston. We came to Somerville when my father . . . got sick."

"Oh?" He made an inquiring face, but the waitress returned with their coffee just then and Beth Marie let the subject drop. She had told Norton something about her father, but ordinarily she didn't talk about him.

"But you grew up here, went to school and all."

"High school. Actually, I live in Point Blank, a not very wide place in the road about ten miles east of here."

"That's where you got pushed off the fire tower."

"Yes. Well, not pushed exactly."

He waved the qualification aside and leaned over his hands toward her. "Know anyone that works for the prison system?"

She lifted her shoulders slightly. "It's hard not to in Watson County."

He leaned back, studying her face closely and silently. Beth Marie stirred uncomfortably and started to speak to fill up the gap, but he suddenly dropped his eyes and spoke himself.

"I guess it's obvious from the question that I'm doing a piece on the prisons. Not exactly original, I know, but every couple of years we have to hit the prison system or our readers think we're not doing our jobs. The hard part is coming up with a new angle every time. We've done death row, women, juveniles, and the reforms from both sides. What else is there?"

His eyes flicked unexpectedly up to her face again. She blinked and made a murmuring noise of vague sympathy. He leaned forward, lowering his voice slightly. "Then I heard about some kind of religious program they have going in a few of the prisons. Not some big-time evangelist, you understand. Our kind of readers wouldn't be interested in that. This is strictly local. People go into the prison and do some kind of touchy-feely weekend. A sort of encounter group for outcasts.

There's a chance our readers might buy that 'just folks' angle."

Beth Marie held her cup with both hands in front of her face and looked down. Amazing. He must mean the very thing Mindy had called her about that morning.

Geoff Granger leaned back again and slid down a little in his chair. He crossed his arms and propped his chin on one fist, grinning at her. "And I've got a confession to make," he said.

Beth Marie looked up, startled.

"I did some research on you, after I saw your piece the *Chronicle* carried. I almost feel like I know you already. I knew you went to school here. Even that you went to college in Somerville for a couple of years. I feel like a voyeur in a way. I had to tell you that. You seem like such a decent person. I was beginning to feel sleazy sitting here, pretending I knew nothing about you."

She put her cup down suddenly, sloshing coffee onto the table. Flustered, she reached for a napkin to mop up the mess.

"Here. I've got it," he said, spreading his own napkin over the spill. "I'm sorry. I've upset you."

She shook her head. "No. Really. I mean, that's what reporters do. Find out information. I'm not shocked or anything. It's just that . . . I mean, why me?"

He tossed both the damp napkins onto the next table and looked at her steadily again. "Fate. Let's say fate. Unless you want to call it providence. There you were in the paper. An obvious link to Somerville and the prison. You work for the paper. You know the territory. Then, when I started checking into your background, I find out you're a member of the local Episcopal church here. St. Barnabas, isn't it?"

"Yes." The word came out sounding breathier than she'd intended.

He nodded in exaggerated encouragement, at the same time grinning at her as if they shared a secret. "So?

I figured maybe you'd know someone involved in this touchy-feely thing for the prisoners. See? I am sleazy."

She laughed. "And you want me to find you a way in."

He cocked his head to the side. "A way in? You've got a way in? To the prison? I thought only men went on these things."

"Oh. I thought you knew. You seem to know everything else." She raised one eyebrow as she tried to keep from smiling.

"Knew what?"

"About the closing."

"Closing?"

"On Sunday afternoons, after the Kairos, what you call the touchy-feely weekend, they have a closing service. Other people can go to that." She laughed in spite of herself. "Even women."

He sat back, his lean body curved pretzel-like in the chair, and appeared to study her, his eyes narrowed. "Woman, you are a veritable gold mine. Where have you been all my life."

He pushed his chair back abruptly and stood up. "Let's get out of here. We need to be someplace more exciting than this to plot an assault on a state institution. You choose the spot. Drinks and dinner. I owe you."

And before she had a chance to answer, he had dropped a couple of dollars on the table, pulled her to her feet, and was steering her toward the door, his hand firmly under her elbow.

# CHAPTER • THREE

AS IT TURNED OUT, GEOFF GRANGER'S idea of exciting fit none of the places in Somerville. Dropping off Beth Marie's Toyota in the *Courier* parking lot, they took his car, a restored '68 Mustang convertible, east over the slow, reptilian river that marked the boundary of Watson County. Clouds of white cattle egrets rose from the still green marshes of the bottomland, while great blue herons stood unperturbed in the shallows, contemplating the silt-darkened water.

"I know a place back along the river that you'll love," Geoff said, smiling at her from behind his iridescent dark glasses.

Beth Marie tried to keep her own smile from looking tentative. He hadn't mentioned the prison again, but she knew sooner or later he'd want to talk about the story. Why had she blurted out the information about the closing service? Should she tell him she was going to one this weekend? No telling where that might lead.

On the far side of the river, they pulled off the highway onto a gravel road. Swags of grey Spanish moss hung from the oak trees, half bare now in early November. Dusty yaupon underbrush crowded to the edge of the road.

"You ever been out here?" he asked, glancing at her again.

Beth Marie shook her head. She'd seen the hand-painted sign on the highway plenty of times. "Belle's Marina—Catfish and Cajuns." The place had a bad reputation in Watson County. Its customers occasionally ended up in the emergency room with a knife between their ribs, and it wasn't the sort of place a woman came alone. In fact, Beth Marie knew her mother wouldn't have approved of her going there under any circumstances. Nor would Norton have brought her. Only his duties as deputy sheriff would take him to a place like Belle's Marina. Its clientele came not just for the catfish and zydeco music but for gambling on outlawed cockfights out behind the big corrugated tin building.

"I did a piece on cockfighting once," Geoff said as they bumped over a mudhole in the road. "That's how I found out about this place. More money changes hands here over chickens than in all the Kentucky Fried stands in the state."

Beth Marie smiled but said nothing. She felt foolish. It took an outsider to show her the sights in her own neighborhood. Not that she actually wanted to see a cockfight. But reporters were supposed to be inquisitive, curious, at least aware of their own territory. School board meetings and county commissioners were about as exciting as her work got. She wasn't allowed to cover drug busts or car thefts. Not that the *Somerville Courier* would print a piece on cockfights at Belle's Marina anyway. The editor promoted what he called "a positive image" of Watson County. Otherwise, advertising from Chamber of Commerce members dried up. Readers of a slick periodical like *Texas Times* might think cockfighting a bit of racy local color, but citizens of Somerville would not find it amusing.

Geoff angled the Mustang around a thicket of pine saplings, and they came out into a clearing. The sun had dropped behind the long, low building to the west, burnishing the river water a coppery pink.

"Let's walk out on that pier," Beth Marie said, reluctant to leave the last shreds of light. "I've lived near this river almost all my life, but I've never looked at it from the eastern bank before. Not close like this."

"Sure," Geoff said and followed her over the broken caliche of the parking lot, his fingertips stuck in his jeans pockets again.

A number of aluminum rowboats, ready for renting, bumped against the pilings of the pier. These and a couple of powerboats tied up at the end of the long wooden walk constituted what the owners called the marina, she supposed. It smelled like fish and mud and green algae.

Beth Marie walked to the end and took a deep breath. The coppery water was turning gold now. A breeze moved the languid tatters of moss on the trees arching over the water, then lifted the fringe of fine hair on her own forehead. She turned and smiled at Geoff, still standing on the shore. "I love it," she called. "Sometimes I wish I could make it stand still like this. But then—" She shrugged and turned back, feeling foolish.

She felt even more foolish in her heels and businesslike jacket when they went inside. At one end of the long, open room a neon-lit jukebox was playing Beau Soleil and at the other end a pool table was illuminated by a shaded hanging lamp.

Geoff tilted his sunglasses up and steered her to a table closer to the pool table. "I think we can talk better here," he said, pulling out a hide-bottomed chair.

A woman with black hair, red nails, and a butcher's apron started toward them with menus, but he held up a hand. "We know what we want," he said. "Longnecks and blackened cat." The woman nodded and headed back to the bar.

"Do they know about the article you wrote on cockfighting?" Beth Marie asked.

"Got it pasted up behind the bar there," he said, grinning.

"They weren't upset?"

"Of course not. It doubled their business. At least for a couple of months. Helped the Renfreaux make it through last winter."

"The Renfreaux?"

"The owners."

Beth Marie looked around the room. It hardly looked like a thriving business. Other than themselves, the only customers were a couple of youngish men playing pool and a group of old men in caps and straw hats shuffling dominoes around a formica table close to the door. A small television set that no one was watching showed the evening news.

"Not much going on now," Geoff said apologetically. "Of course the weekend is when it gets lively."

"That's when they have the cockfights?"

He looked at her sharply. "Let me guess. You're an animal lover."

"Well, I—"

"I should have known. Wow. Stupid of me. I'm sorry, Beth Marie. Forgive me. This is probably a real affront to you."

"No, no," she said, holding up her hands. "I mean, yes. I guess I do love animals. I mean I probably wouldn't *enjoy* watching a cockfight. They're pretty grisly, aren't they?"

He nodded. "They are. And I can't explain or defend the fascination. I don't know what it is. You hate yourself for being there, for getting excited. That is, I do. The good old boys never give it a second thought, of course. It's terrible, really. But it works. I mean it has just the effect everyone says it does. Your heart starts pumping and there's this weird kind of identification with the birds. Man, they're fierce. It's the gladiator thing all over again—only with feathers." He gave a chagrined little chuckle and sat back. "You think I'm terrible, I know."

"Well," she hesitated. "No. It's not that. I mean, *you're* not terrible. In fact you seem like a very nice person. I guess that's what's so surprising."

"A nice person?" he laughed. "Give me a break."

"No, I mean it," she protested.

"Beth Marie. Take my word for it. No man wants a woman he's asked out to dinner to think he's a 'nice person.' It could spoil the whole evening. Try to pretend you think I'm at least slightly dangerous, okay?"

More than slightly, she thought as the black-haired waitress arrived with a tray. She exclaimed with too much animation over the smoke-crusted catfish, hoping to redirect the conversation. But Geoff had already decided to get down to business.

"So tell me more about this Kairos thing. Especially the . . . what did you call it? Closure?" He was juggling a hot hush puppy to cool it before he popped it into his mouth whole.

"Closing."

"What does the name mean, anyway? Kairos?"

"As I understand it, it means 'time.' But not regular time, not chronological time."

"*Chronos*," he said.

"What?"

"*Chronos*. Greek for time. I think one of the gods was named that. I'm not familiar with this other term though."

She creased her paper napkin nervously with her fingernail. She felt out of her depth here. "I'm not really sure, but Father Kamowski says it means a particular time or a special time."

"Father Kamowski?"

"The priest at St. Barnabas. At least for now. I don't know how long he'll be there. He wants to retire."

"Is he involved with this Kairos thing?"

"Oh, yes. He's the one who got some of the people at St. Barnabas involved."

"What about you?"

"Me?" The word almost squeaked out.

"Yes." He watched her closely. "These closings, for example. Have you ever gone to one?"

How had they gotten there so quickly? She thought she'd kept the conversation on a general level, but before she knew it, he had zeroed in on the very thing she felt uneasy about telling him.

"No," she said.

He tilted his head to the side and frowned at her.

"Not yet anyway," she added.

"You're kidding," he said, putting down his fork and leaning back with his arms folded across his chest.

She started to shake her head with a smile, as though to dismiss the subject, but he went on, laying his forearms along the edge of the table and leaning toward her intently.

"But you've got to," he said, and she noticed for the first time that his eyes were a pale grey, the dark pupils like nailheads.

She shook her head. "I don't know."

"Sure you do. Look at it this way, Beth Marie. What if you hadn't come here tonight?" He waved his arms to encompass the room. "Maybe you don't like all this. Maybe you hate it because of the cockfights and stale beer smells. But now at least you've *done* it. Now you know. I think you're the kind of person who wants to *know*, Beth Marie. Just for the sake of experience, if nothing else. You don't want to go through life shying away from things other people warn you about. I mean, how do *they* know? Don't you want to find out for yourself? Don't you want to experience life? What else is it for? How else can you say you've lived?"

He sat back suddenly and laughed, as though to apologize for his intensity. "This isn't just to talk you into the prison thing, though God knows you shouldn't pass up that particular chance. I sound like I'm trying to convert you or something. Sorry. You just seem like that kind of person to me. One who'll be sorry if you miss out on things." He looked up almost sheepishly, then reached over and covered her hand with his. "Don't let that happen, okay?"

Beth Marie could feel herself slipping, could feel her own pulse jerk and stagger, just as it had when she'd first looked up and seen Norton filling the doorway with the light behind him. She knew she ought to pull her hand away. If she didn't, he'd see it as consent, even encouragement. But if she did, he'd feel awkward. And then there'd be his embarrassment to deal with. Besides, it wasn't as though she minded. In fact, when he squeezed her fingers gently and then let them go, she was curiously disappointed. Maybe he only pitied her.

They ate in silence for a few minutes, the wooden balls on the nearby table clicking in a slow syncopation. The jukebox, unfed, had fallen silent too.

"Do you like Emily Dickinson?" she suddenly asked.

He looked up and blinked, for once taken off-guard. His eyes drifted to the side of the white crockery plate and then up again. "Sure. I guess so."

"I didn't really mean do you like her. You don't have to say you like her. I really just meant do you know her."

He seemed more cautious now. "Of course. Nature and death, right? Wrote about snakes and birds and things?"

She leaned toward him, not liking him to be cautious. "Do you know the one that starts, 'My life had stood, a loaded gun'?"

His eyes shifted to the side of his plate again and his mouth tightened slightly. "No. I can't say that I do."

*Just like Norton*, she thought. Men don't like to be asked about things they don't know. She smiled across the table and lifted the amber bottle, looking at him while she drank. "It doesn't matter," she said.

It wasn't until they were driving back to Somerville—the wind had come up out of the north and he'd had to put the top up on the convertible—that the subject of the Kairos closing came up again.

"You won't pass up a chance like that, will you? I mean, if it comes up?" he asked as they pulled into the newspaper parking lot.

She considered whether to tell him then that she had already been offered the chance. But something held her back. She merely shook her head in answer to his question as she got out of the car. It wasn't until she looked back through the glass door of the office—she had to finish up her story on the VFW parade plans—and watched the taillights of his Mustang disappear down the dark street that she realized why she hadn't told him. "A chance" wasn't the way she had thought of the closing. Not, at least, until she met him.

# CHAPTER FOUR

**B**EFORE HE LIT THE CANDLE STUB on the lid of the toilet bowl, Ignacio checked the towel he had wedged into the space between the screen and the glass of the small bathroom window. The glow from the candle was dim, but he couldn't risk anyone noticing a light coming from the camping trailer. He had shared the abandoned trailer with Gordo until a week ago when the other man had been laid off from his job at the horse farm. Ignacio hadn't been sorry to see him go. He had been frightened that Gordo, who was careless and often drunk, might do something to give them away.

But what could he say? Gordo, after all, had lived in the trailer first and had in fact brought Ignacio home with him when he discovered him sitting on the curb outside a convenience store in Somerville. "*Hombre. No siente se a la encinto!* Not in this town."

It was lonely now without Gordo, but safer. Homesickness had made the other man frequently reckless. He was probably home in Mercedes by now, broke but happy. The horse farm where he'd worked had gone under and sold off all its stock. The foreman there probably had known Gordo was living in the trailer someone had disposed of in the gully about a quarter of a mile behind the barn, but he would have pretended ignorance if the county health inspectors came around. And now that Gordo was gone, Ignacio wanted the trailer to appear completely deserted.

They had stored water in plastic jugs that Gordo filled from a hose at the barn. They cooked over charcoal piled in a rusty iron skillet on top of the tiny stove. Not that they cooked much. Mostly they opened cans of beans and mackerel and ate their food cold. Ignacio was always hungry now. It made him angry to find the woman's kitchen so empty day after day. He had risked taking a spoonful of peanut butter from a jar in the cupboard several times, but he was afraid any more than that might be noticed.

He only had to walk about a mile every morning to work in the woman's flowerbeds. He left the trailer very early, before anyone from town might come to check on the empty horse barn, and waited behind the woman's garage until he saw her through the kitchen windows moving about downstairs. Then, concealed by the garage, he made his way back onto the road and around to the front of the house. He always knocked on the front door to tell her he was there. He had watched the black people, how they went to the back door to talk to their employers. Even the Anglo workers did that. He refused.

She always opened the door looking as if she were surprised to see him. Why should she look surprised? Didn't she believe he would come back each day? She had asked him once what kind of transportation he had. He told her he had a friend who dropped him off on the highway on his way to work. When she asked where he lived, he said with a friend. He considered telling her he stayed at the mission in Somerville, but she might check on that. Last week, when the weather turned cooler, she asked if he had a jacket. He had lied and said yes.

He knelt down before the candle now and felt his

heart loosen as he looked at the shrine he had made there on the toilet lid. In the soft glow and shadows it was beautiful. In the ravine where the foreman and horse trainer had dumped their garbage he had found a piece of aluminum foil large enough to cover the back of the toilet tank so that the candlelight reflected and shimmered in its crinkled folds.

It had taken him a long time to find a picture to attach to the foil, however. The women in the magazines almost never showed the proper seriousness or purity in their faces. They smirked or smiled, and their shoulders too often were bare. Or their hair fell around their faces in blond cascades. But finally he had found the right one. He knew he was meant to find her when he read the caption under the picture: "Heiress Acquitted on Drug Charges." The woman was walking down the steps of a courthouse, ignoring the reporters pushing microphones into her face, not smiling. Her dark hair was pulled back into a knot at the back of her neck. His mother would have looked like that too. Like a queen. Only she had not been acquitted.

Alongside the candle, on the towel that covered the toilet seat, lay a holy card the priest in Pharr had given him. On it was a picture of the Virgin in a blue mantle. Unlike the woman in the photograph, she was looking down, modest and gentle. She would want no harm to come to him, he knew. Nor would his mother, who perhaps was more like the Virgin than the Heiress. It was hard to tell. When he remembered her now, she was always covered with a blue mantle, though he knew that was impossible.

The last time he had seen her . . . he squeezed his eyes tighter, trying to remember . . . they had let her come home once before the trial. A woman in a uniform had stayed beside her. A man with a pistol on his hip stood by the front door, his hands behind his back. His mother was changing her clothes in the bedroom she shared with Rosa, pulling out the drawers of the dresser, looking for something. Ignacio, who slept in his grandmother's room, stood in the doorway as though afraid to cross the boundary, staring at her. She had been crying.

"You won't need that," the other woman said. "They won't let you take it."

His mother dropped whatever it was back into the drawer and shut it. She sat down on the bed. He could hear it creak. Her dark hair fell forward around her shoulders like a veil. Then she looked up and saw him standing in the doorway. She raised her arms and held them out to him. "*Hijo!*" she said. He ran to her and crushed his face against her as she held him, rocking him back and forth. Little beads of sweat hung like small jewels on the skin above the whiteness of her slip. He closed his eyes as she crooned to him, "*Mi caro, mi hijo.*" He could smell the warm scent of her body that was like sun indoors. He kept his eyes closed and never looked up. If he didn't open his eyes, she would never go away.

But after a while his grandmother came and separated his arms from her neck, making wet, coaxing noises to him and shaking her head at his mother. His mother's arms loosened and fell away. They carried him from the room. And he never saw his mother again.

That's why it was so hard to picture her now. All he could see were the drops of sweat on the swell of her skin above the slip, though he could hear her voice over his head. When he had closed his eyes to keep her from disappearing, that must have been when the blue veil descended on her. Now he could not see her at all. The only photograph he had of her he had left in Pharr, not wanting to chance losing it. But it was not completely in focus, and her face was half turned from the camera. She had been very young when it was taken, before she had even met his father.

Ignacio sighed and sat back on his heels. It had happened a long time ago. No one else remembered. His grandmother was gone. Rosa, she was gone now too. There was only him now. Even the other women, the ones who had been at the Bromley Unit where they had enslaved his mother, had been moved. Men lived there now. Terrible men. Beasts more than men. It was as though the force that had buried his mother in that prison had tried to obliterate every trace of her existence there, as one would obliterate the scent from a game trail. Even the iron prison bars she had grasped had by now been defiled by the hands of bestial men.

They had received two letters from her while she was in prison. Their grandmother had read them to him and Rosa. He had left the letters behind in Pharr, too. They were short and he had memorized them long ago.

*Be good children, mis hijos. Obey your grannie. Say your prayers, remembering to pray always for your mother. One day we will be together again, if only in heaven.*

The second letter came about a year later, when she was in the prison infirmary. *I am very sick. I may not live to see you again. But I will see you in heaven, my angels. Pray for your mother and remember she always loved you.* It had been enclosed with a letter from the prison chaplain, telling his grandmother that her daughter had been diagnosed with breast cancer in its latter stages. It said she was being treated in a hospital in Galveston and that they could come and see her there if they wanted to.

His grandmother—his father's mother—had no money for the trip. They lived on the welfare check she got every month for caring for him and Rosa. She kept the letter to herself, refusing to tell the Hidalgos about their daughter. After all, they had made it clear that they no longer considered his mother their daughter. In fact, ever since she had run away at sixteen and married Alberto Mascarenas they looked upon her as dead. One day his grandmother had pointed out to Ignacio the long white Lincoln that carried his mother's family into town. Then she spat after it.

Ignacio began to watch for the automobile to appear at the post office, at the IGA store, at the bank. He would hide and peek around corners, trying to catch a glimpse of those proud and distant people. They were short and not very handsome, yet they frightened him. Their heavy lips protruded and their large noses jutted out like hawks' beaks. Maybe his beautiful mother wasn't really their child. Maybe they had stolen or bought her as a baby. She had probably always wanted to escape them. That was why she had run away with his father.

There were plenty of pictures of his father in his grandmother's tiny stucco house. And not small snapshots, either, but studio portraits. His father in a football uniform, his helmet balanced on one cocked hip. His father in a grey tuxedo and a pink ruffled shirt beside a girl—not his mother—in a yellow, wide-skirted long dress. His father in a military uniform. But there was no high school graduation picture and no wedding photograph.

Something about his father's pictures had always worried him. The face was handsome, but oddly asymmetrical. One eyebrow hooked upward; the other drooped down. His mouth was off balance in the same way. This disturbed Ignacio, made him feel uneasy and off balance himself. He remembered the man only dimly, and the memories were of a presence rather than an image. He could *feel* what it had been like for the man to be in the room but he could not picture him. His mother or grandmother had been with him always, but his father was rarely at home. He came and went suddenly, and mostly at night. After he had been there, his mother always cried. That's when Ignacio began to hate him, the man they said was his father. Even before it had happened.

Ignacio rocked forward on his knees now and rubbed his hands together between them, trying to keep them warm. Maybe he should have let the woman give him a jacket. It was going to be the coldest night he had yet spent in the trailer. Gordo had rolled up his blanket and taken it with him when he left, advising Ignacio to steal one from his employer. But he refused to be in her debt in any way. He desired to maintain his honor, not for himself, but for the sake of his mother.

He held his hands to the flickering candle flame to warm them, then pressed them together and began to sing softly. "*O Maria, madre mia, O consuelo del mortal . . . ampararnos y guiarnos a la puerta celestial.*"

Then he prayed, also in Spanish. In his mind that was the language of the Virgin. She understood why it was necessary that he undertake this task. It was the duty he owed his mother. To clear her name. A poor girl whose own mother and father had cast her off. But he would never desert her. He would give his life to restore her lost honor. Then she would no longer be a shameful memory to the Hidalgos. The headlines of every news-paper in the state would say "HEIRESS ACQUITTED, TWELVE YEARS AFTER HER DEATH." Everyone would see she was innocent. She was not the one who had pulled the trigger on the gun that killed the deputy that night. She had been by her husband's side, but that was the duty of a virtuous wife. She had always done what was right. And she had suffered for it. Now it was time for someone else to suffer. Not for revenge. Ignacio knew that the Virgin would not condone revenge. But for the truth, so that the truth could triumph.

"Where were you last night? I tried to call you."

"I had to work late." Even as she said it, Beth Marie wondered why she was lying to Norton.

"Really? I came by your office around five. Thought you might like to get some dinner before you drove back out to Point Blank. You weren't there then."

"No. You must have just missed me. I went out to grab a bite to eat before I came back to the office and finished up."

"Sandy said you left around three."

Beth Marie sighed heavily into the phone. "Well, let's see. Yes. I guess I did. I had an interview to do. Then I got something to eat."

"I mean, it's all right." He had begun to speak even before she finished her explanation. "I just came by on the off chance. I had an hour to kill."

Without warning, Beth Marie was suddenly angry. "Well, you know I'm working, Norton. I can't just always be *available*."

She took a deep breath and sighed again, though not so heavily this time. "I'm sorry. What about tonight? I'll have to come back and finish a story afterwards though."

"Well, I don't know. Let me check my calendar here."

"What?"

"Just kidding. Sure. Unless there's a jailbreak or a bank robbery between now and five, I'll pick you up there. Casa Pedro okay?"

"Sure," she said. And added to herself as she put down the phone, "Isn't that where we always go?"

Later, as they sat across from one another at Casa Pedro, she noticed the way Norton sat in the booth, leaning on the edge of the table but not passing an invisible boundary he seemed to acknowledge both in front and on either side of him. He never moved outside that boundary. She couldn't imagine him, for instance, lounging back with one arm along the upper edge of the booth. Nor sliding sideways, facing outward. That kind of casualness would never come easily to Norton. And never, ever would he wear a ponytail. She could have predicted what he ordered too. The Acapulco Special. Two enchiladas, a taco, two tamales, and beans and rice. She had ordered chicken fajitas, no sour cream.

He was frowning as he scooped salsa onto tortilla chips. "Something's bothering you. Besides the job, I mean." He reached for her hand and waggled it gently.

She popped a chip in her mouth and studied the serape hanging on the wall. "I don't know. It's just—well, everything seems so ordinary here. Don't you ever wish for something exciting to happen? Something unexpected?" It was the most honest thing she'd said to him all day.

"Exciting?" He leaned back, allowing her hand to slip away. "No, thanks. In my line of work, when something unexpected happens it can be life-threatening. I stop a car for an insurance check and the driver pulls a gun on me. Surprises I can live without." He looked at her closely. "But what are you feeling like this for? You just started a new job. Isn't that excitement enough?"

The waiter appeared, a college kid with a long blond forelock who told her to watch the pewter platter, so hot the chicken was still sizzling. "Looks wonderful," she murmured, smiling up at him.

Then, ignoring Norton's question, she lifted the cover on the tortillas and said, as if determined to be cheerful, "So. It's almost the weekend. I have to work tomorrow morning, but I could fix dinner tomorrow night." She had intended the offer as a goodwill gesture, but picturing herself in the light-filled kitchen, engulfed in steam and good smells, she actually began to warm to the idea.

It was a moment before he spoke. "Oh, yes. I think I may have forgotten to mention to you—"

"Mention what?" She was daubing the contents of all the little containers surrounding the platter onto the warm tortilla. This was really the part she liked best. It reminded her of playing tea party as a child. Maybe she'd even offer to cook again on Sunday afternoon. Then, well, maybe she wouldn't go to the closing after all.

"This weekend. I have to go down to Houston. A computer training session on Saturday morning. Then the sheriff wants me to stay over and bring back some prisoners from the Harris County jail on Sunday."

She paused only a moment, then continued rolling up the tortilla. "I see." She didn't want to be stupid about this.

"Sheriff Dooley. You know how he is."

She looked down. "Sure. It was just a thought."

He took a deep breath and glared at the people in the next booth.

Afterwards, when Norton took her back to the office, he pulled her to him before she could reach for the door. "Sweetheart. I really am sorry about the weekend." The scanner made crackling noises at their knees.

Grateful that patrol cars didn't have bucket seats or cumbersome gearshifts, she dropped her head back on the edge of the seat. "It's okay," she said, running her fingertips over the bristles on the back of his neck. "I understand." Maybe she should save the VFW parade for the Sunday edition.

Just then the background clutter on the scanner was interrupted by the dispatcher's voice. "Unit one-four-three. Read me? Code fifty-one."

Norton's head jerked upright as he grabbed for the speaker. "Location?"

Beth Marie reached for the door handle. The VFW would get their story tomorrow.


It was after ten when she pulled into the driveway. She got out of the car and stood for a moment, staring upward. There was no moon yet and the stars seemed very bright and close. Then she shivered and went inside.

Upstairs she sighed and sat down on the bed, slipping her shoes off. So much for loaded guns, she thought. If a loaded gun went off in the forest, would anyone hear it? She lay back and contemplated the ceiling and the empty weekend. Maybe she would go to the closing Sunday afternoon after all.

She sat up, then padded across the floor to the little desk with her appointment calendar. She had slipped Geoff Granger's card inside the back cover. Pulling it out now, she studied it, considering. Maybe she'd call and let him know she'd decided to go.

# CHAPTER • FIVE

**B**ETH MARIE!"
She turned toward the woman calling from the far side of the visitor's parking lot, grateful for the sound of her own name in another person's voice. She could have wept when she saw Mindy waving to her; the weekend had been that bad.

She couldn't comprehend the overwhelming loneliness that afflicted her like a disease these days, coming over her in cold waves she sometimes wasn't sure she'd survive. Nor could she understand why, after living alone in relative happiness during the years following her mother's death, she should now find that solitude almost unbearable. She loved her house in Point Blank. It was almost like her own body, her attachment to it was that great. She loved the light in the kitchen, the feel of the bannister sliding beneath her palm as she went up the stairs, the creaks and groans it made at night as it cooled.

But lately she had begun to dread going home alone at night. She'd never felt like that till she met Norton.

One of her favorite memories from childhood was of lying in bed on summer evenings, the twilight still silhouetting the tree branches outside her bedroom window. From below, the household noises and her parents' muted voices would float up to her, along with the cries of children playing in the vacant lot beside the Baptist Church or out in the road. She had imagined this was how God felt after a good day, the world humming and murmuring itself to sleep. Even as a child she had been aware of the depth of her pleasure.

But now, as late fall turned to winter, the windows were all shut against outdoor sounds, and no one moved about downstairs making comforting domestic noises. She felt abandoned. There was no other way to put it. And Emily Dickinson's poems about the virtues of solitude were no longer convincing. More often than not she found herself crying into her pillow, ashamed of her weakness, yet desperate for another human being to mediate the silence and space that swallowed her.

No doubt that was what had prompted her to call Geoff Granger Saturday morning, especially since she knew Norton would be gone the entire weekend. She had only gotten a machine at Geoff's work number, so she called the number he'd scrawled on the back of his card.

A machine answered, but halfway through the message she was leaving, a rumpled voice cut in. "Yeah. Beth Marie. What's up?"

"I'm sorry if I woke you," she started meekly.

"No trouble. What is it?" She thought she could hear another voice in the background.

"Remember the service I told you about? At the prison."

"Yes?" His voice was suddenly alert.

"Well. I'm going to one."

"Going? When? Where?"

"Tomorrow afternoon. At the Bromley Unit."

There was a pause on the other end while he coughed and muttered indistinctly. Then he said, "Think you could get me in too?"

"I don't imagine. They have to run a security check on you first."

"And you're already cleared?" She was sure she heard another voice now.

"Yes. I have a friend. She's been wanting me to go."

Another pause. It sounded as if he was lighting a cigarette. Then he laughed. A low, throaty chuckle. "You've been holding out on me here, Beth Marie. Haven't you? You didn't mention this the other day."

She sat down and crossed her legs, resting her left wrist on her knee, just as if he'd been in the room with her. "No," she said, feeling suddenly equal to the challenge in his voice. "I hadn't decided when I talked to you. My friend had asked me earlier in the week." That was technically the truth. "I gave her my license number and told her to go ahead and run the check. Just to placate her really. I had no intention of going then."

"Then I told you about my story."

"Then I ended up with nothing to do this weekend."

He laughed again. "If I didn't know Somerville, I'd think you were putting me on, Beth Marie, someone like you. But all right. If you can't get me in, at least do this for me. Meet me afterwards, okay? I don't suppose you can get a tape recorder inside?"

"No. In fact, all you're allowed to take in is your driver's license for identification. Not even pencils and paper. No purses even."

"Mm. All the more reason to meet right away. Holiday Inn again?"

She hesitated. "Actually, the Bromley Unit's out east of town."

He couldn't have delayed his response more than two seconds, but it was enough to let her know he was taking in the implication. "Toward the river?"

"Yes."

"All right. What about Belle's Marina then? Now that you know how to get there. A good place for plotting all kinds of mischief."

"Fine," she had said, with a good deal more confidence than she felt.

"Mindy!" she called now, hurrying across the asphalt expanse and pulling her coat around her against the November wind.

"You've emptied your pockets, haven't you?" Mindy asked, turning her own back to the wind and dancing up and down in tiny steps to generate some warmth. "We hand over our keys and licenses to the guard after we get inside."

They hurried after the knot of people already on the far side of the chain-link fence. It clanged and locked after them. Another guard was holding open a steel door on the side of the building. Obviously they weren't going in through the visitor's entrance. Probably, she speculated, to avoid contact with inmates' families who'd come for a weekend visit.

Beth Marie recognized most of the people in the bare room as members of St. Barnabas, though there was also a sprinkling of people from other churches in town. As they milled around, taking off their coats and making nervous jokes, it struck her how much they looked like late arrivals at a church potluck. Even the stark room looked remarkably like a parish hall.

"I'm glad you wore that," Mindy said, looking at Beth Marie's skirt and turtleneck. "I forgot to tell you it's not a good idea to wear anything that—" She finished the sentence by making swishing motions with her hands. "You know. Sort of flutters. Or anything low cut. They don't actually whistle or anything because the guards are there, but you can feel them looking at you. They're only a few feet away." She rolled her eyes.

"What do you mean?" Beth Marie asked nervously.

"Come on. You'll see. We're going in now."

A barrel-chested guard with oily hair was standing at

the far door, collecting driver's licenses and keys as the group filed through one by one. He muttered the same instructions to each person as he checked their features against the pictures on the licenses.

"Keep right to the center of the corridor. Don't speak to the inmates. Keep your hands at your sides, but not in your pockets."

Beth Marie stepped through the door into a long corridor lined with barred cells. Yellow lines on the floor about two feet out from the cells marked what was obviously a boundary that prisoners were not allowed to cross. As they made their way down the corridor, a line of white-clad men faced them inside the boundary on the left. Further down, half a dozen men on the right waited for them to pass. Any of the men could have reached out and touched them as they walked by.

She had not expected that they would be so close to prisoners, except perhaps in the chapel, and then only with those who'd participated in the retreat. Why hadn't someone warned her? She tried to stare straight ahead at Mindy's back, but her eyes kept sliding off to the faces of the men on her left. Whether their features were sunken or swollen, their expressions were uniformly shut down, masked. Walking between the yellow lines was like running a gauntlet. Each man against the walls fastened his eyes on the people in the middle as if memorizing their faces. Her flesh felt seared. She wished she still had her coat on.

As they passed, a low murmur rippled along the boundaries. The guard paid no attention.

They came to the end of the block of cells and waited as another guard unlocked the steel doors. Beth Marie noticed a sign stenciled on the wall to the side of the crash gate: "Hostages will not be allowed beyond this point. Threats of violence will not alter this policy." No one had told her about that either.

They must have passed through three such segments

of cells, the gate behind them being locked each time before the one ahead was unlocked. Finally they arrived at the chapel, a windowless room with lights recessed behind panels of colored plastic meant to imitate stained glass. The men who had taken part in the weekend retreat were already there, seated in the front rows, inmates on the right, free world on the left. One row of pews was roped off to leave a buffer zone between the retreatants and the new arrivals for the closing.

Mindy caught Beth Marie's arm and pulled her into a pew just as Father Kamowski ambled to the podium. Beth Marie had found him a peculiar sort of priest for the bishop to assign, even on an interim basis, to a parish like St. Barnabas, made up mostly of old-timers with a scattering of younger families. Obviously the vestry was having a hard time finding a new rector willing to come to Somerville.

In the prison setting she could see more clearly just why Father Kamowski seemed so out of place at St. Barnabas. The man appeared to occupy an ill-defined region separating the prisoners from what Mindy had called "regular people." He reminded Beth Marie of someone like Kit Carson or Natty Bumppo in *The Last of the Mohicans*. He was a scout, an interpreter between the settlers and the Indians, knowing the ways and the language of both but belonging fully to neither.

Beth Marie had seen his wife one of the few times she had attended services in the old hardware store on the square that was temporarily housing the St. Barnabas congregation. The woman was sitting at the far end of the pew two rows in front of her now, her improbable red hair set in a 1940s pompadour and pageboy. Beth Marie had the distinct impression that without her, Father Kamowski might have retreated from his neutral zone and joined the prisoners. Immense, gruff, barely civil, he obviously found it an ordeal to stand at the door of the hardware store after Sunday morning service, shaking hands and making pastoral small talk as the parishioners filed out. Here he seemed in his element, however. The inmate argot came easily to him, and he gave up that painful striving for grammatical correctness that strained his sermons at St. Barnabas.

"I won't take up much of your time today," he began. "I already know what *I* think. I wanta hear what you guys got to say about what's been going on here this weekend. So we're saving most of the time the state of Texas gives us for you to talk.

"There's just one thing I wanta say to you though. And it's a warning. Now I know you guys are used to people giving you warnings, even if you don't pay no attention to them."

A low rumble Beth Marie took to be agreement rippled across the front pews.

"The warning is this," he went on, his face settling into a wooden mask of gravity. "There's some guys in this lockup decide to take what's called the Jesus Road. You know what I'm talking about. Their eyes get sort of glassy and they repeat themselves a lot. They say the same things over and over like they're trying to convince themselves that they believe what they're saying. And if you don't agree with them, well, they'll tell you right now where you're headed. As if you wasn't already there.

"Now I don't wanta put down any of our brothers in white. There's plenty of people already got that job. The guys that take the Jesus Road, what they've found is a way to cope. A way to do their time. Like self-hypnosis or something. A way to protect themselves from what you can't escape in this place.

"That's okay. Don't make fun of those guys, and don't think I'm making fun of them. They're doing the best they know how right now. And it's better than some other things they could be doing. But I want you to realize there's a difference between what they're doing and what we've been doing here this weekend. We're not talking about coping. We're not talking about just finding a way to do time. We're talking about something even scarier than that. Scarier than what those guys on death row up there at The Walls are looking at."

He paused and let his eyes rake the first few rows on both sides of the aisle. Several men shifted uneasily in the pews.

"I know. You think death row's the worst thing that can happen to you, that there ain't nothin' scarier than dying. Even locked up here, there's always the possibility some guy could put an ice pick between your ribs in the shower some fine day." Here he moved around to the side of the podium and leaned one elbow on it.

"Maybe dying is what you *think* you're most afraid of—" here he lifted his gaze to include the back rows, "but that ain't it. I'll tell you what we're all most afraid of, convicts and free world both." He walked back behind the podium. "Love," he said. He paused, then repeated the word and snorted suddenly. "I mean look at you. I say the word and you start cutting your eyes over to the side. Can't even look me in the face when I mention the word."

He looked down and shook his head, smiling to himself. "I gotta admit, it scares me too. Somebody lays this love stuff on you, it makes you nervous. You start thinking right away, what do they want, what are they trying to get out of me? And not until you figure out what that is can you relax. Then you feel like maybe you've got everything under control again. Because when you know what they want, then you can decide whether or not you want to give it to them, you know what I mean?"

There were some distinct snickers from the front row.

"Right. I see you do. But what if there was somebody you couldn't do nothin' for? They already had it all. You couldn't give 'em money or sex or even make 'em feel more important." He stopped abruptly as though to allow them time to ponder this. "That don't make sense, does it? For one thing, don't nobody you know fit that description. Everbody wants something. Even the people say they love you. Even your *mama* wants something. Don't she want you to straighten up and get out of this place?"

That brought a smattering of nervous laughter.

The priest slapped the podium with his huge palm and stood up straight. "Well, I ain't gonna play mind games with you. You know who I'm talking about. The one person you can't do nothin' for or add nothin' to. There ain't nothin' you can do for him. You can't do him no favors. Not to get him to protect you or get you out of here. So if you have any notion you can make some kind of a deal with this dude, keep that in mind."

He leaned toward them, focusing on the front rows again. "But there ain't nothin' you can do to keep him from loving you either. That's the scary part. He's gonna keep on whether you like it or not."

He straightened again, even leaned back from them. "Why? Why does he love a bunch of convicts? Well, don't forget that he was one. On death row too. But that's not the reason either. The reason is," he threw up his hands in a gesture of incredulity, "because he wants to. It makes him happy. He gets a kick out of it, okay? Not because you're good and he feels like he owes you. Not because you're smart or good-looking or believe the right things. Not for anything any of us would even call a reason. That's what makes it crazy. I can't figure it. You can't figure it. Is he crazy? Who knows?"

He took a deep breath. "So that's all I got to say. Don't go for that glassy-eyed stare and start telling the brothers they're all going to hell if they don't fall in line behind you. Don't try to cut no deals with God— because you can't. He's already holding all the cards anyway. So you might as well go ahead and let him do what he wants to—which is love you. It's the only thing gonna make him happy. And you can't escape it, not even if you could break out of the Bromley Unit, or even The Walls, could you escape it. You might as well turn yourself in." The shadow of a grin surfaced briefly on his face. "Then he can get on with his party."

It had to be the strangest homily Beth Marie had ever heard, but what followed was even more unusual. Three inmates, each sweating as he made his way up to the podium in turn, made labored speeches. The format had evidently been supplied for them by the retreat team. Each described his condition when the weekend began, then told what he had expected to happen. Finally, he explained what he was taking away.

While the first two inmates were speaking, there was constant traffic up and down the aisle from the front pews to the restroom at the rear of the chapel where a guard was stationed. Beth Marie furtively searched the prisoners' faces as they made their way down the aisle, some shuffling, others swaggering. They looked like either boys or old men to her, though these categories weren't necessarily related to age. It had to do with the way their eyes moved. Some shifted their eyes quickly and uncertainly from face to face, at once eager to draw forth a response and ashamed of their own appeal. Some kept their eyes on the floor as if resigned to their fate. Others raked the faces in the pews with an indifferent, even stare in defiance of their failure.

Much of the speeches were patchworks of clichés from childhood, rambling soliloquies drawn from church memories. But the last man, small with a corrugated, monkey-like face, obviously had no grab bag of sentiments to draw on. He began slowly, his speech coming in short explosive bursts, sometimes half-suppressed expletives, as he searched for words adequate to his experience. He had been abandoned as an infant, lived in a series of foster homes, become a petty thief when he was barely in his teens. He'd served his first sentence at seventeen.

"I been bitter a long time," he said. "My life's been like a yo-yo. Up and down, up and down. I wasn't gonna let you people hook me. But I don't wanna be danglin' on that string no more. Like the guy here says about God not lettin' you go—" he jerked a thumb toward Kamowski, "I don't *want* to be let go no more."

He stopped, his breath catching in his throat as if he were strangling on some unpronounceable word. Finally he continued, almost too low for them to hear. "If you see me break down, don't tell, okay? I been locked up a long time and I can't hold nothin' back."

Last year Beth Marie had helped a pregnant friend who had gone into labor while her husband was out of town. With only a half hour's instruction in Lamaze techniques, she had panted and huffed through the ordeal along with the mother until the baby had dropped, glistening and slippery, into the doctor's hands. By then she was exhausted. That's how she felt now, watching the man labor with his words.

"How does an animal become a man?" he said, looking up sharply. "That's what I want to know. All I know is, I gotta go back to my animal cage when this is over." He jerked his head in the direction of the cell blocks. "But just because I live in a cage, don't mean I wanna be an animal no more. Used to, I wanted to be a tiger—the meanest one I could. But a tiger's still just an animal. A human bein's something different. He can say yes, he can say no. Made in God's image, you people tell us. Me? I don't know." He paused to chuckle nervously. "I'd hate to think God looked like me."

"But this guy—" he nodded in Kamowski's direction again—"when he says how we can't escape, that's something I know about. And it don't make no sense, but I like that—not being able to get away from God. 'Cause if I have to be on good behavior the rest of my life, then I know already I ain't got a chance. Hell, I can't even get enough good time to make parole." A prisoner on the second row laughed suddenly, then broke off. The monkey-faced man went on, not seeming to notice.

"I never thought I could be anything besides an animal before. Maybe when I was two, three years old. Been a lotta water under the bridge since then. Now, maybe, well." He ran his hand through his thinning hair and shook his head. "This's the first time in a long time I ever even thought about it—being a human instead of an animal. I don't know. But if he wants me to be one—" He jerked a thumb upward now, though he kept his head down. "And if he ain't ever gonna let go—" He looked up suddenly as if he had just thought of something, the folds of his creased face stretching. "If I could die, if I could just die wanting that—" His hand dropped to his side. Then, turning his back to them, he slid into his space on the bench, his head still down.

A trio of guitarists down front began strumming a background accompaniment to fill the gap the man's voice left when he broke off. Beside Beth Marie, Mindy began humming. Meanwhile, another man in white stood up and began speaking, like a terrier with a bone between his jaws, determined to worry the meaning out of his words. It appeared that he was an alumnus of a previous Kairos retreat, speaking as a veteran to recruits about the necessity to keep meeting together as a group. His head bobbed forward every time he emphasized a point, and his palm smacked the pew back sporadically. A younger inmate, making his way toward the rear in a loose, loping gait, slowed momentarily to listen to him, then catching Beth Marie's eyes on him, moved quickly past.

How did you know, she wondered, which ones meant it and which ones didn't—who was just using the retreat as a way to get off work detail or to lighten the boredom? Come to that, who meant it at St. Barnabas? And herself. What about her? What was she here for after all? Hadn't she come to mentally record all this for Geoff Granger?

The thought of the reporter waiting for her opened yet another Pandora's box. How could she possibly translate for him all that she'd witnessed here? Not just the prison—he was already familiar with that. But the fear that had made her own heart constrict as she watched the inmate nursing his fragile and imperiled hope. She would be the one struggling with language then.

Geoff Granger, she sensed, only had faith in his own talents. It was the kind of faith that didn't allow for hope. If you had to *hope*, you knew you weren't good enough. You'd lost already. He would only be capable of hearing the inmate's sweaty confession through the filter of irony. How could she ever make it real to him?

# CHAPTER • SIX

THE QUESTION WAS STILL PLAGUING her as the free-world people filed out of the chapel and made the trek back through the cell blocks to the visitors' room. As they were slipping into their coats, Mindy asked if she'd like to join the group for dinner at Casa Pedro. "Arnold Showalter's coming," she added, indicating with a discreet nod a middle-aged CPA—divorced—who was following Mindy's husband out the door.

"I'd love to," Beth Marie said, making a disappointed face, "but I've already made plans to meet someone."

Mindy winked. "Sure. I understand."

No, Beth Marie wanted to say. You don't. You have a husband here with you and two children at home, not a big, empty house waiting to swallow you up. However, being paired with some unsuspecting accountant wasn't her cup of tea, either. Even if Geoff Granger hadn't been waiting for her she would have wanted to escape.

Still, she felt a twinge of guilt as she hurried back to her car alone, listening to the clamor and exclamations of the others as they emerged into the cold November night. She knew Mindy meant well. She was eager to see Beth Marie enjoying the same domestic contentment she did.

But contentment wasn't exactly what Beth Marie was looking for right now. She had been contented before she met Norton, before Geoff Granger. It was something else she wanted now.

She noticed her hands were shaking as she put the key in the ignition. As soon as she'd stepped through the prison door, everything had suddenly seemed to speed up. An internal eruption deep inside her, something she didn't quite understand and wasn't sure she wanted to, was sending out shock waves she could feel reverberating through her body. Just as she got to the river bridge, she looked down at the lighted dashboard and saw she was doing eighty.

She should slow down. Even pull over and give herself a good talking to, get herself under control. What had gotten into her anyway? A part of her was frightened. But another part was even more afraid to stop. She felt as if she were escaping—though what she couldn't say. And she was afraid to look back.

On the east side of the river she pulled off onto the shoulder and edged along until she saw the unlighted sign for Belle's Marina. She made the turn onto the dirt road cautiously, creeping along over the rutted bumps. Her headlights caught the red eyes of small animals off in the underbrush and lit the bare branches of trees from beneath, making the overgrown road look like a stage set. She licked her lips and then clamped her tongue between her teeth.

Finally she rounded the last thicket and came out into the open space covered with chunks of white caliche that served as the parking lot. This time it was crowded with cars and pickups. A knot of men in hats and boots were crowded around a van parked near the woods, their collars turned up against the wind and hats tilted forward over their faces.

Beth Marie tried to pick out Geoff's Mustang, but the parking area was too crowded and dark. She found a spot as close as possible to the circle of light thrown by an outdoor spot above the entrance to the long barnlike building and turned off the engine. Looking in the rearview mirror, she ran her fingers through her hair, fluffing it up as much as she could after the wind had tangled it. Then she got out, being careful to lock the car door, and pulled her coat around her.

At least I'm not wearing heels this time, she thought as she hurried toward the entrance, but no jeans either. I look like a schoolgirl in this skirt and turtleneck.

Stationed just inside the door this time was a wedge-shaped fellow in a tight T-shirt, his bulky arms folded across his pectorals. He stared at her as she stepped to the opposite side of the door, scanning the room for the reporter. The place was full. A woman sat beside the muscle-man on a high stool, leaning on his shoulder. She looked at Beth Marie and frowned slightly.

"You need some help?" she asked flatly.

"I'm looking for someone," Beth Marie said. She spoke too low and had to repeat it before the woman could hear. "Geoff Granger," she added. "I'm supposed to meet him here."

The woman made a face and raised an eyebrow. "Geoff, huh?" Then she scanned the room methodically. "There. At the bar," she said, pointing a long red nail. Then she looked down at Beth Marie again. "Want me to get him for you, honey?"

Beth Marie hesitated a moment, then said, again too low, "No thanks," and started across the expanse of bare pine flooring, conscious of being the only person in the place wearing a skirt.

Geoff was talking to the bartender, leaning far over the counter in his characteristic way. No invisible glass walls around him, she thought. She touched his elbow lightly and he turned.

"Beth Marie!"

She hadn't expected him to sound so pleased. "Here I am," she said, her own voice catching his eagerness.

"Something for the lady," he called to the bartender who had already turned away. "This is great! You're here in time. I wasn't sure you'd make it." He put his hand on her shoulder in a gesture half-protective, half-possessive.

"For what?" He didn't seem to be in a very business-like mood tonight. It appeared he'd already had a couple of drinks.

His mouth brushed her ear as he whispered, "Cockfight tonight." Then he pulled away and looked at her, smiling crookedly. "I swear, I didn't know. Not till I got here tonight." He glanced over at the bartender, who gave him a cautionary look.

"Not a regulation fight. Just sort of a friendly trial, I guess you could say." He'd lowered his voice so that she had to tilt her head to catch the words. "You don't mind, do you? Who knows? It might be your only chance." His breath was warm and damp in her ear.

She lifted her shoulders in a small shrug. "Okay. I guess. But if it gets too bad—"

"Just say the word. Whenever you want to leave," he promised, taking her hand and pulling her after him through the crowd. "Out back here. It may have already started."

They emerged into the cold air again through a back door set at the end of the partitioned-off entry to the restrooms. About fifty feet from the main building she could make out something that looked like an enclosed pavilion. A narrow band of light showed around its upper rim, deflected by an uneven roofline. Beth Marie could hear muted noises coming from the pavilion now that she was outside, though no one in the big tin building would have noticed.

They slipped into the pavilion, drawing stares from the men crowded close to a wooden railing that circled the hardpacked dirt in the middle.

"Up here," Geoff said, steering her with a hand on her shoulder up several rows of bleacher seats past men in down vests and hunting jackets hunched forward over their knees. The surprise in their eyes when they spotted her was quickly hooded.

Two small clusters of men were arranged on opposite sides of the open pit. In the one nearest them, a teenager was holding open a canvas bag that sagged to his knees. The other two men, older and obviously in charge, were frowning and looking into the bag. At some direction from them, the boy hoisted the bag up into his arms and reached slowly inside.

At first, Beth Marie thought it was a snake his hand had drawn from the mouth of the bag. Then she saw that it was the head and neck of a black cock, its feathers trimmed so close that, as it stretched slowly toward the ceiling, the bird looked like a snake charmed from the bag. She was close enough to see now the cock's hard, horny beak, thick and massive at the roots. Instinctively, she grasped Geoff's upper arm. "Why does it look so strange?" she whispered.

"They trim the feathers," he explained. "Around the neck and on the back. See?" He pointed to the far side where the other cock had just been pulled from its canvas bag. It extended its wings momentarily, and she saw that its wing feathers had been cut to less than half their natural length and that the tail had been docked to a stubby, triangular shape. The feathers around the base of the neck had been dressed in such a way as to make the bird's hackles stand up in a ruff.

"Why?" she insisted, tightening her grip on his arm unconsciously. "It makes them look so . . . ugly. Not elegant at all."

"Mostly it's practical," Geoff said. "To keep the other bird from getting a firm hold on the feathers, especially on the back. But I suspect it's more than that. Owners usually make some physical alteration on their sporting animals. Docking their horses' tails or dogs' ears. A sign of mastery probably. Possession." He squeezed her hand on his arm as though to reassure her. As soon as he leaned forward again, she slid her hand away, embarrassed.

Even though they were on the third row of bleacher seats, Beth Marie could clearly see, when the bird on their side of the pit was pulled from its bag, that the natural spurs on the rear of its firm, bony shanks had been trimmed short also. His compact body, its red and black feathers intermingled, looked strong, and his dark blue legs were clean and sinewy. The black, dilated eyes took in everything around him with an arrogant, glittering stare. Even his comb had been cut close, making him look less like a fop and more like a fighter.

"But how is he going to fight?" she asked. "He doesn't even have any spurs."

The man in front of them turned sideways and cleared his throat, frowning.

Geoff slipped his arm around her shoulder, drawing her closer to explain to her in a low mutter. "They're all like that. The trainers cut the natural spur back and fit them with metal spurs."

She widened her eyes and covered her mouth with her hand.

"Actually," he went on, pushing a wisp of hair back over her ear with one finger, as if to make sure she could hear him better, "it's much cleaner that way. Hardly anyone does naked-heel fighting anymore. Too dangerous for the birds. And not really fair. There's too much variation in their natural endowments. The fiercest birds don't always have the longest spurs. Using standard artificial spurs makes the competition more even, more sporting. And," he added, turning back toward the pit, "like I said, there's less chance of infection. The wounds heal faster with metal spurs."

He leaned forward now to stare across the pit, and

Beth Marie's gaze followed his to the other handler who was raising his bird over his head, examining with another man—probably the owner—its beak, wings, and legs. The bird was gold with black-tipped wings, rather slight, but elastic and muscular. At the sight of his antagonist, he stretched his wings and craned his neck upwards.

Geoff smiled back over his shoulder at her tense face. "Charles the Second gave Nell Gwynn a pair of silver cock spurs once. The seventeenth century's notion of a lover's tribute, I guess." He turned back to the pit where the two cocks were now chuckling defiantly at one another from across the pit. The handlers were smoothing their feathers and whispering to the birds. The man nearest them licked his fingers and then used them to moisten the bandaged ankles where the spurs had been fastened.

At a nod from the man who had taken up a position in the middle of the ring, the two handlers advanced with their birds, still stroking them, but tightening their grips. The man who was evidently the referee spoke briefly to both the handlers and watched as they allowed the birds to strike at one another with their beaks. One of the handlers, the one from the far side, laughed shortly. Then the referee backed up to the edge of the pit, holding what looked like a stopwatch in his hand. The handlers stooped down and placed the birds on the floor opposite each other. Then, hands raised, they both backed away.

The two cocks rushed forward, and, for a few moments, stood with their beaks touching. Slowly the birds both raised their heads, stretching toward the roof of the pavilion, each one trying to get an advantage in the first cut. Then in an instant they had sprung high into the air, a flurry of wings and feathers in one furious, confined mass. Their ascent sounded to Beth Marie as if a large wet umbrella had suddenly been forced open.

When they settled to earth again, she could tell that one of the birds, the yellow one from the far side, had already been hurt. It staggered across the pit as though unable to regain its bearings. Its handler advanced into the ring and picked it up carefully, stroking it again. The other handler took up his bird also. It still looked full of fire and irritated courage.

At a signal from the man with the stopwatch, the two handlers brought their birds to the center of the pit again and set them down, then backed away to the pit's rim. This time the red and black cock rose in the air, suspending itself for a moment over the back of the yellow one, who stretched his wings in a display of dazed defiance. Then the red and black cock settled deliberately from the air, driving a spur through the neck of the other bird.

Beth Marie caught her breath in a muffled scream and turned her head against Geoff's shoulder. He kept his eyes fastened on the two cocks but laid a hand on her knee, as though to steady her. She could hear the birds rise again, flapping, then a restrained cry from the men ringing the pit. She looked.

The red-and-black looked fiercer than ever, but the ginger-colored bird was drooping, hardly able to rock forward from its tail onto its legs again. Blood was trailing from its beak. In one mighty rush the black-and-red sprang upward again and swiftly drove its silver spurs up to their hilts into the back of his opponent. Beth Marie moaned and once again turned her head against Geoff's shoulder. He sat back, sliding his arm around her and exhaling the pent-up air from his lungs. "It's over," he said.

She followed him down the bleachers, feeling the men eyeing her furtively. As she stepped onto the hard-packed dirt, Geoff took her arm and steered her outside into the sharp night. Neither of them spoke. The blood, the ritual animal savagery had shaken her. She kept her eyes on the ground, concentrating to keep from stumbling as they made their way back along the path.

Just before they reached the pool of light thrown out into the darkness from the rear door of the tin building, Geoff turned and pulled her against him. Then he kissed her, not urgently but solidly. Beth Marie felt her knees were giving way, but he was already turning away and pulling her through the door.

She stumbled after him, her senses so heightened now that all the motion and noise inside the bar threatened to overwhelm her. Sliding into the chair he'd pulled out for her at a table against the wall, she took a deep breath, trying to regain her composure while he went to the bar to pick up a drink.

For crying out loud, she told herself, pull yourself together. You're acting like a teenager.

He dropped into the chair across from her, then leaned toward her across the table; his elbows, spread outward, almost reached the edges. He looked at her intently, then dropped his eyes quickly as though guarding what was there. At that moment the amplifiers at the other end of the long room whanged to life with a screech.

With sudden inspiration she smiled at him and said, trying to make her voice sound as natural possible, "We can't talk here. Come on. Let's go to my house. It's on your way back to Somerville."

Geoff looked up and laughed. "Sounds like a good idea. Let's go," he said and downed the rest of his drink.

As they passed the bouncer at the door, the woman on the stool caught Beth Marie's eye. "Leaving so soon?" she asked, arching a black eyebrow and shaking her head in mock dismay.

Behind her, Geoff made some reply under his breath, but Beth Marie couldn't make it out. The woman laughed and jabbed one long red nail playfully at his shoulder. Beth Marie pushed quickly through the door, glad to feel the sharp November night bracing her senses.

Geoff followed her out onto the low porch of the building, but as he stepped off the edge, he seemed to trip. Swearing under his breath, he steadied himself against her shoulder.

"Why don't we take my car," Beth Marie said. She wasn't sure just how much he'd had to drink before she arrived. "I don't mind bringing you back later."

His fingers on her shoulder tightened, then relaxed. "Tactfully put," he said. "Sure. Why not?"

But as she started to unlock the door of the Toyota, he stopped her. "Just a minute." He was looking from the knot of men still gathered around the van at the dark edge of the parking lot to his own vintage Mustang, not far from the group.

"You're worried about leaving your car here?" she asked.

"I hate to be crass," he said, "but I know how these good old boys are. Would you mind? I don't think they'd bother yours. It's in the light. Can we leave it and take mine? Here. You can drive."

She took the keys he handed her, and they made their way back to the darkened row of cars beyond the van. A couple of the men stared at them, then turned back to their companions. There was a detonation of laughter and a hoot. Beth Marie unlocked the door on the passenger side first and Geoff got in.

"Thanks," he said in a subdued voice as she slid into the leather seat. "You're a good person, you know that, Beth Marie?"

She started the car. "Is that as bad as 'a very nice person'?"

It took him a moment to recall the way he had rejected her earlier description of him, but when he did, his frown disappeared and he laughed. "No," he replied. Then he sighed and laid his head on the seat back, closing his eyes. "A good person, a genuinely good person, is a rare thing." He opened his eyes again, staring upwards a moment, then rolled his head so that he was looking at her, and added, "I may not be nice, but I'm not good either, Beth Marie."

# CHAPTER • SEVEN

**A**LTHOUGH THEY DIDN'T SPEAK AGAIN during the drive back to her house in Point Blank, Beth Marie wouldn't allow her mind to think. Not to sort or assess or evaluate or speculate about the consequences of what she was doing.

The steering wheel and gear shift of the Mustang were loaded with chrome, and it winked at her in the green glow from the dashboard. She thought she could even smell the sharp, cold scent of the metal, mingled with the thicker odor of the leather seats. She glanced over at Geoff a couple of times, but his eyes were closed and she thought he might actually be asleep. She noted again the vertical lines along his mouth, and a sudden surge of pity added itself to the emotions she was resolutely refusing to name.

She turned her attention back to the road and the narrow tunnel of light piercing the November night. She had never driven so carefully and with such complete concentration.

When she pulled into the drive behind her house and turned off the motor, she had to jiggle his arm to rouse him. "Geoff. We're here."

He opened his eyes, looking dazed at first. Then he sat up abruptly. "Right."

Beth Marie went ahead and unlocked the door to the kitchen, not allowing herself to think that it had been Norton who had insisted she develop the habit of locking her doors. She flipped on the lights, and, hearing Geoff coming up the steps behind her, said quickly, "I'll make coffee." She dropped her coat over the back of a chair and started running the water to keep from looking at him.

She heard him pass behind her and make his way through the alcove at the bottom of the stairs and into the living room. As she waited for the coffee to brew, she could feel the silence adding its weight to a mounting pressure, like water behind a dam. She ran hot water into two mugs to warm them and then arranged them carefully on a small tray with sugar and spoons. She could feel some part of her brain whirring furiously, but she still would not allow herself to read it. She filled the cups and picked up the tray, feeling her pulse beating in her throat.

Geoff had turned on a lamp at the end of the sofa and sat now in his characteristic wedge-shaped sprawl at the far end, his face shaded from the amber light.

Beth Marie put the tray on the coffee table and lifted one of the cups toward him wordlessly. He slid forward and took it, nodding his thanks. She picked up the second cup and sat down on the other end of the sofa, slipping off her shoes.

The face he turned to her now looked tired, almost irreparably so. "Are you all right?" she asked him.

"Just tired," he said, raising his cup and smiling wanly. "I keep wired all the time. This is the most—settled—I've felt all week. This is a great house you've got here. Like something out of a book. *Little House on the Prairie*. I didn't know people really lived like this any more." He laughed mirthlessly. "Sometimes I don't go home for days. Afraid I don't take very good care of myself, Beth Marie." He looked up at her, then dropped his eyes quickly as though guarding what was there.

"You all right?" she asked again. Was he trying to tell her something?

"Sure." He gave a short, deprecating little laugh. "Sunday evenings are the pits though, aren't they? The rest of the week when you're working, it's okay. But it's like there's this hole in the universe that opens up on Sunday afternoons and the vacuum outside sucks out all the energy." He looked up now. "You ever feel like that? About Sunday afternoons, evenings, I mean."

Then before she could answer, he sat back suddenly and laughed again, louder this time. "No, of course not. I forgot. You've been out doing good works, haven't you? I guess that's the answer, isn't it? If I weren't such a self-absorbed son-of-a-bitch I wouldn't be moping around. I'd be out helping the homeless or something, right?"

"Look," she said, feeling a little nettled, "you're the one who wanted to know about the closing."

"You mean you wouldn't have gone to the prison otherwise?" he broke in. "If I hadn't ask you to?"

She stopped and stared at his grey eyes with the dark, nailhead pupils. Then her gaze faltered and slid sideways off his face. "I might have," she said stiffly.

He nodded. "Okay." He leaned back into the corner of the sofa, one arm laid along the back, and stared at her steadily. "So say you never even met me, and you decided to go anyhow. But grant me this. It would have been at least partly to avoid that Sunday afternoon slump, wouldn't it? That stale taste in the mouth or however you want to describe it." He lifted one long finger and tapped her arm. "Maybe you've got better ways of handling it than I have. But tell me I'm not the only one who feels that way." He plucked at the sleeve of her sweater in a mock-pleading gesture.

She forced herself to look directly into his eyes. He stared back, suddenly serious. Until now, she had been a little afraid of him. His experience was so much larger than her own narrow world. But however large his world was, it evidently had holes in it. And he was admitting that to her.

"No," she said, thinking of how she had come to hate going home alone to her house in Point Blank. "You're not the only one." She put her own hand over his, feeling the long bones of his fingers as she had wanted to ever since she met him.

He gripped her arm as though to pull her toward him, then closed his eyes and said in a flat, subdued voice, "Let's get this other matter over with first." Then a grin flickered across his face. "Business before pleasure."

Beth Marie, who seemed to have lost all ability to move, tried to focus on the mug in her lap in order to slow her breathing.

"We'll do this the easy way," he went on briskly, reaching into the pocket of the denim jacket he'd thrown across the back of the sofa and extracting something. "My electronic memory. Never leave home without it." He placed a small black plastic box on the sofa between them. "Speak right into the microphone, Miss Cartwright," he said, straining for a joke. "Take your time. You don't have to rush. It's voice-activated."

Beth Marie stared at the small machine. "Where should I start?" she asked hoarsely, and heard the machine whir into action. "I'm afraid you'll have to help me. I've never been the interviewee before."

"You like being the one asking the questions? The one in control?"

She shrugged. "Don't most people?"

"Probably." He looked at her from under his eyebrows as he adjusted the volume control on the recorder. "But some things you can only experience by yielding control."

He waited, and she knew he was watching the vein pulsing in her throat. She dropped her eyes to her lap.

"Now then," he said, glancing at the little machine, "I think that should be about right. Let's start at the beginning. Don't go too fast. We'll take it easy. I'll prompt you if you need it."

So she began at what she took to be the beginning, telling him about arriving at the Bromley Unit, about Mindy and the other members of the group, about the long prison corridors and the sign about hostages. She described the chapel and the men who had been waiting for them there. Father Kamowski's homily. The response of the small, monkey-faced man. She felt herself struggling to find not just any words for him, but the best, the plummiest, the ones most laden with texture and taste, words that would be equal to the reality she'd found there.

When she would pause or turn away in frustration, Geoff would lean toward her, murmuring something, the meaning of which didn't matter as much as the urging she felt in his voice. When she had finished she sat back and took a deep breath, feeling slightly disheveled and exhausted by the effort.

"That was great," he said, leaning back into his corner of the sofa. He was smiling, but his eyes had narrowed as though he were already thinking of something else, speculating. "You won't mind if I transcribe this, will you? Use some of your own words?"

"No. Of course not. Why should I?" The surge of energy she'd been coasting on made her feel bountiful, extravagant. She picked up the tray with their mugs. "I'll make more coffee."

"Do you want anything to eat?" she asked from the doorway.

Geoff smiled crookedly and shook his head.

There were no blinds or shades covering the many windows in the kitchen, and the cold had seeped in through the glass. Beth Marie shivered as she spooned coffee into the filter and ran the water. She kept her eyes on the coffeemaker as the dark liquid ran into the glass container, afraid if she turned to look at the table she might see Norton there. Or her mother. She took a deep breath and held it. Then suddenly she felt, not what she had been anticipating, but something like a hiss, as though the atmosphere were leaking away through a small fissure. She shivered again.

When she brought the tray back into the living room, she found Geoff stretched out on the sofa. His face was turned to the side, but she could tell from his steady breathing that he was asleep. She stood looking down at him for a moment. The small recorder had disappeared. She took the tray back into the kitchen, lowered it carefully to the counter, turned off the light, and went upstairs.

Methodically she undressed, washed her face, brushed her teeth, staring at her face in the mirror. "What a fool you are," she said. For the first time it occurred to her to think about the other voice she'd heard in the background when she'd talked to Geoff on the phone that afternoon.

What happens to *her* on Sunday afternoons? she wondered.


The cold had penetrated the metal skin of the trailer so that Ignacio could not sleep. He had put on all the clothes he had—a couple of T-shirts, a flannel shirt, a pair of khaki pants over his jeans—still he could not get warm. He was afraid to light the charcoal for a fire. Gordo had told him of a man he worked with once who had died from the fumes of a charcoal fire he kept burning under his bed in a bunkhouse.

Finally he got up and went outside to look at the stars shining like shards of ice caught in the bare arms of the trees. They seemed to speak directly to him.

This is why I could not sleep, he thought. They had something to tell me. Do not be afraid, Ignacio. Set your heart like a splinter of ice in the sky. Then nothing can touch you. You will shine. Everyone will see your brightness, but they will not be able to reach you or tarnish you. You will shine with a clear brightness.

"*Si*," he whispered aloud. "*Las estrellas del hielo*." Then he started walking down the path that led away from the trailer.

It took less than half an hour to reach the house in Point Blank, but as he approached it from the field across the road, he sensed something different and stopped, frowning. He bent under the fence wire and made his way across the gravel cautiously. The shadow in the driveway. That was it. It was longer than usual, and lower. As he came closer, he could make out the details of the car. His frown deepened. It was not the automobile he knew, not the *senora's*, but another. He tilted his head slightly, listening, but heard nothing. Even the crickets were quiet in this cold.

Slowly, he crept all the way around the Mustang, running his hand along the doors and fenders. Long, he thought, but not as long as the white Lincoln of the Hidalgos. He looked at the house. It was completely dark.

He made his way to the garage. The woman never put her car in the garage, not since he'd been there, but he edged the door open far enough to slip inside. Empty.

The dark seemed closer here, even warmer. In the back corner, he knew, was an old quilt, used to wrap pipes to keep them from freezing. He pulled it down from the exposed rafter, wrapped himself in it, and lay down on a piece of scrap plywood. Gradually he grew warmer.

His eyes had only been closed a few minutes when he heard the back door open carefully. Ignacio lifted his head, then stood up, still clutching the quilt around him. Creeping to the small window, he looked out. The door of the automobile opened, the light inside came on, and he saw a tall, thin man slide into the driver's seat and pull the door shut quietly. He started the engine and backed out of the driveway. The lights of the car did not come on until it was almost to the highway.

Ignacio hunched the quilt over his shoulders and lay down again. Gradually the frown faded as he stared up at the ceiling. The man he had seen leaving, he had been with the woman in the house that night. A smile relaxed the muscles of his face. He need not have been concerned. "*Puta*," he said with grim satisfaction.

# CHAPTER EIGHT

CECELIA RAMSEY HAD BEEN THE one person Beth Marie felt she could call the next morning to take her across the river to Belle's Marina so she could retrieve her car. Some time before dawn she had heard Geoff Granger's Mustang start up in the driveway, and then the sound of its engine growing gradually fainter in the distance. She had pulled the comforter over her head to shut out the growing light, feeling stuck someplace between disappointment and relief.

Cecelia Ramsey was seventy or better, an old friend of her mother's who had taken on Beth Marie as a project when Catherine Cartwright died. But unlike Beth Marie's own mother, Cecelia never demanded explanations.

On the way to the marina, she told Cecelia only that she'd been working on a story there with someone Sunday evening who'd had car trouble. Then she stared pointedly out the window, knowing Cecelia wouldn't ask any more questions if she made it evident they weren't welcome. Instead, the older woman chattered over-brightly about the upcoming Thanksgiving dinner at the Baptist Church, put on every year for the Point Blank community.

"I'd love for you to come, honey. That is, if you think you have time. I know how busy you are now at the paper. That piece you did on the Disabled Veterans came out this morning. It looked real good."

Beth Marie mumbled her thanks and rubbed her forehead. She already had a splitting headache. It got worse when she remembered the note she'd found on the kitchen counter. *Thanks for your help last night. Sorry to have to leave like this but I've got a deadline in Houston.* It was signed "GG." She'd crumpled it and thrown it in the wastebasket under the sink.

"Where is that turn, honey?" Cecelia was asking now. "I've never been over here to La Belle's Marina before. It used to have a real bad reputation, you know. I guess it's not like that anymore," she added quickly. "Someone told me they used to have cockfights there. That was probably before they outlawed them though. They don't still have cockfights there, do they?"

Beth Marie shook her head and shrugged simultaneously, then stared steadily out the side window. She hated to lie outright to Cecelia.

"I don't think I could stand to watch one, do you?" Cecelia continued. "Or a bullfight either. Men are so strange, aren't they, sweetheart?"

"I just had to meet someone there. About a story," she repeated.

"You mean like on TV? Where reporters have to get information from contacts in the underworld?" Cecelia looked at her anxiously.

"No, no. It was nothing dangerous," Beth Marie said, forcing herself to smile. She patted the older woman's shoulder as they drew up into the caliche parking lot where the Toyota sat marooned. "Thanks for bringing me, Cecelia. What would I do without you?"

On the trip into Somerville, however, she found herself pondering, not just life without Cecelia, but more generally, life without the boundaries she'd lived within for over thirty years. If she could only be like her mother—not caring what other people thought, setting her own standards, always certain she was right. Beth Marie had never resented the tall, erect woman who had always stood like an immovable marker amid the turbulent current of life. At least not since junior high. But she wasn't sure she wanted to cling to that stable point any longer. The sensation of turning loose, of being whirled away downstream, seemed more and more desirable. *Some things you can only experience by yielding control,* Geoff had said. How could she ever find out unless she let go?

A small sheaf of pink telephone messages waited on her desk. She flipped through them hurriedly, searching for a Houston area code in the "call back" slot. They were all local. She dropped her briefcase on the floor by her chair and sat down heavily. Why was she already disappointed in a job that only last week she'd been excited about?

She flipped the switch on the computer terminal and, while she was waiting for it to boot up, flipped through the phone messages again. A school board member. The AARP secretary. Someone whose unusual name the receptionist had underlined three times—which must mean it had been spelled wrong in the paper. A note that her Girl Scout cookie order was in. And one message with a number that seemed vaguely familiar. After the number was scribbled "Fr. K?" It must be the number for St. Barnabas.

For some reason she put that slip aside and returned all the other calls first, even the one from the disgruntled reader whose name in a list of pallbearers had been misspelled. Finally she looked at the remaining pink patch on her desk, sighed, and stabbed out the number.

Father Kamowski answered on the second ring, mumbling the church's name so indistinctly she wouldn't have recognized it if she hadn't already known what he was saying.

"This is Beth Marie Cartwright," she said, "from the *Courier*."

"And St. Barnabas?"

She hesitated. "Yes," she said more sharply than she'd intended. For some reason, the query irritated her.

"Just making sure. I was wondering if you might be free for lunch today?"

"Let me check," she said matter-of-factly, staring at her appointment calendar, blank so far. "Yes. If it's not too early."

"What about one? The Texas Cafe on the square."

It had absolutely the worst food in town. It was also the first place she'd gone with Norton. "Why not?"

"Good. I have a favor to ask," he said just before he hung up.

"Of course," she said to herself, putting down the receiver. "That always goes with lunch, doesn't it?"

She worked so intently throughout the morning that she almost forgot about the appointment and arrived at the Texas Cafe a little after one and slightly out of breath.

The priest scraped back his chair and stood up, looming over her till she sat down. He already had a hamburger the size of a Frisbee in front of him.

"Just a glass of milk," she said to the waitress who had shuffled to the table.

"You gotta eat more than that," Father Kamowski said. "Busy as you are. Probably don't cook much at home either, do you? Here. Have some french fries." He shoved a plate with a tumbled grid of potatoes toward her.

She picked one up, pointedly pressed it against the paper napkin to remove the excess grease, and bit it in half.

Kamowski shook his head. "I don't understand you modern women," he said. "How do you keep body and soul together?"

"Just trying to keep healthy," she said, forcing lightness into her tone.

He picked up his hamburger, letting the juices drip onto the plate before he raised it to his mouth. "How'd you like the closing last night?"

So he had noticed her there. "It was—" she groped for words— "an interesting experience."

He looked at her bleakly, his mouth working like a cement mixer.

"I mean I'd never been inside a prison before."

He shook his head, swallowed, and ran his tongue between his upper lip and gums. "Really."

Feeling as if she'd offended him in some way she added, "Your sermon, homily, whatever, it was very good."

He nodded once and took another bite.

"And the man who spoke at the end."

"Nightstick."

"What?"

"That's what they call him on the inside. Nightstick."

Beth Marie looked down, turning her glass slowly. She wasn't about to ask why.

"Quite a bunch we had this time," he went on as if not noticing her silence. "Boss Man. Pronto Bronco. Ultimate Warrior."

"Pretty tough bunch, huh?"

"Tough?" He swallowed half his cup of coffee while he considered. "I guess. If you mean would they kill you in a fight, sure. Being tough is their only defense against terror. It's harder for them guys to trust somebody than to kill 'em. When you don't feel like you can trust anybody and you think everybody is out to get you, tough is all you've got to fall back on. Get the other guy before he gets you. They're only tough because they're scared."

She shivered. "I'd be scared too."

He wiped his mouth, then put the napkin down

deliberately. "You wouldn't last long then. Not if you showed it. You either gotta get tough or get on the other side of the fear."

She looked up at him, wondering what he might mean by that.

"You still single, Beth Marie?"

She stiffened and sat back in her chair.

"Sorry. I guess that wasn't very polite." He pushed his plate to one side and folded his beefy forearms along the table's edge. "I was just curious. I mean now that I'm the priest at St. Barnabas, at least for a few months, I'm trying to get to know the parishioners."

Deliberately, she kept silent and waited.

"When you didn't come along to supper last night, I thought you might have a prospect."

"A prospect?"

"Mindy said you were meeting someone."

"It was professional."

"I see. Well. You have to excuse an old dinosaur like me, putting my foot in it. I guess it's as hard for me to understand young folks today as it is for you to understand prisoners." He shuffled the salt and pepper shakers to the opposite side of the table and cleared his throat to signal a shift in direction. "What I'd like to know is if you'd do a feature on St. Barnabas's building campaign. Ordinarily I wouldn't ask this kind of favor, but the vestry's been on my back to do something, get us some free publicity."

"I'd say St. Barnabas has had more than its share of publicity lately. What else could they want?" She felt a small surge of pleasure at turning the tables on him suddenly. Actually, she was only vaguely aware of the scandal surrounding the previous rector who'd been killed in the fire that had destroyed the church. Since she'd met Norton, she'd lost touch with what was going on at St. Barnabas.

"That's not the kind of publicity that helps raise

money for a building fund. The vestry wants to be able to hit up the bigwigs in town. I guess they want their image shined up a little before they go around holding out the hat to local businessmen." The priest looked sideways out the window, as though to disavow any personal involvement in the project.

"How long do you plan to stay at St. Barnabas yourself?" Beth Marie asked abruptly. She wasn't even certain how long Father Kamowski had been serving as the interim priest at St. Barnabas nor had she taken much interest in the plans for a new building.

The priest looked back at his plate and shrugged. "Till the bishop tells me to pack up and move on, I guess. I came to town to do a funeral, and I've been here ever since. Like the man who came to dinner." He shook his head and reached for several limp french fries from the cold plate.

"How do you like it here?" She noticed herself slipping into the interviewer mode. Geoff was right. She was more comfortable asking the questions.

He jerked his head sideways to indicate relative indifference. "It's a job."

She blinked at this.

"You expected maybe a holy answer?" he said, sitting back and smiling. "So what's not holy about a job?"

The waitress shuffled up to the table. "Anything else I can get you folks?"

Beth Marie, feeling maybe it would be worth her while to talk longer with the priest, ordered soup.

"I guess you're right," she said when the waitress had gone. "I just never heard a member of the clergy describe it that way before."

"You never heard them at home then." His massive chest heaved in a silent chuckle. Then he asked suddenly, "What about your work?"

"Mine? You mean at the paper?"

"Sure. What do you do it for?"

She made a disparaging face. "It pays the bills."

"What paid the bills before?"

"I used to keep the books for the Water Board in Point Blank. There're not many bills. I inherited my mother's house there. My father died when I was twelve and left me a small trust." She looked up. "You're right. I don't do it just for the money. I guess it's as much for the excitement as anything."

"Excitement?" he echoed, his tone indicating he found it hard to believe there could be much excitement connected with the *Somerville Courier*.

"Compared to Point Blank, yes," she said a little stiffly.

"Okay. So write a nice story about St. Barnabas. But don't make it too exciting. The vestry wouldn't like that either."

They both laughed, and she felt the tension between them ease momentarily.

"You probably got some other excitement going in your life too." Kamowski's statement was really a question.

Why did he have to keep coming back to that? "Not really." She kept her eyes on the table as the waitress slid a bowl in front of her.

"Somebody told me you're dating a deputy sheriff here in town."

She picked up her spoon carefully. "Yes."

"Not much happening there, huh?"

She looked up now, her face flushed with anger and embarrassment.

"Sorry," he said immediately. "I mean it's your business, of course," he went on clumsily. "Maybe you don't want to talk about it."

Beth Marie didn't know whether to laugh or get up and leave. If he had seemed more priestly, had displayed some pastoral aplomb, she might have taken the occasion to confide her confusion to him. As it was, she only felt vexed. Next he'd be telling her he didn't understand young folks today. She was used to the older people in Point Blank expressing their bewilderment at what they called "the modern world." Hadn't she stayed there so long herself because she felt out of place anywhere else? But a priest—he might have been her own father—should do better than bungle his way through this clumsy conversation. He was no help at all.

"I'm sorry," he mumbled again.

"We're not engaged, if that's what you mean."

"But you want to marry this deputy?" He asked the question with as much candor as a child.

She laughed outright. "Why? You think you can arrange it?"

He shrugged and made a comic face.

"Anyway," she dipped her spoon in her soup, "I'm not sure I want to."

"Marry him?"

"Marry anyone."

"There. You see?" He slapped the table suddenly with a hamlike palm. "That's what I don't understand. I mean, if it's a career you're after, I can understand that. But what is it you want?"

She looked up at him evenly. "That's the point. I'm not sure what I want, all right? I've only just begun to explore my options. I've lived all my life out in the boon-docks. Now that I've just started to break out, why should I lock myself up again? I feel like I'm only beginning to experience life."

"Experience life?" he echoed, apparently undismayed by her outburst. "What've you been experiencing up till now?"

"Okay. A different kind of life."

"How is it different? I mean, just because it's different, well, there's all kinds of different. Life in prison is different. You want to experience that too?"

"No. And I wouldn't jump off a ten-story building

just because my friends do," she said in a singsong voice and stabbed the spoon into the soup, splattering red liquid onto the tabletop.

The priest reached over and began mopping it up in a preoccupied way. "So what kind of different do you mean?" He appeared not to have noticed her pique.

She thought for a long moment, then said, "Exciting."

He looked up quickly. "I see. And you think this deputy might be too dull. You want to test him out against some others. See how he measures up before you commit yourself."

"He hasn't committed *himself* yet."

"But even if he did—"

"If he did . . . well . . . wouldn't I wonder the rest of my life?" She looked out the window, pondering. "When I first met him, I guess I would have married him on the spot. I was absolutely overwhelmed. But—" she turned back to the table, "now he just seems to have settled in and gotten comfortable. Like he expects me to be there."

"And you are."

She looked away quickly. "I know. But what am I supposed to—" She stopped abruptly and picked up her spoon again.

"You might try telling him."

"Tell him what? Issue him some kind of ultimatum? Marry me or else? Great. I mean if he can't come up with the idea on his own—"

"But as things stand now, why should he?"

Beth Marie stared at the fleshy, drooping folds of his face. "Well, maybe he's not even the one I want anyway. After all, he's so—" She fluttered her fingers as though extricating them from something sticky.

"Law-abiding?"

She made a face. "I guess so. I guess that's it."

The priest sat back, shoving his chair slightly away

from the table so that he could cross his long legs. "I see," he said. So. It wasn't the deputy who had been waiting for her last night.

Beth Marie got back to the *Courier* around three with a couple of sheets of smudged paper the priest had shoved into her hand as they parted. It appeared that someone on the St. Barnabas vestry had already written up the kind of story they wanted the paper to print. She dropped it onto the desk of the reporter who normally did the religion page on Saturdays and tried to put her meeting with Father Kamowski out of her mind.

She went to the restroom, splashed water on her face, and patched up her makeup. Then she shook her head vigorously to make her hair look tousled, sprayed it in place that way, and went back to her desk. She'd just turned on the computer terminal to begin work when Sandy, the receptionist, called from the front desk.

"A surprise for you, Beth Marie," she said coyly.

Beth Marie hit the standby key and made her way through the maze of other desks to the foyer. Sandy handed her a long white box. "The florist just delivered them. You must have an admirer."

Beth Marie looked through the cellophane window. Roses. Yellow ones. At least a dozen. She smiled weakly at Sandy, and took them back to her desk.

On the small card inside was written in an awkward, round hand the message that must have been dictated over the phone, "With both my gratitude and apologies, GG." She wished it had been in his own spiky writing. Then maybe she could have read between the lines.

# CHAPTER • NINE

ON THURSDAY IGNACIO FINALLY decided to go to the food bank in Somerville. He had hoped to take enough food from the woman's kitchen to sustain the two of them for at least a week, believing that she would soon restock her nearly empty shelves. But the days came and went, and still the woman seemed to live on air. No new cans appeared on the shelves, no milk or egg cartons in the refrigerator. She must do all her eating in town, he decided. At fancy restaurants where her lovers took her.

She had paid him the previous weekend and told him he had now completed all the work she had for him. She had looked worried as she told him this, not realizing that he had intentionally spaced out the cultivation of her flowerbeds and fruit trees so that his tasks would be completed according to his own schedule, not hers. He had received both her money and apology with equal coldness. I do not need the pity of a whore, he thought as she counted the bills into his hand.

Already he had taken quilts from the unused bedroom on the second floor of her house, hoping those had not been contaminated by unholy love. In the closet of that same room he had found a pair of men's shoes which almost fit him. He had taken them, the soles of his own boots having worn through so that he had to patch them with cardboard. The shoes in the closet were coated thickly with dust as if they had not been worn in many years.

The mission that housed the food bank was only a block from the looming red walls of the prison in Somerville. A farmer had picked him up on the highway, and Ignacio could feel the blank face of the block-long building watching him as he climbed down over the tail-gate of the pickup. It was not the prison that had held his mother, but Ignacio felt it knew somehow what his intention was, though it could only watch him mutely.

Inside the white frame mission, the air was stuffy. A woman at a desk took his name, checked it against another sheet of paper, then led him down a hallway to a larger room where the walls were lined with cans of food and clear plastic packets filled with flour, sugar, and pow-dered milk.

"How many?" she asked, turning toward him. "How many in your family?"

He stared at her, startled by the question.

"Do you have a wife?"

He continued to stare.

"*Tiene esposa? Una chica?*"

He dropped his head, unable to meet the woman's eyes. She must have taken this for a nod of affirmation because she set about methodically dropping cans and packets into a paper bag. When she had filled it, she turned to him again. "*Muchachas?*"

He shook his head quickly.

"Good," the woman muttered to herself. "I hate to think of little ones cold and hungry."

He took the sack from her and left abruptly, too embarrassed for gratitude. Down the street was a Dairy Queen. He went inside where it was warm and began transferring the items in the sack to the string bag he had brought with him. He knew the paper sack would not hold up for the trip back out to the horse farm. He could hitchhike most of the way, but he would still have to walk a couple of miles.

"Hey!"

Startled, he looked up at the man leaning across the counter and then around at the empty tables.

"No, you. You want to order something?" The man's tone was harsh.

Ignacio stuck his hand in his jeans pocket, feeling for the money.

"You want to order something, okay. Otherwise, you get on out of here, you understand? This ain't no halfway house."

At that moment the glass door swung open again and a man in a blue windbreaker came in. He was huge, and it wasn't until he unzipped his jacket that Ignacio saw he was a priest.

Raising one large palm in greeting, the priest said, "How's it going, Jack? Got any coffee been made this week?" The man behind the counter turned toward the coffee machine.

The priest caught Ignacio's eye and nodded. It was only a brief glance, but Ignacio felt the eyes probe him just below his collar. He dumped the rest of the sack's contents hurriedly into the string bag. He wanted to get out; the priest made him nervous.

Unfortunately, one of the plastic packets of sugar missed the bag and tumbled to the floor. It must have caught the sharp edge of the table. When he picked it up, a white stream poured from a rip in the side.

"Hey you!" The man behind the counter shoved a styrofoam cup toward the priest with one hand and pointed the other at Ignacio. "I already told you. Either you order something here or get out. *Comprende?* Vamoose!"

The priest frowned, swinging his big head toward Ignacio. Then turning back to the counter he said, "Pour me another one, Jack," and moved toward Ignacio who had dropped to his knees, trying to scoop the sugar back into the plastic bag.

"Here." The priest set the cup of hot coffee on the table. Then he went back to the counter and waited till the man in the apron poured another cup and slid it across to him. The man did not look pleased, but he said nothing.

The priest looked up at the faded menu over his head. "I'll take one of those basket things too," he said. "Chicken fingers. If you got 'em."

The man behind the counter muttered something else, and the priest pulled his wallet from his hip pocket, opened it, and left a single bill on the counter while he went back to Ignacio's table and slid onto the bench on the far side. He was not smiling and he did not offer to help, but merely watched as Ignacio twisted a plastic strip around the hole in the packet.

"*Habla ingles?*" he asked.

Ignacio, his eyes darting from the bag to the priest's face and then down again, jerked his head sideways once to indicate no.

"Too bad," the priest went on. "I don't speak Spanish either. But sit down anyway. *Siente se.*" Ignacio's eyes darted from side to side. Then he slowly lowered himself onto the bench across from the priest.

The priest moved the extra cup directly in front of Ignacio and nodded toward it. "Drink up."

Ignacio stared at the cup for a long moment, then raised it to his mouth.

The priest leaned forward over his beefy forearms. "I see you been to the mission. You staying there?" He nodded at the string bag beside Ignacio on the bench. "*La mision. El Buen Past*or."

"*Si,*" Ignacio said, and looked down.

The priest covered his mouth with a large hand and raised one eyebrow.

Ignacio could smell the hot grease from the grill behind the counter. He kept his eyes down so that the man across the table could not tell how much the smell affected him. It made him dizzy, it had been so long since he'd had any hot food. He took a sip of the hot coffee. He knew he should leave now. He should not stay here where people could look at him and fix his face in their memories. He started to stand up.

"Wait!" The priest spoke sharply. "I got you some food coming here. *La*—damn, what's the word?—*comida. La comida. Por tu.* It's been a long time since you've had a hot meal from the looks of you. But you ain't staying at the mission either, son. They don't give out sacks of staples if you're staying there. That's only for people living somewhere else." He put his big hand across his mouth again and looked at Ignacio closely.

The cook was coming from around the counter carrying a red plastic basket fluted with paper. Ignacio could see rectangles of crisp fried meat sticking up above the paper. The aroma made him weak. He stood up. He didn't look at the priest. "*Gracias*," he said and picked up the string bag.

Kamowski watched as the door swung closed behind the boy. A slip of paper lay on the floor where it had fallen out of the boy's sack as he transferred the food to his string bag. Kamowski picked it up and examined it—a form filled out at the mission. He glanced at the name, then used the slip to sweep the spilled sugar from the table.

The cook set the plastic basket down. "Don't fool with that. I'll get it. Dirty Mes'cun. How long you reckon it'll be before he's back inside? Getcha anything else, padre?"

Kamowski shook his head and stuck the paper in his shirt pocket. He was watching the figure with the string bag make his way across the parking lot and then cut behind a defunct carwash down the street. He knew, though he did not want to say this to the cook, that the boy had not been in prison. The man might want to argue the point, and Kamowski didn't want to explain how he knew.

Beth Marie hadn't seen Norton since the yellow roses arrived. He had called the office several times that week, but she had either been out or just leaving. Wednesday evening there had been a message from him on her machine at home, but she was tired and went to bed without returning his call. There was no message from Geoff.

Thursday morning she sat at her desk, chewing on a pencil and staring into space. Should she or shouldn't she? In the back of her mind she could hear her mother's voice—*girls don't call boys, Beth Marie. Not young ladies, at any rate.* But that had been almost twenty years ago. Young ladies did a lot of things now that Catherine Cartwright would never have approved of. Beth Marie picked up the phone.

It rang three times, and she was on the point of hanging up before the machine could answer when a voice—a man's, but not Geoff's—said, "Hi. I'm on my way now."

"Excuse me?" Beth Marie said.

"Oh, I'm sorry. I thought it was Geoff. He's waiting for me—well, never mind. Who is this? What can I do for you?" The voice was bright, even effervescent.

"This is Beth Marie Cartwright. From the *Somerville Courier.* Geoff and I were . . . working together on a project. I tried his office first—" It was a necessary lie, she told herself.

"Yes." A short pause. "He said you might call."

"I just wanted to thank him for the roses. They were beautiful."

"He sent you roses?" The voice on the other end sounded amused. "That's nice."

"Um. You don't know when he might be in, do you?" She could hear her voice begin to falter.

"Yes," he said, and stopped.

"Well, I'd, uh, like to thank him. That is, if he'll be in later this evening," she forced herself to go on.

"Why don't I just tell him for you, honey? We won't be in till quite late. And we won't want to be disturbed then." The bubbles of cheer had evaporated, and there was an edge to his voice now. "Believe me, it would be better that way."

"I don't understand—"

"No, you don't, do you? I was afraid you might not. A regular little Laura Ingalls Wilder there in your little house on the prairie. Or is it the big woods. Well, this is the big city, honey. Let me spell it out for you."

And he did. Not in great detail, but enough to make Beth Marie slowly lower the receiver to the cradle and sit staring at it for several minutes. Then she buzzed the front desk, told Sandy she'd be gone for about an hour, and left by the back door so that she wouldn't have to speak to anyone.

She drove around aimlessly for a while—out toward the interstate, then north on a farm road, and finally back into town through Gospell Hill, what had been the black section of town since the Civil War. Downtown, she circled the square, noting the old storefront St. Barnabas was currently using, then veered off into a side street. Finally she ended up in the parking lot at the sheriff's department.

She had only intended to see if Norton's patrol car was there, but just as she pulled in, he came down the back steps of the building. Edging the Toyota alongside the curb where he waited, hands on his hips, she rolled down the window. He bent down, bracing his arms on the car roof.

"Hello, stranger," he said in the stiff way that meant he was smarting from her neglect but would never admit it.

"Hi." The single syllable came out sounding more forlorn than she'd intended.

"What's up?"

All of a sudden she couldn't speak. She looked down at her hands in her lap, praying she wouldn't start to cry.

"What's the matter, Beth Marie?" There was rising concern in Norton's voice, and when she didn't answer but merely shook her head, not looking at him, he jerked open the car door. "Here. Move over. Tell me what's wrong."

She started to say that it was nothing really, that she was all right, but he already had one hand on the steering wheel and was motioning her peremptorily across to the passenger seat. She had to climb across the gearshift panel, feeling awkward and foolish. Then, as she collapsed against the passenger door and saw Norton looking as alarmed as if there'd been a death in the family, the absurdity of the whole situation hit her and she began to laugh.

How could she ever tell him that she was upset because the romance she'd daydreamed about all week long had turned out to be a chimera? How could she tell him that she hadn't returned his calls because she'd been fantasizing a love affair with a sophisticated city reporter who, as it turned out, wasn't interested in women at all? How could she ever explain just how ridiculous, how mortified, she felt? All she could do was laugh.

Norton stared at her. "What? What is it?"

She kept laughing, putting one hand vertically over her mouth, grimacing and shaking her head to indicate that she was powerless to stop. Finally the tears started to come. At first it was a matter of laughing until she was crying. Then she was simply crying. Her head drooped and her shoulders started to shake.

Norton reached across the car and took her by the shoulders. She could tell he was restraining himself from shaking her. He gripped her shoulders tightly through her coat and then pulled her toward him. The gearshift was still between them, but she buried her face in his shoulder.

"It's going to be all right, Beth Marie," he said. "Whatever it is, it's going to be all right." He reached into his pocket and pulled out a handkerchief for her, still taking care to keep her head cradled against him.

When she had finally stopped inhaling in sharp little gasps, she sat up and blew her nose.

He glanced darkly at her, then put the car in gear and pulled out of the parking lot.

"Where are we going?" she asked, still sniffing.

"My place."

She started to protest that she was all right now, but he ignored her, and a couple of minutes later they were pulling up in front of his apartment building. He came around the car, opened the door, and half-lifted her out.

"Norton, really, I'm all right," she said, but he took hold of her arm and guided her up the stairs ahead of him.

He unlocked the door and stepped aside for her to enter first. Sweeping newspapers off the sofa, he gently forced her to sit and then disappeared into the kitchen.

She knew this determined mood of his. What should she tell him, she wondered, listening to him run water in the kitchen. The truth was out of the question, not just because it would make her look so ridiculous, but because it would be painful to him. She couldn't possibly tell him she'd been infatuated with someone else—especially someone who turned out to be gay.

Norton came back from the kitchen with a glass of water and a couple of aspirin. "Here," he said, sitting down beside her. "Take these. You always get a headache after you cry."

She glanced at him, surprised that he would remember a detail like that, then swallowed the tablets.

"I'm sorry, Norton." She sighed heavily. "I don't know what got into me."

He said nothing, though his eyes never left her face.

"I . . . I've been under a lot of strain with the new job. I'm not sure if they like my work."

He still said nothing.

"I, uh, had a tiff with Sandy, the receptionist." It was all she could think of on the spur of the moment.

"The receptionist?" His tone sounded incredulous.

"Yes. She failed to give me an important message. It meant that I missed an important interview." Where in the world had that come from?

Norton shifted a little on the sofa and frowned. "An important interview? How important can any interview in Somerville be? Are you sure you're not overreacting? Who was it with anyway? That kind of thing can be fixed. Just reschedule."

"Yeah, well." She closed her eyes and leaned back on the sofa as though she were wearily resigning herself to being misunderstood. Maybe he wouldn't ask her any more.

"No. I mean, really. Who was it with anyway? Can't you fix it?"

She opened her eyes and stared at the ceiling. "That's not the point, Norton. What I don't understand is why Sandy didn't tell me this fellow had called back. And no. It can't be fixed. It's not like it was a city councilman or something." The story was gradually taking shape in her imagination now.

"Come on, Beth Marie. Are you sure you're not being paranoid? Isn't it possible that the receptionist just forgot? Surely she's not out to get you. And who in Somerville has such a full schedule that he can't work you in somehow?"

She lifted her head and managed to look offended. "Maybe it's not someone from Somerville, Norton. Has that occurred to you?"

He sat back now, smiling. She could tell he was relieved she was getting over her agitation. And if he had only been content to leave it there, the complications that arose later might have been avoided.

"So who was this mystery man?" he laughed. "A hog

farmer from Point Blank? The Dodge dealer from Masonville?"

She sat up and slid to the edge of the sofa, stung by his comments. "You put me in a difficult position sometimes, Norton. I can't always reveal my sources, you know. Particularly not to you."

"What? You mean this is some criminal you were supposed to meet?"

She stood up and walked to the window, aware that she was being dramatic now. With her back to him, she even smiled. "I just can't say any more about it."

She heard him snort and mutter something. She held her breath, hoping he would believe this, the perfect dead-end to his inquiries.

Another minute went by in silence. Then he exhaled dejectedly, and she could tell she'd won.

"Okay, Beth Marie. I know it won't do any good to try to talk you out of whatever it is you're up to. But be careful. Sometimes you imagine life is a lot more romantic than it is. And there's nothing romantic about criminals, believe me." He stood up and came to the window where she was looking down at a pair of mockingbirds flitting in and out of the pyracantha bushes below.

He was so close she could feel his breath stir the wisps of hair on the back of her neck. She recalled how Geoff Granger had kissed her after the cockfight, and once again she felt a scalding wave of humiliation sweep over her. The reporter had seen how fascinated she'd been with him—she'd made it pretty obvious—and he had used that, used her. The image of the defeated ginger rooster flashed into her mind, and she caught her breath sharply.

Norton put a hand on her shoulder. "You're sure you're all right?"

She nodded. Then, with a sudden inspiration, she turned to him. "Absolutely. It's just the stress I'm not used to. Tell you what. Why don't you come out tomorrow evening. I could cook. Wouldn't you like that? Then we could just relax."

It was her ultimate gesture of goodwill. She knew Norton loved her house, and liked it when she made dinner for him occasionally. He was, she had learned, a homebody without a real home. His mother had died when he was eight, and he and a younger brother had grown up as best they could, moving from one rented house to another with a vagabond father who'd named his sons Burlington and Great Northern for the railroads he still missed. Norton had told her how he'd feared his dad might move on one day and simply forget to take him and his brother along.

His hand was still on her shoulder. The concern on his face began to lighten, and he started to pull her toward him. Then he froze, and his eyes went to the window again, frowning.

"What's the matter?"

"I've got to go out of town tomorrow."

"Again?"

He looked down guiltily. "Yes. Another seminar. The sheriff pulled some strings to get me into this one. DNA matching. At the U of H."

"All weekend?" she said flatly.

"Yes." He caught at her hand and she let him take it, limply.

It was all she could do not to cry again. What am I, some kind of pariah? she thought. Then suddenly she looked up at him, her face hopeful once more.

"What if I went with you, Norton?" she asked softly and reached up to finger the collar of his shirt. "We could stay someplace really nice. The Galleria. That would be close for you, and I could shop."

He raised her hand to his lips, kissed it, and held it against his cheek. His eyes were locked on her face. "You mean that, don't you? You're not just teasing."

"Yes." She felt ready to collapse.

He lowered her hand slowly, keeping the tips of her fingers in his grasp. His eyes didn't waver. "I'd give my right arm to take you, Beth Marie. But Sheriff Dooley's going too. He's already got us signed up to share a dormitory room at the university."

She pulled her hand away and tried to smile. "Of course." She wanted to sound offhand, as if it truly didn't matter, but her voice was rougher, harder than she could help. "I understand." She turned away. "I've got to get back now. Thanks, Norton. You're always—" She fluttered her hands, indicating some vague quality, "helpful," and started toward the door.

"Beth Marie!" He caught the doorknob before she could turn it. "Look. You've got to believe me. The weekend after this we'll—"

"It's fine, Norton, really. Please. I understand. It's no big deal." She kissed him lightly on the chin. "Now really, I've got to get back."

Norton stood in the doorway watching her trip down the stairs and stride purposefully across the parking lot to her car. He'd have to call someone to come pick him up and take him back to the department now, but he hadn't dared to remind her of that. Something in all this wasn't quite right; something wasn't fitting. Beth Marie was a strange combination of caution and recklessness, but she had never made such an offer before. Going away for the weekend together. What had prompted it now? Was she really getting mixed up in something dangerous?

But this worry gave way to the vision of what might have been if only he hadn't volunteered to go to the seminar, or even if he hadn't talked the sheriff into going too. Then he and Beth Marie could have had their weekend together, away from the prying eyes of all her Point Blank neighbors.

"What a fool I am," he said aloud. It wouldn't be the last time he thought that.

# CHAPTER • TEN

NEVERTHELESS, WORRY NAGGED at him the next morning, so before he left town he called Beth Marie at the *Courier*.

"I'm sorry, but she's out of the office right now," the receptionist said. "May I have her return your call later?"

Norton pondered a moment. "This is Sandy, isn't it?" He sounded as though he'd be exceptionally pleased if it were.

"Yes." A pause and then eagerly, "And this is the sheriff, isn't it? I mean the deputy. Norton?"

"Sure is, Sandy. Say, could you just leave a message for Beth Cartwright from me?" He knew she'd dropped her middle name at the paper.

"Of course."

"Just say I called and that I'll get in touch as soon as I get back in town Sunday evening."

A conspiratorial chuckle on the other end made him feel he'd built enough rapport with the receptionist to say next, "And I hope she won't be doing anything dangerous while I'm gone."

"Dangerous?"

"You know. Secret meetings with underground agents. That kind of thing." He kept his tone light.

The receptionist laughed. "I don't think that's very likely. The garden club and the historical society are about as dangerous as Beth's assignments get."

"No calls from muttering men obviously trying to disguise their voices?"

"Hardly. Not unless you count the VFW representative and the Episcopal priest."

"Just checking up," Norton said.

"Well, there was the reporter from the *Texas Times* last week." She added this quickly, as though she were reluctant to end their conversation.

"Oh?"

"And then he—oh no. I guess I shouldn't say anything about that."

"About what?" The question came out sounding sharper than Norton had intended.

"Nothing, nothing. She'd kill me."

Norton hesitated, but decided not to press the young lady, even though she so obviously wanted to be pressed. He thanked her, putting extra warmth into his voice, and hung up. That was the trouble with women, he told himself. Half the time they meant something different from the words they used to say it.

He picked up his duffel bag and headed to the patrol car where Sheriff Dooley was waiting for him. Maybe he should have swallowed his pride and let the receptionist tell him about that reporter. He vaguely remembered Beth Marie mentioning last week some Houston reporter who was sniffing around some prison program her church was involved in. But the prison system was a political football reporters were always trying to find a new angle on. He hadn't paid much attention. Had there been more to it than that?

Stopping halfway down the steps to the parking lot, he considered going back to his office and calling the *Courier* again. But what would Sandy know about it? And he could see the sheriff waiting in the patrol car with the motor running. He went on down the steps, jerked the back door of the car open, flung his bag onto the floor, and crawled in front beside the sheriff.

"What's the matter, Norton?" Sheriff Dooley asked, grinning.

Norton muttered something indistinct and noncommittal.

The sheriff laughed, as though relishing his deputy's discomfort. "Don't forget this trip was your idea. I probably ain't gonna understand a word them professors say. They hadn't even invented this DNA stuff when I was in school. As best I remember, I didn't even pass high school chemistry."

Then he frowned and caught the deputy's eye in the rearview mirror. "But they is *some* chemistry I know about, Norton. I know you better get that little lady of yours tied up. Neither one of you getting any younger, you know that?"

Norton didn't answer. He was going to have a talk with Lurline, the dispatcher. She had relatives in Point Blank and somehow managed to keep the whole department updated on his personal life.

"When I was your age I already had two kids in school," the sheriff went on. "That Beth Marie, she may be a late bloomer, but let me tell you, she's ripening fast. That's the kind of chemistry I know about, Norton." He settled back and eased his boot down on the accelerator as they pulled onto the interstate. With a satisfied smile, he added, "Yep. You can talk all you want about this DNA malarkey, but it's the chemistry of life that counts, son."

Beth Marie got back to the office around four that afternoon and found Norton's message, faithfully recorded by Sandy, on her desk. She was sorry she'd made up the story involving the receptionist and, in a surge of remorse, considered suggesting the two of them go to a movie. But the prospect of spending the evening with someone ten years younger didn't appeal to her. It might not appeal to Sandy either. And, she thought, I certainly don't feel like any more rejection right now.

On the way home she stopped at the supermarket and, on a whim, filled up a basket with all the things she would have fixed for Norton if he had stayed in town. Maybe he'd get back early enough for dinner Sunday evening. No. She wasn't going to let herself think about that either. She'd only be setting herself up for disappointment.

As she carried the grocery sacks into the house, she briefly considered going someplace alone that night. What if she went to Belle's Marina by herself? She'd like to see Norton's face when she casually dropped that into the conversation next week.

—*So what did you do while I was gone?*

—*Oh, not much. Went out to Belle's Marina for a while. Danced with a couple of crazy Cajuns. Don't worry. I came home alone.*

But would she? She didn't know if she could trust herself anymore. Sometimes she imagined herself an arrow that had already been fitted to the string, the bow bent, ready to be launched on some dangerously erratic trajectory. She felt propelled by some force over which she had little control.

She set the sacks of groceries down on the kitchen counter with a sigh, recollecting what Geoff had said about giving up control. There were moments when that sounded like what she really wanted. To be the arrow in the hands of the bowman. If she could go on flying forever. Fly and never fall to the ground.


He had swept the floor as well as he could with the stubby broom he'd found in the abandoned horse barn and carried all the empty cans and bottles outside, where he'd dumped them on the pile behind the trailer. Then he'd spread out the quilts he'd taken from the unused bedroom in the woman's house. Keeping only one for himself, he laid the other two along the bench seat meant to serve also for the trailer's bed. The cushion had disappeared before the trailer had been pushed into the ravine, but the bench provided a sturdy surface and more warmth than the cold floor. She would not be able to say she hadn't been treated to the best he had to offer. As a last touch, he turned the corner of the top quilt back in a triangle. He had always found comfort in the way his grandmother turned his bed back for him.

He put the food from the mission in the tiny cabinet over the sink. Maybe she would cook, he thought, as he sat down to survey his housekeeping. This was the kind of place, a little playhouse, he had dreamed of sharing with Rosa when they were children. Or like a house in the stories the Anglo teacher had read to them in school. The flying boy and the children who had run away from their parents. The stupid bear who made up silly songs. The family who lived in a tree house. Ignacio had dreamed that he and Rosa would someday run away and live in a small house in the woods also.

That was before he even knew what "woods" were. When the only stands of trees he had seen were the citrus orchards along the Rio Grande. He remembered how, when he first came here, he had felt smothered by the tall, dark pines blocking out the sky around him. The somber shade among the trees, both frightening and concealing. But later he recognized this as the place that had been intended for them, the place where he and Rosa should have had their small house. In these woods. It would have been a real house, of course, not a discarded metal trailer. The house would have been made of white limestone, or maybe logs. And quite small, hardly bigger than the trailer. Small windows with only four panes, so that they could see out but no one else could look in.

Rosa would keep it shining and beautiful. Maybe she would even plant flowers around it.

The muscles around Ignacio's mouth twitched. Planting flowers was a woman's job. A man might work in the fields, but a woman should plant flowers. At night he went to sleep seeing the dead corpses of the flowers he had dug up that day from the woman's beds. He knew the dreams came because he was doing work meant for a woman. It worried him, seeing the dried seedpods of the marigolds scattered across the upturned earth. What would happen to them? Would they simply rot there, or dry out and turn to dust, impotent on the surface of the earth? These questions caused him pain. He felt somehow responsible to the seed scattering wantonly around his feet as he carried the stalks to the burning pile behind the house.

Ignacio sighed and dropped his head between his knees. He was tired. The trip into town had been stupid and had exhausted him. The red brick walls of the prison watching him and the man in the Dairy Queen yelling at him had awakened a terror that siphoned his reserve of energy. And he would need to be strong tonight.

He lay down on the quilt he had spread for himself on the floor, pulled it around him, and closed his eyes. He would rest now for the test that lay ahead.


Geoff Granger stepped out onto the balcony of the Galleria Hilton, hoping the chill night air would clear his head. It was being borne in upon him that he'd made a number of bad decisions lately that needed to be sorted out as soon as possible. Starting with that hit of coke right before they'd left for the party. Even as he'd watched the thin white line disappear with his indrawn breath, he knew it had been a mistake.

"You're never any fun at a party otherwise," Brent had wheedled. "How do you expect me to enjoy myself if I have to watch you sitting in a corner positively saturated with melancholy? You know how I soak up your moods. I'm an emotional sponge. I can't help myself."

Geoff had always envied Brent's ability to sustain metaphors—Brent, who was so dyslexic he couldn't hold a job requiring more than his signature. It was Brent's facility with analogies, though he'd never told him so, as much as his cherubic charm that had originally fascinated Geoff. For months now he'd been keeping lists of Brent's casually thrown-off phrases in his computer. From time to time he managed to work one into an article. Brent, of course, never read his work, so there was little chance of discovery. Nevertheless, some vague residue of guilt remained in Geoff's consciousness, making itself felt whenever they had a squabble.

Geoff hadn't wanted to take Brent to the party in the first place. That had been another bad decision. Coming out of the closet had a certain cachet these days, but still it was best not to go too far. Brent was unpredictable. Geoff never knew when he might decide to go into his Caligula act. Large parties like this one—particularly with lots of rich people around—seemed to stimulate him to wild excess. But Brent had been home when the mail came and had opened the invitation, scenting in the thick, creamy paper of the envelope an opportunity to nibble at the delectable borders of affluence.

The aging heiress of two oil fortunes, one from each side of her family, had adopted Geoff for the season. He functioned, in her words, as "the cattle prod to her social consciousness," chosen no doubt because she'd seen his articles in *Texas Times* as she thumbed through its lush ads. Geoff knew, however, that his actual function was more court jester than moral goad. She meant for him to both needle and amuse the guests at her opulent parties. He knew he'd been neither amusing nor provoking this evening, even though there was a New York editor present whom he needed to chat up.

What he really wanted to be doing was working up the notes on the new prison story. He'd listened to the Cartwright woman's tape several times while transcribing it verbatim. Now he was working on incorporating her report into a frame of his own words. After a few paragraphs, however, he had stopped, uncertain whether her words, which he had intended to contrast with his own—the primitive set off by the urbane—were having the effect he had hoped for.

It was a technique he had used often and to good effect. In the cockfighting piece, for instance, he'd gotten wonderful snatches of raw good-ole-boy talk set like uncut gems in his own smooth, sly prose. And there was certainly something primitive in the emotional content of the little Somerville reporter's account of the chapel service at the Bromley Unit, though the language she'd used was hardly elementary. The vocabulary swooped and plunged far outside the range of ordinary journalism, improbable connections were made with audacious metaphors, and the images presented to the mind were deft and precise. He was beginning to see that if he used her verbatim account, the contrast this time would not be to his advantage. And unlike Brent, she would be watching for the piece.

That's what happened when you got mixed up with women. It never failed; they always got the upper hand. He should have found some other angle, some other source. Another bad decision.


Several hours later the stars shining down from the November night over Texas are, as the song states so primitively, big and bright. In fact, they look like lavishly scattered spangles on a velvet painting. Or, seen another way, like birds caught in the hair of trees. In the city where Geoff and Norton sleep—the reporter as immobile as the patient poetically etherized upon the table, the deputy tossing restlessly on an internal sea of more prosaic hormones—the stars are scarcely noticeable, washed out by lights that burn even when people sleep.

Beth Marie in Point Blank, however, found the stars both near and cold as she looked at them from her bedroom window, up through the bare branches of the sweet gum tree. They reminded her of the Snow Queen and the ice shard that broke off and entered the heart of the boy in the fairy tale. Now she lies sleeping, the book that has fallen from her hand not the usual volume of Dickinson poems but a paperback mystery she picked up at the grocery store. Under their lids her eyes dart back and forth, and her lips move slightly from time to time, as though she would call out if she could.

Only Ignacio, walking along the road for what he tells himself will be the last time, sees the stars now. They gather around his shoulders and over his head, casting blue shadows about him and urging him on with crystal whispers. He is both awed and heartened by their company. To him, they are the assembly called to witness his courage and faithfulness.

They watch as he reaches carefully within the garage door, slides his hand along the ledge, and takes the key he finds there. They attend him as he inserts the key into the back-door lock and steadily turns it, then pushes open the door whose hinges he oiled only last week.

But then he is lost to them as he disappears inside, stepping carefully over the squeaking places in the floor that he has mapped in his mind. They cannot see him ascending the stairs, holding his breath, listening for sounds from the bedroom above. There, he is in complete darkness.

# CHAPTER • ELEVEN

CECELIA RAMSEY HAD A REPUTA-
tion for acting on impulse. At least that's
what most people in Point Blank called it.
Cecelia herself would say she was sometimes
prompted by the Holy Spirit, a figure she pictured as ungendered and flamelike, with long hair made
of white light streaming backwards in flight. With the
Holy Spirit's aid, she was frequently able to find her mis-
placed scissors, make her bank statement come out to the
penny, and get home safely even though the needle on
her gas gauge had pointed to empty for the last fifty miles.

As she drove by the Cartwright house early Saturday
morning, she could feel the Holy Spirit prompting her to
stop. Probably to check on Catherine, she thought. Then
with a jolt she remembered. Her friend had been dead—
how many years now?

Cecelia had a hard time keeping that fact fixed in her
memory. For one thing, Catherine had always been such
a *definite* person that it was hard to think of her as even
dormant, much less dead. Even now she seemed to live
on in that tall house which had always been so much like
her—giving the impression of welcome with its well-
tended flower borders while protecting its privacy by
drawing the wide, skirtlike porch around it.

Beth Marie had tried to keep everything just as her mother left it, but every year with less success. This morning the flowerbeds looked bare and desolate.

Maybe, Cecelia thought suddenly, it was Beth Marie the Holy Spirit had meant for her to check on. The child had not been herself the other day when she drove her across the river to pick up her car at Belle's Marina. In fact, ever since she got that new job in town, Beth Marie had been acting funny. Not funny ha-ha, but funny peculiar. Could it be she was in love? She and that nice young deputy had been seeing one another regularly for almost a year now. Cecelia wondered if they were having what her own daughter Lois called a "relationship." Catherine Cartwright, she knew, would never approve of that.

No question about what the Lord thought about such arrangements either, especially the Father part of him, though Jesus might be a little more sympathetic. After all, being a young person these days couldn't be easy. They had so many choices, they couldn't make up their minds what it was they wanted. And such an *innocent* view of the way the world worked—as if you could put your life together the way you made out an order from the Sears, Roebuck catalogue, picking and choosing. Expecting the package would come on time and you'd open it and there it would be—everything you'd ordered, all shiny and new. What they didn't realize was that some of the items would be on back order, others would be discontinued, and what you did get wouldn't look the way it had in the catalogue. And it would all cost a lot more than you'd ever expected.

Take Beth Marie for instance. She used to love Point Blank, never wanted to live anyplace else. But ever since she went to work at the *Courier* in Somerville, her discontent had been growing. That's why she'd gone to Belle's Marina. Honky-tonks like that played on a young person's restlessness and discontent.

Well, she supposed the restlessness was inevitable. She could remember being young herself and wanting things she didn't have. She could still close her eyes and see all the handsome young soldiers in their khaki uniforms. But she'd known even then that for most people life was a pretty ramshackle affair, subject to forces outside your control—like depressions and war. With hard work you might possibly get by, though there were no guarantees. But anything more than that took luck. Or the Holy Spirit.

She sighed, put the car in reverse, and backed up to the front gate of Catherine's house. It appeared to be frowning from its front dormer windows today. Around it, the dead flowers of the past season had been pulled from their beds, and raw chunks of overturned earth lay dark and damp, like narrow graves along the walk. Though the sky was overcast and threatening more rain, the house's eyes stared blank and blind. Cecelia shook her head. The dark windows meant either that Beth Marie wasn't up yet or wasn't at home.

Cecelia paused with her hand on the ignition key. It was only eight o'clock, a little early to come calling. Then, about midway down her windpipe, she felt another twinge.

She switched off the key, got out, and pushed open the gate which was standing half ajar, remembering how Catherine had always kept it not only closed but latched. Rolling from one arthritic foot to the other in a kind of marine motion, she made her precarious way up the walk, across the porch, and knocked on the door.

Cecelia remembered the time when all she had to do was stick her head in and call out, "Anybody home?" And almost always Catherine had been. Later, after Catherine was gone, Beth Marie would answer, sometimes from upstairs, sometimes from the dining room where she'd set up her office for the Water Board. But no more. The deputy had told the girl—and rightly so—that a woman living alone these days, even in Point Blank, needed to lock her doors.

Cecelia knocked again, then looked back at her car on the other side of the low fence and at the brick walk leading around the side of the house. It would be a long, painful journey around the house to try the back door. She wouldn't be able to help noticing if Beth Marie's car were in the driveway, and if it weren't, she'd feel sad all day, knowing Catherine's daughter had not been home that night.

She stood still, her head on one side, listening either for a sound from inside the house or a follow-up prompt from the Holy Spirit. Nothing. After another moment's consideration she went back down the porch steps, leaning heavily on the railing and wincing as she slowly lowered her weight from one step to the next. Then she tottered along the walk around to the back door. As long as she was there, she might as well be thorough.

Just as she had feared, there was no car in the driveway. Pulling herself up the back steps, she knocked on that door also. Silence. She put her hand on the knob and turned. The door swung slowly inward. Sticking her head in, she called out, "Beth Marie, honey. You here?" Her voice echoing in the empty house only seemed to intensify the silence.

She was on the point of pulling the door to again when the ringing silence turned to the noisier ringing of the telephone. Startled, she stepped back out the door, then inside again. She had no business answering it, of course. But then the phone ringing in the empty house suddenly seemed fraught with sinister implications. What if burglars were calling to see if anyone was home? What if Beth Marie had been injured in a car wreck? She tiptoed across the kitchen to the stairwell and picked up the receiver. "Hello?"

"Beth Marie?"

"No. This is a friend."

"Mrs. Ramsey?" It sounded like the nice young deputy.

"Yes."

"This is Norton. Is Beth Marie there?"

"You mean she's not with you?" Cecelia forgot to check the relief in her voice.

"With me? I'm calling from Houston. I thought I'd be sure and catch her this time of morning."

Cecelia grimaced in the dark stairwell. She'd put her foot in it now. "Uh, no. She must have gone into town early this morning." There was a long pause during which Cecelia realized that the deputy might be wondering what she was doing in the house. "I just now got here. The back door was open and I heard the phone ringing," she added lamely.

"The back door open? She promised me—"

"Or maybe she just ran up to the post office or something," Cecelia broke in.

There was a longer silence on the other end. Other explanations for Beth Marie's absence were evidently occurring to the deputy also.

"Well. Who knows?" he said stiffly. "Still, you'd think she'd lock the door, especially if she—were going to be gone any length of time."

Cecelia cleared her throat and looked distractedly around the kitchen, wishing the Holy Spirit would oblige her with a helpful response. "Yes," was all she could say. "She needs to be careful."

He repeated the last word, as though it tasted bitter. Then he added, "Well, leave her a message if you would. Just say I called."

"She'll be glad to know that," Cecelia said, forcing enthusiasm into her voice. But it was too late to console the deputy. He had already hung up.

Cecelia found a notepad on the kitchen counter and carefully wrote out Norton's message, following it with three exclamation points she hoped Beth Marie would find encouraging. It was only then, as she was propping the note against the sugar bowl so that the girl couldn't miss it when she came in, that Cecelia noticed the purse in the recess of Catherine's old pie safe. Why hadn't Beth Marie taken her purse with her?

She hated leaving the door open with the purse sitting there in plain view. Maybe she should lock the door as she left. But what if Beth Marie didn't have her house key with her?

She crossed the kitchen again and picked up the purse. She'd just check to see if the house key was in it. If it was missing, she would lock the door as she left. The key wasn't in the little side pocket, so she unzipped the main compartment and rummaged through the contents. No keys at all, though the wallet was still there with her driver's license. Cecelia frowned. Leaving the door unlocked, driving without her license. What had gotten into the girl?

Retracing her steps across the kitchen, she paused and opened the refrigerator door. A chicken. Lettuce. Fresh corn. Beth Marie must be expecting company.


Norton hung up the phone in a savage mood. In order to get a little privacy, he had waited till Sheriff Dooley went down to breakfast before he called Beth Marie. Now it was time for the first seminar session to start, and it looked as though he wouldn't have time for breakfast himself.

However, he reflected as he rode down on the elevator, he wasn't all that hungry. Not for breakfast anyway. He'd slept badly, caught in some strange nocturnal region between dreaming and imagination where Beth Marie was beside him. Every time he had waked, just for an instant he had believed he could actually catch the woody scent of her skin. Then the disappointment of hearing the sheriff's all-too-real snores instead of her light breathing only served to increase his longing. He punched his pillow savagely. Why wasn't she here?

Being one of those fortunate individuals who ordinarily sleep soundly and deeply, Norton took a sleepless night as a personal affront. Inside the door of the windowless conference room he spotted the coffee urn and reached for a styrofoam cup from the stack on the table, glowering at a boy in a red jacket standing guard there.

"Won't be ready for another thirty minutes, sir," the boy said.

Down in front, a man in a tan suit with western points was making testing noises over the PA system as a hundred or so law enforcement officers trickled in and began to settle into their chairs. Norton looked around the room for Sheriff Dooley, finally spotting him on the far side in the back row with a clump of other good old boys, laughing and nudging one another with their elbows. What was it with them anyway? Their kind always sat on the last row against the back wall, their arms folded across their chests as if daring the speaker to make a dent in their ignorance.

Norton looked away before the sheriff could catch his eye and made for an aisle seat about halfway toward the front. And why did *he* always pick an aisle seat in the middle of the room, for that matter? He knew what Beth Marie would have said—it showed he liked to keep his options open. At least that's the way she would have put it six months ago. He wasn't sure now. More than likely she'd say he was afraid to make a commitment.

He scowled as the man in the western suit introduced the DNA expert from the University of Houston, an academic type in a corduroy jacket. She probably liked corduroy jackets, too. Well, she was a fine one to be talking about commitment. Where was *she* at eight o'clock on a Saturday morning? Not that she was obliged to tell him everything she did, of course. But until recently, that's the way things had generally worked out, without having to talk about it. They'd just sort of drifted into relying on one another. That's the way he would have put it. Relying on one another. It had seemed natural enough. Even comfortable. What was wrong with that? Why complicate things?

As the academic type started flicking slides on the screen in the now darkened room, the phrase kept echoing in his mind from a long way off, like a pebble in a deep well. *Why complicate things?* The words sounded familiar, but he had to close his eyes and concentrate through several slides until the original context of the words came back to him. Who had said that? With a start, he sat forward in his chair. The man next to him glanced at him and scowled.

Sheriff Dooley. He said that all the time—"No need to complicate things, Norton." He said it whenever Norton wasn't satisfied with obvious answers that presented themselves too easily. When his deputy insisted on probing a situation, wanted to consider other points of view, other alternatives. Secretly, Norton had always liked that image of himself as the maverick in the department, the one who wasn't satisfied with the easy answers, the one who didn't mind complicating things. He couldn't remember the sheriff saying that to him in a long time.

He pulled one boot up onto the opposite knee and leaned forward, clearing his throat. He felt thoroughly confused. When had not being afraid of complications turned into keeping his options open? And how did Beth Marie then make the jump from that to his being afraid of commitment? It was all a muddle to him. He never had been able to understand how women thought. Everything got knotted up when you tried to figure them out.

But as the slide show came to an end and someone fumbled for the light switch, one fact—one clear, undeniable fact—hit him. Complications were indeed beginning to annoy him. Not just in his work, but in general. And especially with Beth Marie. He wanted to know where she was, what she was doing. It complicated things when she wasn't where he expected her to be.

It was scary, sitting there in the dark, thinking how like the sheriff he was becoming. *No need to complicate things.* Another year, and he'd be sitting on the back row with his arms crossed, just another Bubba.

When the man in the corduroy jacket asked for questions from the audience, Norton got up and tiptoed to the back of the room. It wasn't time for a break yet, but he had to get some coffee. This was getting to him. His hand was shaking as he held the styrofoam cup under the urn's spigot, and coffee slopped over the edge. The kid in the red jacket smirked and turned away. Norton glared at him and headed toward the back door.

Out in the corridor, he took a large gulp of the coffee, shook the spilled liquid off his fingers, and headed toward a bank of phones by the elevators. If she wasn't at home, maybe she'd gone in to the office. It didn't matter. He had the entire county network of communications. He'd even put an alert out for her car, if necessary. And when he found her, he thought, smiling to himself, he'd show her just how much he could complicate things. Wouldn't she be surprised! The sheriff had been right. It was time.


It wasn't working out. He couldn't get the right slant on the story. Geoff had been awake before dawn, the problem revolving in his head, wearing a groove he couldn't break out of. Finally he'd gotten up, made coffee, and turned on the computer. He'd been staring at the green glow of the screen for an hour now.

He hit the standby key, stood up and stretched, then went to the window to smoke a cigarette while he tried to find the hidden entrance to the story, a crack in the wall through which he could insert his objectifying consciousness. That's the way he thought about articles when he found them resisting him. He tried to make himself invisible, then slide into the picture in his mind he was trying to describe for his readers, an audience already satiated by too much creamy fiction and semi-surrealistic, full-color ads. He'd learned to make his writing stark and cool, like a grainy 1950s black-and-white photograph. That was the only way he could make it stand out in *Texas Times*.

But that meant he had to have some facts to work with. The hard little grains of the photograph. This time he'd had to rely on someone else's report, the plummy oral prose of the Somerville reporter. At first he'd thought he could simply transcribe her tape and then pare it down, putting his own austere stamp on the bare facts. That hadn't worked. It had ended up sounding like a parody of Sgt. Joe Friday.

The truth was, he told himself as he lit a second cigarette, he had no insight into the situation at all. As he had told Beth Cartwright, he wasn't a religious person. He could count on one hand the number of church services he had been to in his entire lifetime. He wasn't even sure he had some of the terms right. He had tried talking about it with Brent, who had always described his childhood as swaddled in the moist molasses bosom of the Methodist Church. Brent, however, had made a point the last few days of displaying exaggerated boredom every time Geoff talked about his work.

"Really, Geoffrey," he said, "if you wanted an adoring little wife to meet you at the door and ask how things went at the office, you should have married one. I love your contacts, but I don't care at all about your work. Conjugal career-concern is something you gave up along with children, remember? You pays your penny and you takes your choice, duckie."

Geoff wasn't sorry about the choice, at least most of

the time. He knew Brent's paranoia about his dyslexia made him resentful of his career. Otherwise, Geoff had nothing to complain about. Generally, Brent pampered him shamelessly. He certainly would never have found a woman as devoted to him while making so few demands. His only substantial irritation with Brent was his jealousy, a problem exacerbated by Geoff's own attractiveness to women. Brent hadn't even liked it when the old cow who gave the party last night insisted on planting kisses on his cheek every time she swooped by.

"It's part of the job," Geoff had told him countless times. "How do you think we'd ever get invited to these parties you love so much if I didn't schmooze the old ladies?"

"It's not just the old ladies," Brent retorted. "It's models, musicians, bulbous secretaries. They're all over you like fire ants on road kill. Can't you see they want to eat you up, devour you with their awful, slavering mouths? Is that what you want, Geoffrey?"

"Don't be silly. They're sources—information stockpiles, nothing more. Think of them as data bases. I can't help it if the juiciest stories get stored in some trash can of a female mind."

"I can't see what information that little hick up in Somerville could possibly have for you. Don't tell me she's just a diskette."

"Don't worry about it, Brent," he said to pacify him. "You're still my hard drive." But from the way Brent had scowled at him, he wasn't sure the figure of speech had worked.

And now it looked as though he was going to have to contact Beth Cartwright again. Maybe he could get some other leads from her. Other people to talk to. Maybe that chaplain, Father what's-his-name. He felt confident he could charm her into that much. She was obviously a woman ready to be charmed. He was constantly amazed at how most women were, even the tough Houston socialites and working girls. It was frightening the way they swarmed a guy with so little provocation. Fire ants on road kill. That was good. He went back to his desk and pulled up the file with Brent's bon mots.

Just then the phone rang. He picked it up quickly. Brent was still sleeping off last night's party.

"Yes?" It was his policy to be gruff when he was working.

"Geoff?" A breathless woman's voice he couldn't quite place.

"Yes." Even gruffer.

"This is Beth Marie Cartwright."

Speak of the devil.

"I'm—I need your help." She sounded as if she were about to cry.

He grunted and waited silently for her to go on.

"Have you ever heard of Angelina Mascarenas?"

"Who?"

"An inmate at the old Bromley Unit when it was the women's prison. She died there seven years ago."

He could hear another voice in the background.

"Her son is here with me," she went on. "He wants the world to know the truth about his mother."

Geoff grabbed a pencil from the jar on the desk and pulled a yellow pad toward him. "Yes?"

"He says she was a martyr. He wants the world to know this. That she was a good woman. Not a criminal. They killed her. At the prison."

The other voice said something again, the tone falling at the end, as though concluding a statement.

"He wants the world to know this. He says it has to be in the papers—tomorrow."

"Where are you?" Geoff demanded. "Tell me where you are."

There was a pause. Then she said shakily, "Or he's going to kill me."

The phone went dead.

# CHAPTER · TWELVE

**S**HE DIDN'T KNOW WHERE SHE WAS when she first opened her eyes. She blinked, waiting for the world to slide into place the way it sometimes did after she'd fallen asleep on the sofa in the afternoon. She blinked again, frowning now.

Then suddenly the memory of the night returned, and a wave of nausea made her shut her eyes.

When she had fallen from the fire tower over a year ago, she'd had no time to feel terror. When she woke on the ground in the dark with dirt in her mouth and eyes, she had been sustained by an unexpected euphoria, the product, they told her at the hospital, of the body's chemical response to emergency. When she'd been attacked later in the hospital, she'd been unaware of what was happening until it was almost over. But last night there had been plenty of time for terror.

She had found herself, before she was fully awake, being dragged from bed, a hand clamped across her mouth. Then she was face down on her own bedroom floor, a knee in her back and her arms wrenched behind her. He had needed both his hands, though, to hold her and tie her arms. She had screamed then, even knowing there was little chance of anyone hearing her.

A cup towel was stuffed in her mouth. Then he pushed her ahead of him down the stairs, still in the dark. Never once did he turn on a light, not even when he paused in the kitchen, keeping the point of a knife pricking into her back while he rummaged in her purse on the hutch. He must know her house well. How had he gotten in? She'd locked all the doors. She would have heard a pane breaking, a door being forced.

The cold had sucked the heat from her body as he shoved her out the back door. She was barefoot, and her nightshirt was little protection against the November night. Jerking the back door of the Toyota open, he had forced her down onto the rear seat, breathing heavily but still saying nothing, and slipped a pillowcase over her head. Her brain was churning, trying to remember details, thinking of ways to defend herself. As the car started, a wave of anger suddenly swept over her, tumbling her thoughts. Where was Norton? She'd done what he said. She'd locked the doors. Now where was he?

For what seemed like hours they had driven over back roads. From time to time she would try to raise her head, but he would reach one arm back between the front seats and shove it down. From the feel of the roads and the lack of light penetrating the pillowcase she knew he was keeping to the country, possibly driving in circles. Maybe he wasn't going to kill her. Why would he try to disguise their location if he was going to kill her?

But why had he forced her out of the house? Why abduct her? She had no family, little money. She wasn't an important person. Was he some kind of psychotic killer? Some ritual sadist? Was it her terror he enjoyed? TV images of police scouting empty fields for corpses forced their way into her mind. After a while she could only huddle passively in the back seat, shivering and exhausted by fear and cold.

Finally the car had stopped, and he got out and opened the back door. She drew herself up against the far side. He jerked one of her ankles, and she shrank further against the door.

"Out." He said the one word, the first one he had spoken, in a gruff unnatural voice. From the tone she was almost certain he had only broken his silence because, contrary to what she had dreaded, he wanted to avoid touching her again.

With her bound hands, she tried to tug the short nightshirt down while backing out of the cramped rear seat, fighting against the shame that threatened to dissipate what little courage she had left. As soon as she straightened up, he prodded her forward with the knife point. She was afraid she might start crying. She couldn't afford to collapse. A show of weakness could trigger his violence.

She counted seventeen small, tentative steps over grass and weeds; then she stumbled against a step. He said nothing to warn her, only prodded her up the step and into what she sensed was an enclosed space. A trailer possibly, since it rocked slightly when he followed her inside.

Now, she thought, tensing again. Now it's going to happen. But he only nudged her another foot or so forward until her knees banged against a ledge. Then, pushing with only the tips of his fingers on her shoulder, he indicated she was to sit down.

She felt some kind of loose padding beneath her, then a covering of sorts was flicked up across her lap. She could hear him breathing heavily nearby, then the floor creaking as if he were sitting down.

She had already managed to work the wadded towel loose from her mouth in the car. Now she spat it out altogether.

"Where are we?" she said, hating the high thinness of her voice. "Who are you? Why—"

But her words were cut short by the knife, this time laid firmly across her throat. Gradually the pressure eased. She didn't try to speak again, and after a moment she heard the floor creak under him as he moved back and sat down again.

She'd sat there shivering for long, silent minutes; then she began working the covering further over her, eventually discovering that there was room for her to lie down. Nevertheless, she tried to keep upright for what must have been another hour. But in the end, overcome by the exhaustion of fear and cold, she pulled her bare feet up onto the shelflike surface and managed to wriggle what seemed to be a quilt over her. He made no move, though she was sure he must be watching there in the dark. Much later she must have dozed off.

All this came back to her as the first light of morning penetrated the pillowcase, only half covering her face now. Not in sequence, but as shards of fragmented memory.

Gradually, she managed to rub the pillowcase completely off her head. She felt her stomach heave, and only by forcing herself to focus on the curved ceiling overhead did she keep from throwing up. Turning her head slowly, she saw an empty, rumpled nest of quilts on the floor. Even more slowly she slid her feet to the floor and sat up, wincing at the pain in her arms and hands, still bound behind her. The trailer was small, no more than fifteen feet long. She could see no one.

She was just getting to her feet when a pale shadow fell across the trailer doorway.

"Ignacio!"

He looked away from her quickly as though half-angry, half-ashamed.

"Why—"

With one bound he was up the step and through the doorway. "Shut up!" he commanded.

She stared at him in disbelief. "What do you mean—"

He slapped her across the face with his open hand, knocking her back onto the bench.

Beth Marie had never been hit like that before. She stared at him, tasting blood in her mouth. "What have I ever—"

He struck her again on the other side of the face with the back of his hand. "*Puta!*" he shouted. "Whore! You think you're better than her, don't you? But you're not. You're no better than a whore!"

She caught her breath, her ears still ringing from the blow. "What do you mean? Better than who, Ignacio?" She was shocked when the words came out in a weak croak, shocked that she kept on speaking, that she seemed, at least for the moment, indifferent to the pain.

He looked at her wildly. "No! Her name is not for your polluted mouth." And he let loose a stream of vituperative Spanish of which she only understood the single word "madre."

She swallowed, keeping her eyes trained on his face, and waited for him to run down. Then she said, as quietly and evenly as she could manage, "I've got to go to the bathroom."


Lurline, the dispatcher at the Watson County Sheriff's Department, was having a mighty fine morning. First of all the call from Norton around nine. Most of the men Lurline dealt with at work were either scumbags or didn't pay her any mind. Norton had always been a real gentleman though. Said "please" and "thank you" and never told smutty stories around her. Not that she didn't get a kick out of some of the jokes the scumbags came up with. But it was nice to know somebody thought she was too good for that. If she ever had any kids, Lurline reflected, she was going to teach them to say "please" and "thank you" and call her "ma'am."

Norton's request had been a strange one, especially considering he was down in Houston. He had wanted her to put out a bulletin on Beth Marie Cartwright. But not really official, he'd said. Keep it off the log. He had sounded like an excited little boy, just the kind Lurline could never say no to.

Lurline thought a minute, counting on her fingers. He'd been seeing that girl for over a year now. Was this supposed to be a romantic way to propose to her? Well, he'd taken his own sweet time about it. They hadn't even been living together, so far as her cousin in Point Blank could tell. What had forced his hand now, she wondered. Was that Cartwright girl pregnant? Too bad he didn't have a taste for women with a little more meat on their bones. She closed her eyes and pictured the way Norton stroked his mustache when he was puzzled.

A few minutes after Norton's call the phone had rung again. This time it was some reporter from Houston wanting to speak to the sheriff.

"Sheriff Dooley's not available right now," she said with satisfaction. The one thing that united all Watson County law enforcement agencies was their loathing of reporters. Especially Houston reporters.

"Okay. So who's next in charge? Let me speak to him."

"That would be Deputy Norton. He's not here either," she drawled. "In fact, they're both down there in Houston at this very moment. At a scientific convention."

There was a long pause. When the reporter spoke again, his voice had dropped a couple of notches in a way that made Lurline picture a masculine figure silhouetted against blue neon.

"So. I guess you're having fun then. With both your bosses out of town." The mysterious figure leaned toward her, offering to light her cigarette.

"Oh, I got plenty to keep me busy," she laughed, tugging her striped T-shirt down snugly over the elastic waistband of her slacks.

"Say. What's your name anyway?" The reporter, who

had sounded brusque at first, now seemed as if he had all the time in the world to while away on the telephone.

She exhaled a stream of smoke toward the ceiling. "Lurline," she said.

"Lurline, huh? Sounds alluring," he said, dragging out the middle syllable of the last word.

Somewhere in the blue neon she could hear a jukebox begin to play.

"This conference your boss is at—any idea where it is? Or doesn't he want you checking up on him?"

"Of course, I know. I've got to know where the sheriff is twenty-four hours a day. I probably keep better tabs on him than his wife does." She giggled.

"Say, you know what? It would sure save me a lot of trouble if I could talk to him while he's in town. You mind telling me where I could find him?"

She hesitated. Dooley would kill her if he knew she'd given out his whereabouts to a reporter. On the other hand, Houston was a big city, full of reporters. Could she help it if one happened to run into him?

"Well. Don't let him know I told you, you hear? It's at the University of Houston conference center. They're staying there on campus."

"Reckon they'll be there long?"

"Till tomorrow afternoon anyway."

"Thanks, Lurline. I won't let him know how I found him."

"Say."

"Yes?"

"You never did tell me *your* name."

"Jim Bob" was all she heard before he rang off.


Ten minutes after his call to Somerville, Geoff Granger was in his Mustang headed north. His first reaction had been to report a possible hostage situation to the sheriff. However, with both the sheriff and his chief

• 128 •

deputy out of town, he hesitated. A bunch of two-bit country cops with no one in charge, itching for a chance to act out their John Wayne fantasies—that could be a disaster. The girl could end up getting killed.

But he also couldn't afford to waste time tracking the sheriff down in Houston. It might even be best if he got there first. Maybe he could deal with this lunatic himself. He'd get to Point Blank, check out the situation, then call in the cavalry. He glanced into the backseat of the Mustang to make sure he had his camera. He smiled to himself. Maybe this was the break he'd been waiting for.


Dan Kamowski lowered his coffee mug and stared glumly out the window at some kind of grey bird nipping red berries off an evergreen bush. Dell, he was certain, knew the names of both the bird and the bush. Nature was something Dan was only dimly aware of, and he liked it that way. It flowed over him like a river. He noticed if the day was hot or cold, whether there were trees or rocks around, but that was about as detailed as his impressions got.

It sometimes bothered him that he didn't "love" nature, not in the way he heard other people claim to. He worried that this failure meant some vital component might be missing from his soul. In fact, he'd once combed secretively through the Psalms, since nature-lovers seemed particularly drawn to them, in hopes of discovering just what it was he was missing. It had been some comfort to him to discover that whoever wrote those ancient songs hadn't been any more detailed than he was. Trees, rocks, mountains. Now and then a "young lion." Well, he could recognize a lion when he saw one.

Nevertheless, he considered Dell's knowledge of bird names another sign of her superior intelligence, a trait he was growing to resent less the longer they were married, especially since he now recognized how essential her wisdom was and always had been to his survival. Besides, generally speaking, she didn't show off about it.

"All I've got for her is a box number," he said. "No street address."

Dell put the back of her hand to her mouth to cover a yawn and stretched her long arms over her head. They'd stayed in bed late that morning, and now he was feeling like he had to make up for the pleasure. Dell was merely languid and unfocused, drifting in her private sea of reverie. She'd always been like that afterward. For forty-some years now.

"You feel like you need to see her?" She stroked her throat contemplatively.

Dan twisted in his chair, trying to work a kink out of his back. "I don't know. Well, yeah, I *feel* like I ought to see her. I don't *know* that I need to. I mean there's no particular reason."

"Didn't you talk to her earlier this week?"

"Yeah. We had lunch. Singletary on the vestry is leaning on me to get some publicity out about the church so he can hit up the town fat cats for tax-deductible donations to the building fund before the end of the year. I thought she might give us some help." He paused and sighed heavily. The birds had deserted the bush outside the window by their breakfast table. "I just don't understand young people today."

Dell lifted an eyebrow and waited.

"I mean what's the big deal? Why don't women get married like they used to? Young. Like me and you did."

She glanced up from the newspaper she had surreptitiously started to scan. "They have other options these days."

"Options?" he snorted. "What kind of word is that? We're talking about life, not the stock market."

"Sweetheart, people don't talk about 'life' anymore. They say 'lifestyle.' Life sounds too—" she fluttered her fingers "—big."

"So? People are big. Lifestyle sounds like you're talking about department store dummies," he said belligerently.

"I'm just telling you what they think," she said, snapping the paper open. "If you have a lifestyle, you get options. It's part of the package."

Another minute went by while he watched her turn to the comics and do the word jumble in her head. Then she added, "I take it you talked about something besides the building fund."

"Well," he picked up his mug again and said with an injured air, "I *am* her priest. At least for the time being."

Dell reached for a pencil and started on the cross-word puzzle. "Options aren't *bad*, are they? Having a choice about whether to marry or not—what's wrong with that? Men certainly seem to like being in a position to choose."

"Yeah, well, maybe men just know what they want and women don't."

"Oh?"

"Sure. Men know what they want and they go after it. They don't worry about all that option stuff."

"Really?"

"Yeah. You see, that's the trouble with women. They never can believe just how simple men are. They expect 'em to be complicated, but they're not. Men know what they want. To them, it's just a simple case of supply and demand. You either get what you want or you don't. You don't worry about options."

"Is that a fact? So what does all this have to do with the Cartwright girl anyway? Is she selling shares? I heard she was seeing some sheriff's deputy."

"She is. Or was. Now I think maybe she's met some-body else."

"Ah. The option." He had her attention now. She looked up, tapping the pencil against her cup.

"There's this deputy sheriff. Mindy Hill says they've

been seeing one another for almost a year, though according to the girl herself, he hasn't made any commitment. I take it that means he hasn't proposed. Not marriage anyway. Is 'seeing someone' the same as 'having a relationship'?"

"Don't be silly, Dan. Go on. What are her other options?"

"Well, there's her job."

"Don't say job, Dan. Career."

"She's expecting some excitement out of that. Which might mean she isn't planning to stay in Somerville the rest of her life."

"It might also mean the deputy's not providing any."

"Any—?"

"Excitement. Or any other reason to stay."

He looked out the window again. Why was the girl worrying him so much anyway? How come he couldn't get her out of his mind? He hardly knew her, yet he sensed she was at some turning point in her life, balancing on a knife blade. He turned back to Dell.

"I got the feeling when I talked to her there might be someone else on the horizon, too, someone she met after the Kairos closing Sunday evening. She said it was 'professional,' but I suspect it's more than that." He took a breath as though preparing to make some further remark, then stopped and frowned at the sun that had just broken through the clouds.

"And?"

"Men may be simple," he said ponderously, as if that had been her pronouncement, "but women are naive. What if this guy—this 'professional'—"

"Yes?"

"I mean she shows up at that closing. Then as soon as it's over she rushes off to a meeting with the guy—"

Dell frowned. "You think maybe—"

He stood up. "I think maybe between her and this 'professional' we may get the kind of publicity we don't need. The warden only lets us come into the prison because I promised him there wouldn't be any publicity. If we get into some Houston newspaper—"

He grated his chair back. A cardinal, just lighting on the birdfeeder outside the window, burst upwards in a flurry of scarlet.

"I think I better go out to the boonies—ask at the gas station for directions, I guess—and have a little talk with Miss Cartwright."

# CHAPTER • THIRTEEN

I T WAS THE QUILTS THAT WERE ALMOST her undoing. The quilts and the shoes. The physical relief of emptying her bladder outside had almost made her feel grateful to him. He had even turned away. But as she started to step back up into the trailer, she'd looked down and noticed the shoes, recognizing them as the pair her father had bought not long before he died. Ignacio had no socks on, and the untied strings hung loosely to either side. She hated him then.

Back inside, he had allowed her to wrap herself in a quilt while he talked, and as she sat listening, trying to concentrate on the details of what he was telling her, her eyes focused on the faded fan-shapes of the cloth, pieced scraps of her mother's and grandmother's discarded dresses. The world suddenly whanged out of its time-locus, bulged its temporal borders, and she was a child again, in bed with the measles, her mind passive and drifting, the pattern of the quilt imprinting memory with the unarticulated meaning of home and comfort. When she lifted her eyes to look at him again, she had to blink back tears.

Ignacio, who had been frowning and intent, suddenly broke off what he was saying and went to the door of the tiny trailer. The sun was coming over the horizon behind him, silhouetting him darkly in the open space. She noted the direction of east, her only information so far about their location. Then she realized he thought the tears were for his mother. Quickly she wiped her eyes on the edge of the quilt. She couldn't afford to weaken. No pity. Not for herself, not for him, not for this woman he'd made into a myth.

The Lower Valley must still be filled with women like his mother—wandering lost in some romantic haze from puberty till their third child. Marrying while they were still in high school, getting pregnant, then losing their beauty and appeal for their perpetually adolescent husbands. His mother, as well as she could calculate, would have grown up during the sixties when the strictures governing that almost medieval society along the lower Rio Grande were giving way. It was inevitable that there would be an Angelina Mascarenas.

This dark, brooding person in the doorway—was he inevitable too? And his hand across her mouth in the darkness, the sickening terror, the cold, the quilts—were they all inevitable? Was there no way to escape her own entanglement in his anger? Was she only a piece in a pattern? She stared at the quilt stupidly, feeling her mind go blank, passive, just as when she'd been a child, sick with measles.

*Don't be ridiculous!* Beth Marie heard her mother say the words as clearly as if she'd been standing before her. Then her mother's unmistakable icy logic formed an answer to the questions in her mind. *If this were inevitable, there'd be hostages taken every day of the week. Think of all the young men in this country today growing up without fathers. Do they all seize unsuspecting girls in the middle of the night? Of course not. This is an aberration. Now get a grip on yourself.*

She sat up straighter and ran her fingers through her hair.

Ignacio turned back from the doorway and looked at her coldly. "Do not waste your tears on me. I am not afraid to die. My mother is dead, my sister is dead. I am not afraid to join them. Only I must finish my mission."

Beth Marie could tell from the bravado with which he announced this that he intended for her to ask what his mission was. She kept her eyes trained on his face but said nothing.

After a moment he went on. "I have not told you all the story yet. My father was no-good. He brought her only sorrow. But she was faithful. Always." He looked at her sternly, as though defying her to contradict him. "He was unworthy of her, yet she loved him and always tried to please him."

His eyes drifted away to look out the door again. "One day he came home in the daytime and went to bed. He was always coming and going like that. He slept all day long. When he woke up in the evening, he told her he wanted her to go with him. He didn't say where or for what. But she was a good wife. She obeyed him." He paused as the muscles in his jaw worked. Then he said, "She never came home again." After a moment he added, "Except once."

"What did he do?" The words were out of her mouth before she could stop them.

Ignacio smiled, as though her response were a small victory. "He took her with him down to Rio Grande City. He said he had to meet a man there who owed him some money. They went to some bar, and the bartender took them to a little room in the back, a storeroom with a little table. Another man came in, a big man with a loud voice, and he and my father began to drink. After a while they started to quarrel. He said it was my father who owed him the money. He said he was going to kill my father if he did not pay. The man stood up and my father pulled a gun from the back of his belt. My mother tried to grab the gun. It went off and hit the man."

He was speaking as if reciting a story. "'Here,' my father said to my mother. 'You want it, you can have it.' And he handed the gun to her. Then he took off. People from the bar came running in. They saw my mother with the gun. They lifted the man from the floor. Part of his head was blown away, but they could see that it was the sheriff of Starr County."

He dropped his eyes to her upturned face. A small muscle in his nostril twitched. "She was innocent. Pure and innocent. He threw her to the dogs, abandoned her. Her family had already disowned her for marrying him. They wouldn't help her then. No one would. The jury said she was guilty."

"And nothing happened to him? Where is he?" She asked this evenly.

He shrugged. "Who knows? In Mexico probably. There's a ferry in Los Ebanos. In hell I hope. He's probably dead by now." He slid his back down along the wall until he was squatting on his heels. Then he pulled out the knife and began to stick it into the linoleum on the trailer floor, making a pattern with the cuts.

"Your sister? You said she was dead too?" She heard her voice asking the question as calmly as if she were interviewing him.

"Rosa," he said, swallowing the name as though it were difficult for him to say. "A car crash. She was with some other kids. They'd been drinking. She was fourteen."

She noted he made no claims for her innocence or purity.

"She was very smart, very beautiful, very popular, even though we were poor. She overcame that. But—" He dropped the knife several more times into the cracked linoleum.

"But what?"

He shook his head. "Then they killed my mother. In prison. They said she was sick. That she had cancer." He laid one hand on his chest as though to indicate the location. "But they were lying."

"Lying?" She said the word very tentatively.

"She could have no cancer in her body. She was too pure. Pure and sinless."

He looked up suddenly and caught her staring at him. His mouth twisted. "You would not understand that, *puta*," he said, daring her to contradict him. "You have lain with men and taken their filth into your body. But she never did. Never."

He lowered one knee to the floor and leaned forward toward her, pointing the knife at her. She shrank back against the bench, clutching the quilt to her throat.

After a moment he gave one short bark of a laugh and stood up. "You are no different from the others. But she was. And now the world is going to learn the truth. That is my mission. They will learn they have killed an innocent woman. One as pure as the Blessed Virgin. They will learn the true story."

He looked down at her, scorn contorting his face, and opened a cupboard over her head. The clothes he pulled from the cupboard, a pair of men's pants and a sweatshirt with a Dallas Cowboys logo on the front, were filthy. He threw them into her lap.

"You work for the newspaper. You will make a phone call to someone—maybe one of your lovers—who can see that the world hears this story. Or else it will be written in your blood."


Lurline had called Howard Satterthwaite in his patrol car in the east part of the county. He was a new deputy-intern who had been training with Norton for the past month. He was still pretty green, but the closest unit to Point Blank. He'd been puzzled by the request to pick up Beth Marie Cartwright, but Lurline had implied Norton might have certain personal reasons for making the request. The sheriff's chief deputy never discussed his love life, though his attachment was common knowledge in the department. Howard, who had decided to go into law enforcement after flunking out of Bible college in Tyler, found the request highly irregular on several counts. On the other hand, who was he to argue with his supervisor's orders?

He had to stop at the Point Blank post office to ask directions to the Cartwright house. Since it was Saturday, the window in the post office was closed, so he asked directions from an old lady who was having trouble getting down the steps.

"Beth Marie?" she repeated, looking at his uniform anxiously. "Is anything the matter?"

"Just routine," Howard answered stiffly.

"Routine? Why isn't—" The old lady broke off her question awkwardly. Then she said, "Why don't I take you there? That might be the easiest."

He followed her at a snail's pace past the Baptist Church and the service station. She blinked to signal a right turn, drove to the next crossroad and turned left, then drew up in front of a two-story frame house in need of paint. He waved to the old lady, expecting her to drive on, but she turned off her motor and waved back to him.

Howard opened the front gate and went up the walk, uncomfortable with her eyes on his back. Why didn't she go on? He crossed the deep front porch and knocked on the glass-paned door, turning his ear to listen for approaching footsteps. He knocked again, then turned and went down the porch steps slowly, trying not to appear indecisive to the woman waiting in the car.

She rolled down her window and called to him. "I don't think she's here."

He stopped on the brick walk and put his hands on his hips.

"I came by earlier this morning and she wasn't here then either."

He frowned. He didn't like civilians interfering in official work. Without a word, he made his way around the house to the back door. A few minutes later he reappeared.

"The back door was open when I was by here earlier," the old lady called to him, "but I locked it when I left."

He walked deliberately up the walk to the front gate so he could talk to her without shouting. Hooking his thumbs in his belt, he said, "Anything else you'd like to tell me, ma'am?"

"Well," she said, her mouth puckering thoughtfully, "you might want to look for yourself, but her car wasn't here then either. Could I ask," the old lady added diffidently, "why you're looking for her? I hope nothing's happened."

"Happened? No." He started toward his car.

"Then what could it be?"

He scowled at her severely, hoping to indicate the impropriety of her questions. She only tilted her head at a more attentive angle.

"Do you have any idea where she might be?"

"No," she said in a drawn-out sigh. "I sure wish I did. I'm afraid—"

"Afraid?"

"Well, this just isn't like Beth Marie. I thought earlier maybe she'd gone for a drive, maybe even to pick up her mail. Her purse was in the kitchen when I came by earlier, but the keys were missing."

His frown deepened.

"Oh, it's all right. I've known Beth Marie ever since she was just a little thing. Her mother was my best friend. Of course, she's dead now. Beth Marie's almost like my own daughter. Well, not exactly. Lois is quite a bit different from Beth Marie, but—"

"Wait, wait." Howard held up his hand. "You went in the house—"

"The back door was open."

"And you went through her purse—"

"Not *through* exactly. I noticed it was there and that the car was gone. That seemed strange to me, so I looked for her car keys. They were gone."

"How long ago was that?"

She lifted one plump hand from the steering wheel and consulted a pink plastic wristwatch. "A couple of hours." Her face brightened. "I was here when Deputy Norton called. He was looking for her too."

"He called?"

"Yes. Do you think—"

But he had turned away, rubbing one hand across his mouth and scanning the horizon as if he expected Beth Marie to miraculously appear across the field. This assignment was beginning to look more serious. So Norton already knew his girlfriend wasn't here. Did that mean this was some kind of test or something? Maybe Norton and Sheriff Dooley had set up this whole thing. Maybe this was one of those simulation games like they did to test paramedics. In that case, he better not drop the ball. They'd expect him to show some initiative, some ingenuity. On the other hand, they'd expect him to follow the rules. He knew he had no legal right to go busting into somebody's house without a warrant. He looked at the old lady again.

"I don't suppose you've got an extra key to the house," he said.

"No," she said, "but I know where one is. I could—"

"Just tell me where," he interrupted.

"In the garage. Right inside the door on the left. There's a cup hook just about shoulder high."

"Fine," he said and turned toward the driveway. Then he stopped and looked back to the old lady in the car. "Thanks, ma'am. I think I can handle this now."

"I'm sorry if I caused any trouble," she said. "If only I hadn't locked the back door."

"Yeah. Well. Don't worry. We'll let you know if anything turns up," he said vaguely. He waited till she'd put her car in gear again and rolled slowly out of sight. Then he made his way back to the garage.

He reached inside the open door, groping along the exposed studs till he felt the hook. Nothing. He stepped inside, waiting for his eyes to adjust to the gloom of the garage, and considered the situation. First he gets this order to pick up the Cartwright woman. She's not here, but an old lady gives him some story about coming by two hours before and finding the back door open, her gone, and her purse still sitting in the kitchen. The old lady locks up the house when she leaves. And the extra house key is missing. If there really was an extra key.

Maybe he should just radio in that the Cartwright woman wasn't there and leave it at that. Or was he supposed to show more initiative than that? What was he supposed to do? If this was a test, they were certainly making it complicated.

Scanning the cluttered shelves under the window on the side wall, Howard picked out a thin scrap of sheet metal, probably used for a patch at one time, and the smallest screwdriver he could find. Then, his mouth set in a resolute grimace, he headed for the back door.

The kitchen looked ominously neat as he stepped across the threshold. He called out, but the silence of the house seemed impenetrable. Tiptoeing into the living room, he was relieved to find homey signs of life—an afghan on the sofa trailed to the floor beside a couple of books, an empty cup on the coffee table. The dining room, however, had obviously not been used in a long time.

He paused at the bottom of the dark stairwell, then started up, listening to each step creak beneath his weight. The door to the right at the top of the stairs was open. He entered, seeing with a surge of relief that the room was empty. Then he noticed the confusion of the bedclothes. The electric blanket, its control light still glowing, had been pulled to the floor, and a pillow, naked of its covering, lay beside it. A water glass had been overturned on the nightstand.

"Don't touch anything," Howard said aloud to himself, already backing out of the room.

# CHAPTER • FOURTEEN

AS GEOFF TURNED THE SECOND corner from the Point Blank post office, he saw a vehicle with a sheriff's star on its side pulling away from the Cartwright house. He tightened his grip on the steering wheel, swore, and kept going. Half a mile farther down the dirt road he pulled into a driveway and turned around. When he reached the house again, the road in front was deserted. He drove into the driveway and parked in back so the turquoise Mustang couldn't be easily seen from the road.

He sat for a moment with his hand still on the ignition key, thinking through the possibilities. The sheriff's department, he could see, was already onto this. Maybe some neighbor or a friend had discovered that the girl was missing. At any rate, there was no longer any need to worry about reporting it.

Wherever she'd called from, she obviously wasn't here now. Why hadn't the officer sealed off the house though? Geoff shook his head. He'd been right not to trust whatever incompetents had been left in charge while the sheriff was away. Nevertheless, the situation could work to his advantage. He could check out the house—if he could get in—before anyone else showed up.

He went up the back steps cautiously, then gently turned the doorknob. The back door swung inward easily. His eyes scanned the kitchen, registering details. The purse he'd seen her carrying sat on the hutch. There might be some helpful bit of information inside, but he'd have to be careful handling it.

Deciding to leave the purse for later, he tiptoed into the two front rooms. Nothing unusual there. He checked the titles of the books on the floor. *The Way to His Heart: Cooking for the Man in Your Life.* Under it was *Final Harvest: Emily Dickinson's Poems.* He noted the color of the afghan trailing from the sofa—colonial blue, he'd call it. Geoff smiled. Great details. Just the kind his readers loved. The grainy stuff.

Retreating to the dark passageway at the bottom of the stairs and taking care not to touch the handrail, he ascended slowly, inspecting each step as he went. The door to her bedroom was open and he could see, even before he stepped through the door, the "signs of a struggle." Phrases describing the disarray of the bed-clothes were already forming themselves in his mind.

He crossed the floor, glanced into the bathroom, then inspected the desk under the window. An appointment calendar had "Norton in Houston" scrawled across the last two days of the week.

He frowned, trying to recall his phone conversation with the dispatcher at the sheriff's department. Norton. Didn't she say the sheriff and his deputy—Norton, she'd called him—were at a conference in Houston? Were Beth Cartwright and this deputy friends? Lovers? His frown deepened. Colleagues? He thought of the cock-fight he'd taken her to at Belle's Marina. She'd seemed almost pitifully innocent and eager. But had she actually been setting him up? He stiffened. Then, careful to handle only the edge of the leaf, he turned to the next week's appointments. At the bottom of the right-hand page, across Saturday, was written "Norton?" He turned back two pages to the previous week. Again, scrawled across the weekend, was "Norton out of town."

Then his eye caught another notation, written more neatly on the Friday square: "Ignacio. Final payment."

Ignacio. Who was this Ignacio? What was she paying him for? He flipped several pages back into the previous month. Ignacio's name was written in three Fridays, along with a modest dollar amount. An informant? A laborer?

He let the stiff pages of the calendar drop back into place, noting with relief that his own name did not appear anywhere in the book. He remembered the mocking name he'd given the dispatcher that morning—had she caught on? If he left now, no one would know he'd been here. Maybe he could find out who this Ignacio character was before he called in his story.

Then he recalled his previous visit to the house. His fingerprints were probably all over the furniture in the living room. Where else? The back door. That might complicate things. The first thing they'd do was dust for prints. That would take a while though. At least they'd find none of his up here in the bedroom.

He was halfway down the stairs when he heard the sound of measured footsteps below, crossing the kitchen. He froze. The police are back, he thought. Of course. They weren't leaving the scene unsecured after all. How was he going to get out of this now?

Before he could think further, a black hulk blocked out what little light there was at the bottom of the stairs.

"Hullo?"

The voice was gruff, but Geoff sensed a strange uncertainty also. This was not a law officer. The reporter straightened and came down the stairs with cautious deliberation. "Yeah?"

"What's going on?" The man stood in the passage-way, blocking Geoff's descent.

"I don't know. I came by on business. I found the

back door open. Beth's not here." Then he added, "You a friend of hers?"

"No," the hulk said, finally backing out of his way. "I'm her priest."

Geoff took the final step into the passageway. This must be the guy who went into the prisons, the one the girl had told him about. "Father—"

"Dan Kamowski," the hulk said. He didn't extend his hand. "What's going on?" he repeated.

"I don't know. I just got here. We were supposed to meet. I came in to check things out. The back door was open. It looks like—" He shook his head and pointed up the stairs as though inviting the priest's inspection. "I don't know. Maybe you better have a look."

The big man pushed past him up the steps. Geoff waited till he heard him overhead, then retreated to the kitchen.

The heavy footsteps descended and made their way first into the front rooms of the house and then back into the kitchen. "We better call the sheriff," the priest said. "You touch anything up there?"

Geoff ignored the question. He didn't like the priest's overbearing tone. "I think they already know. I saw a county car leaving just as I got here."

"And you came on inside? They let you?"

Geoff shrugged. "I'm a reporter," he answered ambiguously.

The priest's eyes narrowed. "You say you were supposed to meet Beth Marie. What about?"

Geoff shrugged again. "It was professional."

The other man appeared to look at him more closely, as if the word, meant to derail further questions, had instead heightened the priest's interest. "You got any ideas about this?" he jerked a thumb toward the stairs. "It don't look good."

Geoff's eyes darted around the kitchen as though searching for something to settle on. "No. No, I don't.

But there's her purse," he said. "We could look in there."

Kamowski's pouchy eyes didn't leave his face. "Yeah, we could," he said slowly. "And maybe we will. But why don't you tell me what you know first?"

He stared at the priest, feigning surprise. "What do you mean?"

Kamowski took a long, deliberate step toward him and laid a massive hand on his shoulder. He fingered the collar of his denim jacket contemplatively. "Because I'm a priest, and when the sheriff comes back and I tell him I found you nosing around upstairs, he's going to believe me instead of you," he said. "If you know anything at all about this girl or what's happened here, I suggest you tell me right now."

Geoff tried to shake off his hand, but the priest only tightened his grip. "All right," Geoff said. "Do you know anybody named Ignacio?"

The priest didn't respond.

"I found the name written on her desk calendar. Along with payments she'd made to him."

Another moment went by. The priest's breathing slowed. The reporter looked up at him. He didn't often have to look up at anyone; this guy must be over six-six.

Kamowski transferred his grip to Geoff's arm. "Maybe I do," he said. "Come on. Let's go see."


As she pulled away from the Cartwright house, Cecelia decided she couldn't go home right then. People would have noticed the sheriff's department car at Beth Marie's and would call her to find out what was going on. She was beginning to be seriously worried about the girl's absence. If that young fellow had been sent out to check on her, something must be wrong.

So instead of going home, she drove. As long as she didn't go home she wouldn't have to answer questions about what had happened. The missing car keys had alarmed her more than she'd let on to the young man. Somehow, she didn't have a lot of faith in his abilities. He reminded her of someone. Who was it? He had a chin like Mason Dugger, the fellow who got run over by a hay mow a couple years ago. But it couldn't be his boy. The Duggers only had two girls. One had moved off to Chicago. The other lived someplace over close to Louisiana. Athens? No, Tyler. That was it. Married a Satterthwaite. Maybe she had a boy, one that looked just like his granddaddy. Whoever he was, surely he'd be contacting the sheriff right away. Surely.

Cecelia felt she had a special duty to Beth Marie. For one thing, she'd promised Catherine—who was probably looking down on them all right now in stern disapproval. But also because, not much more than a year ago, Beth Marie had saved her own daughter from a fate worse than death. What if Lois had actually run off with that Blalock boy? She'd be in prison herself now.

An angry horn blasted behind her. Startled, she jerked the station wagon to the right onto the shoulder to let a red pickup, its body jacked up high over its axles, speed past.

I've got to pull myself together, she thought, her heart racing. Where am I going? I can't just wander around like this, Lord.

She would not have sworn that the answer she received came directly from the mind of God, but a thought did present itself with startling clarity. The sign right in front of her as she sat on the side of the road composing herself said "Belle's Marina." Cecelia read the name aloud, recalling how evasive Beth Marie had seemed about what she'd been doing there when they'd gone to retrieve her car. She eased the car into gear again. At least it was a place to start.

She followed the rutted track leading off the highway with slow deliberation. The place was farther off the highway than she'd expected. When she rounded the last clump of trees, she saw that the parking lot was deserted except for a Budweiser truck backed up to a side door. She pulled up close to the truck and, as she struggled out of the station wagon, smiled hopefully at the young man wheeling a dolly down the ramp. He ignored her.

"Excuse me," she called, squinting against the winter sunshine. "Is anyone inside?"

He braked the dolly at the bottom of the ramp. "Yeah," he said. "Cody." Despite his plain intent to keep his expression impassive, Cecelia could tell he was wondering what in the world an old lady like her was doing at a honky-tonk on a Saturday morning.

She thanked him and made her way up the two plank steps onto the narrow porch, then pushed open the door of the front entrance. It took several moments for her eyes to adjust to the darkness inside. Then she made her way across the bare floor to a table close to the bar where a woman was filling a cash bag.

The woman frowned at her as she approached the table. "We're not open yet."

"No, I didn't expect you would be. For business, anyway. Might you be Cody?"

The woman set her face in the same impassive manner as the delivery man had outside, then zipped up the bag and laid her forearm across it. She had on tight jeans and a black sweater with a neck so low it exposed the upper edge of a black lace bra and a remarkable expanse of freckled flesh. It occurred to Cecelia that the woman was concerned about being robbed.

"I'm looking for someone. A girl," Cecelia said, steadying herself against a chair back. "A young woman, I guess you'd call her."

"We don't serve minors," the woman said, defensiveness giving an edge to her voice.

"Heavens, no. I didn't mean that. I mean, well, her

name's Beth Marie Cartwright. From Point Blank. She works for the *Somerville Courier.*"

At the mention of the newspaper's name the left side of the woman's mouth jerked slightly.

Encouraged by this, Cecelia went on. "She's gone. She disappeared sometime last night."

The woman's eyes slid sideways.

Cecelia tightened her grip on the back of the chair and waited. She didn't know what else to say.

"Who are you?" Cody's voice was deep and rough, though not unpleasant. It reminded Cecelia of water scrubbing rocks.

"Cecelia Ramsey. I live in Point Blank too." She hesitated. "I went by her house this morning—something just told me I should. Do you ever get those kind of feelings, like you were being *led* or something?"

The woman's eyes, still smudged with last night's mascara, narrowed.

"Anyway, she wasn't there. I told the deputy when he called—Norton, that is. And then later when the other deputy showed up to look for her, well, it appears that maybe something is wrong." She knew she was sounding foolishly vague.

Cody frowned up at her. "So? Why did you come here?"

Cecelia took a deep breath. "I knew that she'd been over here recently. She said it was to meet someone she was working with on a story. Have you seen her here? Let's see, she and my Lois are about the same age, about, well, let's say thirty. Nice-looking. She just got a new short haircut that looks good on her, even though it may be a little drastic for Point Blank. Sort of brownish."

Cecelia noticed that the woman's eyes had wavered once more when she mentioned that Beth Marie had been working with someone on a story. She gazed around the large, cavernous room now. "I guess if you could tell me who she met here. To work on the story, I mean. That might be helpful."

The woman picked up a pencil and tapped it rhythmically on the cash bag.

"I don't think the sheriff knows about her coming over here." Cecelia paused and prayed for guidance. She could tell the woman was trying to make up her mind. "You know, I remember when they used to have cockfights out back here. Before they'd been outlawed, I mean. Of course, that was so long ago it would have been before you were even born." She smiled encouragingly.

The woman took a deep breath, expanding her chest so that even more lace appeared over the top of the sweater. She appeared to be considering.

"I know Sheriff Dooley would appreciate any help you could give," Cecelia urged.

"We get a lot of people in here," the woman finally said. "I sure can't keep track of all their names."

"Certainly. I can see it can't be easy for you."

"There may have been someone like that. Short hair, like you say. Most girls come in here have that mall hair, you know? All long and frizzed out."

"And she was with someone?"

The woman hesitated. She ran a chipped red fingernail along the zipper of the cash bag. "There's this guy that comes in here ever now and then. A reporter—"

"Yes?"

The woman frowned at the interruption. "I think his name is Granger. I've seen it in the *Texas Times*."

Cecelia sincerely doubted that Cody ever read a magazine like *Texas Times*.

"Whether they was working on something though—" The woman shrugged to indicate her reservations. "Looked to me like he was working on getting her hopes up, if you know what I mean. Geoff does that sometimes."

Cecelia made a murmuring noise of sympathy.

"However." The woman raised one eyebrow. "Hopes is all she'll get from Geoff. He's got other things on his mind. Only time he gets interested in a woman is if he thinks she might know something he'd like to. I 'spect she's found that out by now. Whatever he was after from her, he's probably got." She picked up the pencil and tapped it sharply once more on the ledger. "But that's the way with men, ain't it? Money, sex, information. They know how to get what they want. I'll say that for them. If I was as good at getting what I wanted—" She broke off with a rueful shake of her head.

Cecelia nodded as if she understood all this. "What would that be?" she asked.

A finely etched furrow appeared between Cody's black eyebrows as she glanced at Cecelia suspiciously. Then, appearing satisfied with what she saw, she leaned back and folded her arms across her ribs like a shelf for her bosom to rest on, her gaze squinting into the middle distance. "Hard to say. Same as ever woman, I guess. Money and a man. Right now I could stand a little security."

"Oh, sweetheart," Cecelia blurted out before she could stop herself, "then you don't want either money or a man. They just get you stirred up."

Cody stared a moment, then laughed, exploding the air from her lungs like a shower of gravel. "I guess you're right. Security and stirring up don't go together, do they? I just can't make up my mind between the two—excitement or security. That's what gets me in trouble all the time." The laugh died away and her face turned serious again. "Well. That's all I can tell you about Geoff Granger and that girl," she said. "I seen 'em in here together, and I could tell she was getting all stirred up about him. But what they was supposed to be working on I couldn't say. But if you're thinking she's gone off with him or something like that—well, I don't think you have to worry."

"Thank heaven," Cecelia said with relief.

"She a good friend of yours, you say?"

"Almost like my own daughter."

Cody tilted her head, studying the stumpy figure holding onto the back of the chair. "She's lucky." Then she stuck the pencil out to Cecelia. "Here. Why don't you write down your name and number for me. I hear anything about her, I'll give you a call."

# CHAPTER FIFTEEN

HOWARD SATTERTHWAITE HATED using the pay phone outside the Point Blank post office, but figured he didn't have any choice. He would tell Lurline that the radio in the patrol car was acting up. If he called in from the patrol car, everyone in the department, plus all the jokers with CB scanners, could listen in.

Howard was more convinced than ever that the situation he found himself in was some kind of test Norton and the sheriff had cooked up between them. He'd been sent on a wild-goose chase, but he had to treat it as if he believed it was real, all the time knowing it wasn't and looking out for ways they might be trying to trick him.

He'd have to be especially careful about not breaking any department regulations. Already he'd broken into the girl's house, but if they asked him about that, he'd say that the old woman had only thought she'd locked it when she left that morning, that it was still open when he got there. He'd been careful to leave it that way himself, in case he might need to get back in.

After he called Lurline and explained there was a

short in his radio, he told her about the old lady and the scene he'd found inside the Cartwright house.

"What? Are you saying this looks like an abduction?" Lurline demanded, her voice rising. "I better get ahold of Norton and the sheriff right away. You stay there, Howard. And keep that place secured. Whatever you do, don't let any more little old ladies go traipsing through there, you hear?"

Howard hung up, his face flushed. She didn't have to tell him that. He knew that. Who did she think she was? Or was Lurline in on this too? He'd just climbed back in the patrol car and slammed the door when an old fellow in grimy quilted coveralls rapped his knuckles on the hood to get his attention.

The old man shuffled up to his window.

"Something wrong, son?"

"No," Howard said gruffly. He pulled a pair of aviator shades from his front pocket and put them on before he looked up at the man.

"You going back up to the Cartwright place?"

Howard nodded, keeping his face immobile.

"Anything wrong up there?"

Howard shook his head and turned the ignition key, gunning the engine.

"Well, you need any help, let me know. I'm just over at the filling station." The old man pointed across the street to a corrugated tin building with a couple of pumps out front.

Howard nodded and raised one side of his mouth slightly in what he hoped was a patronizing smile. Then he lifted his left hand to gesture both thanks and dismissal and put the car in gear. The man, who'd been leaning against the window, straightened and flicked his own hand briefly in an abbreviated wave, as if to acknowledge a kind of fraternal compact between them.

Howard drove slowly back to the Cartwright house, resisting the urge to turn on his rotating lights overhead.

After calling the department in Somerville and telling Lurline to have Beth Marie picked up and brought in, Norton had barely been able to sit through the rest of the introductory session on DNA-typing. This is it, he kept thinking. This is taking the plunge. He leaned forward over his knees, keeping his head down to hide his unmanageable grin and rubbing his hands together. When he caught the man beside him staring in his direction, he cleared his throat, sat up straight, and soberly crossed his arms across his chest.

But then he started picturing Beth Marie again, how surprised she was going to be when some unfamiliar deputy pulled her over on the highway and insisted on taking her in. She'd probably even be a little angry—her nose turned red when she got angry—but then later, when he walked in, looking serious at first, and asked her right out of the blue to marry him, all her anger would dissolve, leaving her suddenly limp. He'd have to catch her in his arms. It was going to be just the kind of proposal Beth Marie would think was romantic. It would make a story they could tell the rest of their lives.

He was pretty sure she'd want to get married as much as he suddenly did. It just made sense. No more trying to juggle their schedules so they could be together—that would do away with most of their quarrels. They could be together all the time except when they were at work. Every weekend. Every night. He made an involuntary noise in his throat but managed to turn it into a cough.

Now that he came to think about marriage—not just as an abstract possibility or an institution, but as real life—it made remarkable sense. Two salaries instead of one. He could get those rattling windows in the house sealed for winter. And the kitchen really needed rewiring. He wouldn't have to take his clothes to the laundromat any more. Maybe he could even teach her to cook. He could already feel the night's tense frustration loosening inside him.

His mind, dimly absorbing the speaker's comments about gene-tracking, had just started to consider the possibility of children, when someone touched him on the shoulder. It was the kid in the red jacket. He motioned Norton toward the rear of the room. The deputy followed him out into the corridor, where the kid handed him a white cordless phone. Norton said his name into the handset, turned his back, and walked a few steps away.

Lurline's voice, pitched higher than usual, poured out the details of Howard Satterthwaite's discovery. "Blankets were all pulled off the bed, laying on the floor. A glass knocked over. And the pillowcase had been stripped off the pillow."

It was as if someone had suddenly cut a cable and he was dropping thirty stories on an elevator. It was a moment before he could speak.

"Who'd you say you sent out there?"

"Howard Satterthwaite."

"That turkey!" Shock was turning quickly to rage.

"He was out in the eastern part of the county. He was the closest one."

Norton took a deep breath and released it slowly. Why hadn't he told Cecelia Ramsey to check upstairs? "Mrs. Ramsey was there earlier this morning. She answered the phone when I called. She said the back door was open."

"All I know's what Howard reported," Lurline said stiffly.

"Okay. Pull every man we have and get them over there on the double."

"Everybody?" Lurline asked hesitantly.

"No, wait. Some yo-yo's bound to screw up something that might be important if they're all trampling around the place." He paused while his mind flailed wildly. "Damn, Lurline. Satterthwaite! What was going on in your brain? Wait. Okay. Just send Larry Rostow. At least he's had some experience. He can keep an eye on Howard. I'll be there in forty-five minutes. But get the techs out there too. The best ones you can find on Saturday."

He lowered the handset while he rubbed at his forehead, trying to think clearly. When he lifted it again, he asked, "The bulletin you put out on her car. Anything come in on that yet?"

"No, sir."

"Well, get on the radio. Somebody's asleep out there. And call the departments in Trinity and Montgomery counties. Harris too, I guess."

"Sure the sheriff'll want that, sir? He doesn't like things to get outside the county if he can help it."

"Don't worry, Lurline," he said. He tried to speak as evenly as he could, but his voice shook nevertheless. "I'll take care of that."

He pushed the disconnect key and stood there a moment, willing himself to think clearly. Lurline was right. The sheriff wasn't going to like it. Was he overreacting?

If Beth Marie hadn't been home at eight o'clock on a Saturday morning—well, there could be other explanations for that. She could have left the house early, met someone for breakfast, done some work at the office. But why hadn't her car been spotted then? Or—he forced himself to think of another alternative—she could have been with someone else last night.

But would she have stayed away overnight or gone someplace this morning and left the back door unlocked? Not likely. And besides, there was her purse. Cecelia Ramsey said it was sitting in the kitchen with the car keys missing.

And the disarray in her bedroom—that indicated she must have spent the night there. Did Lurline's secondhand report of the scene indicate violence? Or an unrestrained encounter with someone else?

Norton shut his eyes tightly, remembering how upset

she'd been when he'd told her he was leaving town for the weekend. And her crying jag that day—what had really caused it? From this distance, it seemed unlikely that a missed phone call would have sent Beth Marie into such an emotional tailspin. What had been going on that he had blindly blundered past?

He had to see that upstairs bedroom for himself. He would know, he felt, the instant he stepped across the threshold, what had happened there.

He took out his pocket notebook, scribbled a message to the sheriff, folded it, wrote "Dooley" on the outside, and gave it to the kid in the red jacket to deliver at the coffee break. Then he headed for the stairs to the parking garage.


She knew they hadn't driven far to make the phone call. It had been very early. And it was Saturday. She told herself it made sense that she couldn't hear other vehicles on the road. Before he put her in the car, Ignacio had tied the pillowcase over her head again, but she had carefully counted the left and right turns they made. Three left and two right. However, for all she knew, they might still be within walking distance of the trailer.

As they drove, Ignacio told her who he was calling and what she was to say. "He can look up the information about my mother, if he doesn't believe you. It was in 1981 they put her in prison. And two years later they killed her."

"You said they were treating her for cancer. People die from cancer all the time. Even with the best care." Beth Marie tried to say this levelly, remembering his earlier, emotional denial.

"They lied. They wanted to get rid of her. They knew she was innocent." The anger in his voice seemed momentarily dulled. She decided to risk a question.

"Where are you from, Ignacio? And your grandmother—is she still alive? The reporter will want to know that."

Suddenly the tires screeched and the car swerved hard to the right. Beth Marie was thrown sideways against the door as the engine stuttered and died.

"You leave her out of it," the boy panted, turning toward her. "I have the knife in my hand at this moment. I could kill you."

Beth Marie's scalp prickled, and she could feel the sweat start on her body. She took a breath and said as calmly as she could, "The reporter will have to find information in the newspaper of your hometown. Then he'll want to talk to your grandmother, find out what she can tell him."

"Let him find the story in the big Houston paper," he said angrily.

"It might not be there," she went on, slowly.

"A sheriff got killed!" He was shouting now. "Don't tell me the Houston newspaper would not write a story about it. Everyone talked of it. Everyone knew. I could not even go to school!"

"Houston has enough murders of its own," she continued in a near monotone. "If it was in the Houston papers at all, it would have been only a short notice of her sentencing. He'll need more information. If you want him to have the whole story."

She held her breath, then felt the car pull forward.

"Tell him to look in the Harlingen paper then. That's close enough. August, 1981. But he must not bother my grandmother. She has suffered enough."

She hadn't been able to say any of that, however, when she talked to Geoff Granger.

Ignacio had not let her get out of the car when they stopped. Evidently he had found a drive-up phone, maybe in a convenience store parking lot, though she still could not hear any other vehicles around them. He stopped the car, keeping the motor running, and got out.

Surely, she thought, if anyone sees me with this pillow-case over my head, they'll know something is wrong. She heard gravel crunching as he came around the car, but she could hear no other sounds, no other cars.

A moment later he had jerked her door open and was fumbling with the cord around her wrists till she felt it loosen. Then she heard the electronic tones of a phone number being punched out. He must have found Geoff Granger's card stuck in her desk calendar. As the phone started to ring he thrust the receiver into her hand. A moment later the car rocked as he climbed back inside. Then the knife pricked through the pillowcase against her neck.

The conversation with Geoff had been over before she could gather her wits. Ignacio told her word for word what to say. Her voice had cracked when she repeated the phrase "he's going to kill me." Then he had grabbed the phone from her, breaking the connection. She could hear him panting. Maybe someone was coming. She could feel him stiffen.

The low buzz of tires on asphalt penetrated the pillowcase as he leaned against her, probably covering her from the view of the passing driver.

Gradually the sound of the tires faded and she felt him relax. He bent across her and tossed the receiver out the window. She could tell he was panicking. A receiver dangling from an outdoor phone. It could be traced. It might save her.

Another moment went by in silence. Then, as if they had shared the same thought, she felt him stretch across her to retrieve the receiver. He grunted once with the unsuccessful effort, then pulled back and twisted side-ways, raising himself on one knee and forcing his other leg across her to reach his arm and shoulders out the win-dow. She heard the receiver rattle as he replaced it on the hook. When he drew his shoulders back inside the car, she could hear him breathing hard.

One of his knees was still between her and the car door, the other leg stretched backward over the gear shift. His right hip had ground into her shoulder as he leaned out the car, but she had stifled a groan. Now as he shifted his weight to move back into the driver's seat, his belt buckle scraped across her face, and she cried out. He froze, as if suddenly aware of the contact of their bodies. Then she felt his thighs thrust against her.

"No!" She screamed and wrenched her head away, pushing at him. She felt the knife slide across her shoulder and down her left arm as he jerked sideways, collapsing into the driver's seat.

His breath came raggedly for several long moments. "You are evil," he finally said, his voice trembling with terror and contempt. She felt the prick of the knife again, the point breaking the skin over her ribs. She stifled another scream, forcing herself not to breathe. Gradually the pressure of the knife lessened. Then she heard the gears engage and she breathed again.

Too unnerved to disguise their location this time, Ignacio must have driven directly back to the trailer, because she counted only three turns this time. Then the Toyota bounced over rough ground, nosed abruptly down an incline, and came to a shuddering halt. Ignacio had thrown open the door, rushed around the car, and jerked her out, prodding her roughly up the steps of the trailer with the knife blade.

Inside, he had bound her hands and feet again, keeping silent all the while, except for his labored breathing. Then she heard him go down the steps and slam the door behind him.

After his sudden departure, she slumped against the bench, exhausted. She was dimly aware that she was hungry and thirsty. The cut on her arm began to hurt, and she could feel where a trickle of blood on her side was slowly drying and sticking to the filthy sweatshirt.

I've got to calm down, she told herself. Got to think.

She tried breathing deeply, and after she felt her heart slowing, she began to reconstruct what she had managed to tell Geoff Granger. Had he understood the danger she was in? Surely by now he had contacted the police. But who would he call? The Houston police? The Watson County sheriff's department? Norton and Sheriff Dooley wouldn't be there.

She was dizzy, almost sick. Everything was out of place, backwards, twisted out of shape. No one was what he seemed. Ignacio wasn't a migrant worker. He'd come to Somerville to avenge his mother. Was she the martyr he claimed? And Geoff Granger wasn't the romantic reporter she'd created from her fantasies. Norton, too. Where was he when she needed him most?

And what about herself? How had she ended up in this mess? She wasn't the kind of person Ignacio thought she was. Was she?

The old Beth Marie had begun to slip away a year ago. After she'd met Norton, she'd felt her whole life expanding as she opened her heart to him, felt herself emerging from the small, enclosed world of Point Blank. She'd believed it was a change for the better. She wasn't limited to being Catherine Cartwright's daughter anymore. And when she'd met Geoff Granger, she suddenly hadn't wanted to be limited by Norton either.

Ignacio had called her evil. Was he right? Who was she?

She felt her throat constrict. I can't cry, I can't, she told herself. I can't lose my grip.

She slid sideways onto the bench and drew herself up into a ball.

*Norton, Norton.* She called the name over and over again in her mind as though sending out a telepathic signal. *Norton, where are you? Help me. Where are you?*

And gradually, as she began to cry, the phrases began to change. *Lord, hide me. Come to my aid. Hide me under the shadow of thy wings. Let me never be put to shame.*

# CHAPTER • SIXTEEN

**T**HE PRIEST HADN'T OFFERED another word of explanation, had only propelled Geoff toward a van pulled up behind the Mustang in the back driveway. "Get in," Kamowski had ordered abruptly, and the reporter had obeyed. It appeared the guy knew something.

Now, however, Geoff wasn't so sure he'd done the right thing. They were reaching the outskirts of Somerville, and the entire ride had been spent in silence.

Geoff had been weighing the advantages of telling the priest about the phone call from Beth Marie. On the one hand, since he hadn't reported the phone call, he could be in serious legal difficulties. The First Amendment wouldn't stretch to cover this situation, especially if anything happened to the girl. Though he might get away with claiming he'd initially thought the whole thing was a hoax, now that he'd been to her house and discovered not only that she was missing but that there were signs she might have been abducted, he'd be skating on thin ice if he stuck to the hoax theory. Especially since he'd said nothing to the priest about the phone call.

But on the other hand, he couldn't bring himself to give away his one advantage. Not until this overbearing bastard tipped his own hand. Being a reporter, Geoff thought of information as investment capital, and he expected to get a healthy return on any he supplied. So far, the priest had not seen fit to reveal why the name "Ignacio" had sent him racing back to Somerville. Therefore, Geoff intended to keep his own ace-in-the-hole a secret.

Naturally, he assured himself, if the sheriff had been available, he would have already reported the call. It was only his fear that the situation might be bungled by some incompetent underling that had kept him from notifying the department already. Besides, he was very possibly on the verge of discovering who had kidnapped Beth Cartwright. This hulk of a priest evidently knew something.

Geoff glanced at his watch. If the priest was able to establish a verifiable connection between the mysterious Ignacio and the name Angelina Mascarenas within the next hour or so, he might still be able to call an exclusive in to the *Houston Chronicle*. Maybe this Ignacio character Beth had been paying off knew the woman who'd died in prison.

The priest, however, was obviously a skilled speculator himself, used to playing his own cards close to the vest. His mouth, set like a granite slab amid the folds of his sagging face, looked as if he never intended to open it again. Geoff was almost sorry now he'd revealed the name he'd found on the desk calendar.

He looked over at the man's impassive face as they pulled into the city limits, hating to be the first to break the silence.

"I take it you know something about this Ignacio character. Are you going to the police or what?" he forced himself to ask.

Kamowski grimaced and swung the van around a corner at the next light. "I gotta check something out here first," he said as he pulled up in front of a white frame building where a flock of nondescript sparrows pecked in the bare dirt between the curb and the front porch.

"El Buen Pastor Mission," the priest said glumly, as if even the name of the place was more than he wanted to disclose, though it was painted on a rickety sign in front. "You better come on in too."

Geoff grinned to himself. He could tell the priest didn't want his company inside, yet didn't want him out of his sight. He noticed the priest slowed his gait to a deliberate saunter as soon as he stepped into the mission.

"How's it going?" Father Kamowski said to a woman with thinning blond hair who sat sideways at a battered desk against the far wall of what, in a former state, had obviously been a living room. Gas fumes from a leaky space heater mingled with a whiff of bacon grease coming from a hallway that no doubt led to the mission's soup kitchen. A piece of pale green carpet, packed and discolored by the feet of countless petitioners, covered the midsection of the scarred wooden floor.

The woman, who'd been fingering through a jumble of files, looked up. "About the same as usual. The poor we have with us always. Volunteers come and go." She dropped the file back in the drawer and closed it. "What can I do for you, Dan?"

"I need any information you got about a guy who came here a few days ago." The priest had taken a seat in an unstable Danish modern chair of fifties vintage.

The woman eyed the chair nervously, then glanced up at Geoff and back to the priest. "You know we don't give out information about our clients, Father Kamowski."

He nodded thoughtfully, then reached in his pocket and pulled out his car keys. Pitching them to Geoff, he said casually, "I forgot to lock the van. Would you mind going out and doing that for me? Pretty rough neighborhood around here."

Geoff started to protest, then shut his mouth abruptly. It was evident the priest thought he could find out more from the woman with him out of the way. He turned and went out the door.

The congregating sparrows flew up into the bare branches overhead when Geoff stepped onto the porch, then settled again as soon as he'd made his way across the naked yard. Opening the van door to push in the lock button, he caught sight of a stack of brochures stuck in the side pocket. "Kairos," the black letters said at the top. Geoff pulled one out, stuck it in his jacket, and rummaged quickly through the other contents of the pocket. A list of names and local phone numbers, many crossed out, some with comments written beside them. Another list of names, computer-printed, each followed by long number sequences. It took a couple of seconds for him to figure it out: these were inmate names and numbers. He glanced at the top of the page. "Bromley Unit" it said in capitals.

He stuck that page inside his jacket too, shuffled the brochures and other papers neatly back inside the pocket, and finished locking up. He made plenty of noise crossing the porch again to give the pair ample warning of his approach. When he stepped back inside the stuffy room, both the woman and the priest smiled blandly up at him.

"Sister Luke has invited us to stay for lunch," the priest said. "How about it?"

Geoff's nostrils contracted. Was this guy crazy? They had a possible kidnapping on their hands and he was thinking about lunch? His own deadline was weighing on him heavier every moment. He wanted to get out of here, find out what the priest had discovered about Ignacio, and get his story called in.

"No thanks," he said, trying to keep the edge out of his voice.

"Sure." The priest nodded, affecting sympathy.

The woman smiled with benign pretense. "Maybe next time," she said and stood up to see them out.

"So what's going on?" Geoff demanded as the priest unlocked the van again.

Kamowski didn't reply until he'd pulled away from the curb. "A guy called Ignacio came here several days ago and collected a bag of groceries from the food bank."

Geoff stared at him. "That's all? What about an address, a phone number? A last name even?"

"People who come to the food bank don't usually have addresses and telephones," the priest said, swinging the van out onto the highway back to Point Blank. "And you can't always count on the names they give you."

The reporter stared straight ahead. He hated this guy. Time was running out. He'd been a fool to leave his car out in Point Blank. Maybe he'd even made a mistake coming up here from Houston. He might have already found out more information using the modem in his office than riding around the Watson County countryside with this cagey priest.

"So what did you find out?" he demanded. "What did she tell you?"

"Not much," Kamowski said with maddening nonchalance. "She said he picked up food for two people. She thought the other one might be a woman."

Geoff opened his mouth, then closed it again. They were both silent as the van rolled on for another mile between walls of dark pine trees, the pale winter sunlight flickering erratically across the dusty dashboard when there was a break in the timber. Then suddenly the priest swung the van off the highway and onto a gravel road marked with a Forest Service sign.

Geoff stared at him. "What's going on?"

The priest was silent until the van bumped to a stop in front of a brown-bordered sign showing a map of the campgrounds, along with a list of state regulations. Then the big man swung sideways in the seat, staring at Geoff impassively.

"The question is *who's* going on. Now either you tell me what you know about this business, son, or you get out and walk. It's five miles back to Somerville and about the same distance to Point Blank. You could probably hitch a ride either way. But the smart thing to do would be to tell me just why you happened to turn up at Miss Cartwright's house this morning, why you were nosing around upstairs, and what this story is you were supposedly working on together. The whole ball of wax. Otherwise you're going to be getting a little unexpected exercise and fresh country air."

"I can't believe this!" Geoff protested. "Have you lost your mind? Just what right do you have to be—"

"Hey!" the priest's voice interrupted his protests like a detonation. "What right do you have to be riding in my van?"

Geoff stared at the priest. Then he struck the van door with the side of his fist. "Damn, I hate you bullying church types. I guess this is your idea of Christian charity?"

"Don't play games with me, son. All I have to do is tip the sheriff off that you were poking around upstairs when I got to Miss Cartwright's house. For all I know, you're the one who broke in."

"Yeah?" Geoff shot back. "And what about you? You think being a priest gives you some kind of special immunity?"

"I could ask the same of a member of the press," the priest returned. "It's obvious you know something about this Ignacio. All I'm worried about is finding the girl. But I have this feeling you've got other priorities on your mind. Some story would be my guess. You say you were working on a story with her. Okay. So what was it about? I suggest you tell me everything you know. Otherwise, you're going to need a good Samaritan to come along and rescue your ass."

Geoff stared at him, speechless with rage.

"Fine," Kamowski said. "Out you go. But keep in mind, I'll be in Point Blank inside of five minutes. So don't be surprised if the first car offering to pick you up has a star on the side."

The defiance on the reporter's face began to fade. There was a long silence as the winter sun played through the pines.

"Okay," he finally said. He turned to stare forward out the window. "I got a call at home early this morning. Must have been around seven."

"Where's home?"

"Houston. It was Beth Cartwright. I could tell someone was with her, telling her what to say. The son of somebody called Angelina Mascarenas. She was an inmate in the Bromley Unit back when it was the women's prison. Supposedly she died there. Anyway, her son wants the world to know that his mother was innocent. A martyr was the word Beth used. He seems to think she was killed—by prison personnel, I take it. Beth was obviously repeating what this other person was telling her to say. Apparently he wants his dead mother exonerated in the eyes of the world. As if the world gives a shit. And I've got to get this in the Sunday papers." He paused. "Or he's threatening to kill her."

It was the priest's turn to stare now. "And you're just now telling me this?" He looked away and then back. "But you've called the police, right?"

Geoff hesitated. Then he said, "Yes and no."

The wind had picked up, and light rippled through the van as the pines bent and swayed across the sun.

"What?"

"I called the Watson County sheriff's office. They told me the sheriff and his chief deputy were out of town." He glanced sideways at the priest. "I had no idea where she was calling from. For all I knew she was at home. I was afraid if I turned this over to some redneck flunky, he might decide to play John Wayne, try to make a hero of himself, and end up getting her and everybody else killed."

"She didn't say where she was?"

"No. The connection broke off suddenly."

Kamowski was silent a long moment, gnawing on a large knuckle. "So you went out to her house. I don't suppose you had any fantasies of playing John Wayne yourself?"

"Sure," Geoff said contemptuously. "Like I keep a loaded assault rifle in my backseat."

"I did notice a camera."

"That's the only kind of shooting I do."

"I see. You think it's better to be a hyena than a tiger. You'd never murder anyone yourself, but you don't mind making money off of one."

"I don't know what you're talking about. The public has a right—"

"Yeah. Well, we don't have time for a discussion of the Constitution right now." The priest put the van in reverse, but kept the clutch in. "Is that all? You weren't able to pick up any hints of where they might be? Or if she was in any immediate danger?"

"No. I think maybe she'll be all right until tomorrow morning when the paper comes out. He's using her to get the publicity he wants. He won't do anything yet."

The priest shifted into low and eased the clutch out, but instead of turning around, he went farther on down the gravel road.

"Hey! Where're you going?" Geoff protested.

"There's a public phone down here," the priest said. "The campground's closed for the winter, but the phone works. You can call from there."

"But—"

The priest pulled the van up in front of a set of cinder block toilets and pointed to the phone on the pole nearby. "Then you can call a cab. Or I'll send somebody back to pick you up. It'll be the car with a star on the side. Now go call in your story."

Norton had had forty-five highway minutes to think. That had been too long. Leaving Houston, he had been forced to concentrate on outmaneuvering the north-bound traffic on I-45, but twenty minutes later when he'd only reached The Woodlands he could feel anxiety rising inside him like a tide that threatened to submerge his rationality. His palms were sweating and sticking to the steering wheel. He wiped them, one at a time, on his thighs and tried talking to himself.

"All right. All right," he said aloud. But then the words stopped. All that came from the chaos inside his head and chest was an incoherent roar.

"Okay," he tried again, "okay. Here's the plan. Best case, worst case." He tried to think of the least frighten-ing explanation for the scene Howard Satterthwaite had found at Beth Marie's. Maybe she had just gone shop-ping or something. Where wasn't important. Maybe she'd been in a hurry, knocked over stuff, left a mess. Not very likely. Not like Beth Marie at all. The best case wasn't a very convincing possibility.

Worst case. He steadied himself against the onslaught of the tide this time, holding it back from at least a part of his mind so that he could think. Un-known intruder comes in through the back door she for-got to lock. Again, not likely. If Point Blank was on a main highway, it might make sense, but being on a back road kept it isolated from that kind of random criminality. It was more likely that she'd known who-ever it was.

Someone local? Again, possible. Point Blank had its share of violent natives. In fact, that's what had brought him and Beth Marie together—when the Baptist preach-er's son had been shot by Cecelia Ramsey's cousin. Beth

Marie herself had almost been killed. But he'd been able to save her then.

He could feel the wave lap over the wall. What about this time? This time he hadn't been there. In fact, he'd left her. He hadn't been paying attention or he would have known she needed him. Or needed something. Otherwise she would never have shown up at the department the other day in the state she was in. She wasn't a girl to come crying about nothing.

As he recalled her near-hysteria in the car, his mind clamped down eagerly on an actual event he could deal with as data, dissect for clues. Something had been very wrong—and it wasn't just a spat with the receptionist. Something she obviously hadn't wanted to tell him about. What had she said later at his apartment? Something melodramatic about revealing a source. He'd made fun of her. He remembered now. And it had made her mad. When she refused to say any more about it, he had suspected it was only because she'd made the whole thing up. Or blown it out of proportion anyway.

"Hell!" he exploded, gripping the steering wheel. And his anger was both at himself and at life in general, the way it slipped up behind you, no matter how hard you tried to be ready for it. "How was I supposed to know?"

It was the tone of voice in which he asked the question that brought him up short. It was the same tone of aggrieved complaint he'd heard so often in the voice of kids he'd shoved into the backseat behind the wire screen of the sheriff's cruiser. It was a question that had to be put aside for the time being.

"Okay," he said aloud again. "Say it was someone she knew. Who?"

It was then that he realized how few of Beth Marie's other friends he knew. Cecelia Ramsey in Point Blank. A couple of people from the paper, though he'd only just met them. The members of her church he didn't know at all. However, he doubted the hypothetical intruder would be one of them.

No, the best bet was still this mysterious "source" she'd alluded to. Possibly some underground connection. Maybe she had in fact gotten in over her head. It would be just like Beth Marie. Living out some kind of story-book fantasy. But who? What? She hadn't said anything specific, hadn't mentioned drugs or gangs or any particular news connection for this supposed informant. No wonder he'd thought she was making the whole thing up.

As he passed the sign marking the Watson County line, he radioed in to Lurline. Still no word about the Toyota, she said. And the sheriff had called. Fit to be tied, she said. Wanted to know what the hell was going on.

"Sorry. I'm losing you for some reason, Lurline. I'll try again when I get out to Point Blank," he said as he turned off the switch. The sheriff would have to wait. Norton couldn't afford to worry about him. If his mind went beyond the present moment, the anxiety began to wash over the top of the dam. Even now, he could feel it eating away at the footings.

He wiped his palms on his thighs again and cursed a pickup that turned out of a side road in front of him. The palpable fear sank slightly inside his chest, as though some of the pressure had momentarily escaped in the outburst of anger.

"All right," he said again. A plan. He had to have a plan. With any luck, Larry Rostow would be there by now and have the situation stabilized, the site secured. If Satterthwaite hadn't already destroyed some essential information they would need. He heard himself saying, "Please, please," and wondered fleetingly who the appeal was meant for.

As he turned the final corner to her house, sliding sideways on the gravel, he saw the two official vehicles— a patrol car and the technicians' van—parked along the fence. Good. Larry had at least kept any tracks in the back driveway clear. He slammed his own car to a halt so it would block the entrance.

It was then he spotted, at the end of the drive, the vintage turquoise Mustang looking like something that had materialized straight out of Beth Marie's daydreams. He couldn't have been more certain.

"The source," he said.

# CHAPTER · SEVENTEEN

**A**S SOON AS THE TRAILER DOOR slammed behind him, he had set out running. He knew he had to get as far away from the woman as possible. He could see now she was a witch, a *bruja*. She had cast a spell on him, caused him to feel things, do things that he, the true Ignacio, did not want to feel or do. Not the true Ignacio.

He crossed his arms across his chest and gripped his shoulders as if to defend himself or, rather, to hold himself together. A false Ignacio, the one she had conjured up, was inside him, threatening to take over. He knew it was her creation because it grew powerful within him whenever she was near. Demanding, voracious. It wanted to do things the true Ignacio had never wanted.

But the true Ignacio, the one who, without crying, had watched the big white Lincoln of the Hidalgos drive past him, the one who prayed at the shrine he had built in the trailer, what had happened to him? Where did he go when the false Ignacio wanted to do brutal things to the witch? He remembered how her flesh and bones, pressed against him in the car, had felt at once hard and soft. It had taken his breath away. Then she had cried out, frightening him. He had wanted to sink the knife into her then. Plunge it deeply into her flesh. Just the prick he had given her had made her tremble. Ah—to make a witch tremble! He hugged himself tighter.

Suddenly his left foot sank in a mole burrow, and he pitched forward into the dry stubble of the field, rolling over and over, feeling the hard winter earth defining the circumference of his form. Sensing the boundaries of his body restored him instantly to sanity. He thought, this is the true Ignacio. This is. She will not get through again. I will not let the witch through.

When he came to rest at the bottom of an incline, he lay on his back, staring up at the sun, almost at its apex in the southern sector of the sky. He took a deep breath and let it out slowly. It was warmer today than yesterday. The wind had stopped. He felt his muscles gradually relaxing. He had had little sleep. The scents of the warmed pasture rose around him—the dark, damp earth, the dry grasses crushed under his weight. He closed his eyes, and slowly his fingers unclenched from his shoulders, dropping curled against the ground.

He was on the ferry down below Rio Grande City, across from Ciudad Camargo on the Mexican side. They had just released a lot of water from Falcon Dam up above, and the raft floated high and easy in the river. He lay on his back, feeling almost as if he were flying. Shading his eyes from the sun, he looked down along his glistening body and saw that he was naked. He turned on his side and saw on the bare sand across the river his mother. Her hair was down and loose and she was stretching out her arms to him. He sat up, looking for the guide-rope that attached the raft to the pulley overhead, but it was gone. Then, suddenly, near the raft, shooting from the water like a geyser, rose a woman. The witch!

She balanced her briefcase on her head with both hands and laughed at him. Then, lowering the leather case onto the water as if it were the surface of a table, she snapped it open. The lid flew up and out stepped his father onto the raft. He glanced down at Ignacio lying there as if he didn't see him, or if he did, as though it was no more to him than seeing an empty can beside the road. He flexed his powerful shoulders—they were furred with black hair—and dove into the water.

The witch laughed again and swam toward the raft. He watched her coming closer, frozen with horror. He looked across to the far side of the river. His mother had disappeared. The witch raised her hands, dripping from the water, grasped the edge of the raft, and started to pull herself from the river. He jerked away.

"No!" he heard himself shouting. He was kicking her. Hard. In the face. She was bleeding into the water. The whole river was turning red, tinged with her blood. "No!"

Suddenly he was sitting up, staring around at the empty field. He turned back toward the trailer at the top of the rise. A thin cloud blurred the sun. He started to shiver. He made a noise in his throat, high and despairing. Then, scrambling to his feet, he began to run again.

Cecelia's driving had not been improved by her encounter with the woman at Belle's Marina. Her mind kept drifting back to the conversation, and the station wagon would drift onto the shoulder of the highway or into other lanes. More than once she was startled out of her reverie by an angry blast from a horn.

Deep down inside that Cody was a nice girl, Cecelia decided. But like most girls today, she was probably too obliging. Why was that? Girls like Cody worked at honing themselves, just like sharpening a knife, so they'd be hard enough to keep harm away, not get taken advantage of. Then, first thing you knew, they'd turn right around and go to any lengths to humor the first no-good, low-down rascal who caught their eye. Her daughter Lois was like that too. That's how she'd got mixed up with Finney

Blalock. Well, she hoped Cody got herself another job before the sheriff found out about the cockfighting that still must be going on out back. Meanwhile, at least she'd found out the name of that reporter Beth Marie had been working with.

Cecelia pictured the two of them working together like children, their heads shining in the lamplight as they bent over their tablets at the kitchen table, struggling through their homework. Maybe that's where Beth Marie was now. If she'd gone someplace with this Geoff Granger, she sure wouldn't want anyone checking up on her. Cecelia knew what Lois would say. *For crying out loud, don't you think I can take care of myself?* Not long ago Beth Marie might have only laughed when she found out her friends had been worried about her, and even thanked them for their trouble. But now? Cecelia wasn't so sure.

What kind of a story was she working on with this Houston reporter anyway? She'd never mentioned it, not even when they'd gone to pick up her car the other morning. And why would Beth Marie have left her purse at the house?

A horn blared and tires squealed as Cecelia wandered into the left lane again. Shaken, she pulled off onto the grassy shoulder and swallowed drily, waiting for her heart to stop pounding. A woodpecker drilled on a pine tree close to the road. She felt like she was battering her own head against a hard surface.

"Well," she said aloud to herself after a few moments, "the Lord wouldn't have sent me out to Belle's Marina if he hadn't had a reason."

She put the car in gear again, but, deciding she'd be safer off the main highway, she turned onto a back road angling toward home. At the next blacktopped road, she turned right, her hands maneuvering the steering wheel in jerky increments. Once she got home, she decided, she would call the *Texas Times* in Houston and try to find this Granger person. It was all she could see to do.

The road, one she hadn't been on in a long time, meandered through a patchwork of cleared pastures and reforested sections of timber harvested periodically by paper companies. At one time, Cecelia had known the owner's name of every field she passed. But now she couldn't tell who half the land belonged to.

A sinking corrugated tin shed marked the site of what used to be the Gilpin place. A pole corral, its cedar posts green with moss, was where the old Czech used to load up his spring calves for market. And beyond the next stand of evenly spaced pines was the MacGruder place. Bud Wylie had told her some fellow from Houston had bought it to raise horses on, but had lost it for back taxes recently. The new, white gentrified buildings he'd put up were already turning grey with neglect, the prancing wrought-iron horses on the weather vane beginning to rust. And he'd left his trash behind too. From the road she could see discarded building materials poking out of a wash behind the Dutch-roofed barn. Even an old camping trailer had been tipped into the ravine. Such a shame. No telling who would take over the place now.

Another stretch of timber in regimented rows crowded the road for a couple of miles. Then, as her station wagon topped a hill, a long stretch of pastureland spread out on both sides of the road, land that had belonged to her dead husband's family for four generations. Her own part of it was a mere five acres, for which she was glad. Land was a weighty responsibility, and she hadn't been sorry when her young cousin Archie had inherited the bulk of it. Old Bud Wylie was doing a good job managing it for him; nevertheless, it would probably end up in the hands of speculators eventually.

She was almost within sight of her own little house when she saw the boy bending down to crawl through the barbed-wire fence. The wire had snagged the back of his plaid shirt. Still bent, he spotted her, jerked the shirt loose, and struck off across the field, headed back toward the timber in the direction from which she'd come.

Cecelia frowned, trying to recall where she'd seen the boy before. Was he the one the Gorlack sisters had hired to clean the chimney this fall? No. That wasn't it. It must have been at Beth Marie's. Yes. That was the boy Beth Marie had hired to work Catherine's flowerbeds. Cecelia remembered the girl saying she felt sorry for him because the horse farm where he'd worked had closed. Cecelia had tried to think of some jobs she might give him too, but she knew eighty-year-old Loomis, the handyman she'd more or less inherited from her Aunt Min, wouldn't like an outsider coming around.

She wished she'd recognized him quicker. She would have offered him a ride. She glanced in the rearview mirror at his diminishing figure. How was he surviving? Maybe she ought to get Bud to go over to the horse farm and check on the boy. What if he was cold and hungry? Right there under their noses?

She'd write it down, she thought as she pulled into her driveway, so she wouldn't forget. But first of all she had to call that magazine fellow in Houston.

She paused only long enough to jot down "Boy—Beth Marie" on a pad she kept beside the phone in the kitchen, not even stopping to take off her coat. Then she looked at the square black plastic box beside the phone, said "Drat!" and banged her large, heavy handbag down on the kitchen table. The red light on the black box was winking at her like an evil eye.

Cecelia hated the contraption. Like some kind of alien animal it guarded the instrument that had previously been friendly and companionable. She still didn't completely understand how to use the machine. However, Lois had bought it for her last Christmas, and she couldn't afford to seem ungrateful where her daughter was concerned. She couldn't simply disconnect the thing and put it away in the closet because Lois might call while she was away, and if the machine didn't answer, her daughter would know she wasn't using it.

As long as the eye glowed a steady red, Cecelia could live with it, even though she didn't like it. But when it began to wink, her brain went into spasms of anxiety. That meant it had captured a message between its mechanical paws and didn't intend to give it up without a fight.

Often Cecelia simply ignored the winking light until someone came over who could operate the machine for her. Usually the messages weren't very important anyway. Today, however, the message might be from Beth Marie. She couldn't afford to ignore it.

She sat down and tried to compose herself first. She took a deep breath, closed her eyes, and prayed. Then she held out one plump finger, watched till it stopped trembling, took another deep breath, closed her eyes, and stabbed at the array of buttons.

There was a whirring noise, then a click, and finally a high, thin voice. "Miz Ramsey, this is Lurline at the sheriff's department. Deputy Norton would sure appreciate it if you could meet him over at the Cartwright house in Point Blank. It looks like—well, I'll let him tell you about it. Anyways, he's going to need your help, I think. Thank you. And have a—"

The machine clicked again, cutting off the voice, then whirred as the tape rewound. When Cecelia opened her eyes, its eye was no longer winking. But by then it had already done its damage.


Norton went down the drive carefully to avoid stepping on any tracks and walked all the way around the Mustang. Larry Rostow was coming down the back steps by then.

"We've already got an I.D.," he said, joining Norton by the car. "Harris County. Belongs to a Geoffrey Granger."

"Anything on him?"

"An address is all. Just off Westheimer."

Before he could stifle the reaction, a grimace flickered across Norton's face. Westheimer was an area of Houston noted for trendy restaurants, boutiques, and what Sheriff Dooley would call deviant behavior. What was somebody like that—someone who would drive a vintage Mustang—doing in Point Blank? What was Beth Marie doing knowing him?

He headed toward the house, Larry following him. Entering by the back door, he found a couple of technicians sorting through the contents of the garbage pail they'd dumped on a plastic sheet in the middle of the floor.

"We got started down here," Larry said. "But we haven't done anything upstairs yet. I figured you'd want to look around first."

Howard Satterthwaite was talking on the phone at the bottom of the stairs. Norton stepped across the plastic sheet and stopped at the bottom of the stairs. He stood waiting, hands on his hips, till Howard hung up the phone.

"Just checking again with Lurline about Miss Cartwright's car," the intern said nervously. "Still no word. She said to tell you she couldn't get Cecelia Ramsey, but she left a message on her machine."

Norton turned to Larry. "Get the county map out of the van. I'll be down in a minute." Then he started up the stairs alone.

At the top of the stairs he hesitated. The door to Beth Marie's bedroom was open, and through the north window he could see the hood of the turquoise Mustang below in the driveway. What kind of a name was Geoffrey Granger anyway? Why hadn't she said anything about him? Was this the interview she had been angry with the receptionist for messing up?

His stomach tightened as he stepped into the room.

Forcing himself to stand still a moment, he let his mind absorb details. He had learned his brain would do that—blot up data and store it away until he could process it later. The white filmy curtains, for instance, at the window where she had her desk. The briefcase he'd given her lying closed on the chair, just as she'd probably set it down when she came in from work the night before. The bookcase beside the desk, packed with old college textbooks and newer paperbacks. Photographs of both her parents in oval frames on the wall. And a snapshot she'd taken of him last summer at the lake stuck in the mirror over the dresser. Nothing along that wall appeared to have been touched.

But in the middle of the floor lay the stripped pillow. The water from the overturned glass had soaked into an embroidered doily on the bedside table. The glass itself was lying by the baseboard on the far wall. The bedside lamp leaned askew against the bed's headboard. And the sheets and blankets, pulled loose from the foot of the bed, had been dragged halfway off the mattress. It looked like the aftermath of violence all right. Stark, not sensual. The missing pillowcase clinched the matter. It had been taken for a purpose. To put stolen items in? But the room wasn't torn apart in that way. Maybe to cover her head. His shoulders jerked involuntarily.

Stepping carefully across the floor, he nudged the bathroom door open with his shoulder. Nothing out of the ordinary there, but he didn't want to risk touching any of the surfaces. A white towel that she had thrown over the shower-curtain rod brushed against his ear. Before he could stop himself, he had buried his face in its rough texture, breathing in deeply, filling his lungs with the smell of her skin. He dropped the towel on the floor, went back through the bedroom, and down the stairs.

The sight of Satterthwaite's thin face staring at him anxiously at the bottom of the stairs provided him with a focus. Nothing would have pleased Norton more at that moment than to dislocate the kid's collarbone. But he had to be careful here. He was aware that in Howard he was working with inferior material. If the kid were too frightened, he would either lie or forget something important.

"All right," Norton said, keeping his voice down as he led him into the living room. "Start from the beginning."

Howard, who'd had the presence of mind to break and fray a wire on the radio phone in the patrol car before Norton arrived, had gotten to the part where he'd called Lurline from the pay phone outside the post office when they saw another vehicle pull up in front.

"Wait here," Norton said to the intern. When he stepped out onto the front porch, he saw that Larry had already stopped the big man who was climbing out of the Ford van. Norton strode down the walk, in a glance taking in the clergy sticker on the van's back window and the priest's collar.

"Investigation underway," Larry was saying.

"I need your name," Norton said preemptively, stepping up beside him. He had already figured out that the guy was Beth Marie's priest, though he hadn't expected him to look like an aging linebacker.

Kamowski hitched up his belt and lowered his bull-like head at the deputy. He looked nervous. "Dan Kamowski," he said.

"St. Barnabas?" Norton asked.

The priest nodded, but seemed strangely impassive in the face of all the official commotion. He took a deep breath and said, "Actually, Sheriff, I've come back. I was here earlier."

Norton tried to match his impenetrable demeanor. "When?"

"Around ten-thirty."

"What were you doing here?"

"Making a pastoral call on Miss Cartwright."

"And?"

"She wasn't at home."

Norton frowned up at him. "So what brought you back?"

The priest appeared to ignore the question. "Someone else was inside when I got here."

"The Mustang in back—"

"Belongs to the man who was here."

"What was he doing here?"

"He was upstairs." Kamowski paused. "I saw the car, the back door of the house was open, so I just stepped in. I heard him walking around up there. He said there were signs of a struggle."

"Did he say why he was here? Where is he now?"

"He'd gotten a phone call from Beth Marie early this morning. He said he wanted to check it out, make sure it wasn't a hoax."

"A hoax?" Norton echoed.

"He's a reporter. Supposedly someone has the girl and wants him to write a story for the paper. About his mother. I take it she was an inmate at the Bromley Unit when it was the women's prison."

Norton stared at the priest a moment longer; then his eyes wavered. The source. A reporter. Westheimer neighborhood. "He called the Houston police? Our department didn't—"

"No. He didn't contact the Houston police. Instead he phoned your office, but he didn't tell the dispatcher about the call from the girl—"

"What are you saying?" Norton broke in. "You mean—"

"He said the sheriff here was out of town and he was afraid what might happen if some local yokel got wind of it."

"He thought he'd handle this on his own?" Norton's voice was rising. "Where is he now?"

"Just off the highway into Somerville. That state campground. I dropped him off there to use the telephone—"

"The telephone!"

"He had a deadline. He had to get this story into Sunday's paper."

Norton's consternation had reached the level of speechlessness. He stared at the priest, waiting for him to go on. The big man seemed strangely uneasy, shifting his gaze from side to side before he answered.

"I guess the deadline is important. The girl's life may depend on this story being in the paper tomorrow."

Norton called back over his shoulder to the priest as he headed for the car. "Stay here. I'll be back. Don't leave."

Kamowski looked back at his van and scowled. Then, head lowered like a balky bull, he followed Larry Rostow inside.

# CHAPTER EIGHTEEN

CECELIA DIDN'T KNOW WHEN SHE'D felt so tired. Her arms and legs felt heavy as logs. You're too old to be running around the countryside, a nagging voice complained. They ought to know that. If the sheriff wants to talk to you, he ought to come to you. And Beth Marie. What could she expect but trouble, traipsing around to honky-tonks on back roads with degenerate reporters from Houston.

Cecelia recognized the voice. It came from a place in her head just behind her left ear, most often when she had spent all her energy. Fortunately, she had learned to slide a little window shut to muffle the complaints; then she could use the rest of her brain to think about other things. Such as the fact that she'd had nothing to eat all day. Most likely that's why she was feeling so crossways all of a sudden.

Dragging herself from the kitchen chair, she went to the refrigerator and took out a pitcher of orange juice. After she drank half a glass, she felt able to pull out a loaf of bread and smear peanut butter across a slice. This she ate standing at the counter, washing it down with the rest of the orange juice. Then she rinsed the glass, poured it full of milk, and took it back to the table where she sat drinking it slowly and contemplating the note she'd written to herself: "Boy—Beth Marie." For the life of her, she couldn't remember his name.

When she finished the milk, she lifted the shutter over her left ear a crack. The voice was only grumbling now in a low monotone. Good. It wouldn't take long to run over to Beth Marie's. She felt like she could make it now. Later she could rest.

But as she drew up in front of the Cartwright house, the sight of the sheriff's department vehicles unsettled her again. She opened the door of the station wagon slowly, trying to sort out the scene. Where was Norton? Lurline had said he would be waiting for her.

The young fellow she'd run into earlier at the post office came out the front door and made his way down the walk toward her. She studied his chin—the spitting image of Mason Dugger's.

"Mrs. Ramsey?" He touched the brim of his hat in an abbreviated gesture of courtesy.

"Norton sent for me," she said.

"Yes, I know." He closed the car door for her and offered his arm. "He's, uh, had to go check something out. He should be back soon. Till then, you just make yourself comfortable inside."

She allowed him to lead her up the front steps and into the living room as though she were a stranger to the house. As she stepped inside, a figure on the sofa rose, so startlingly tall that she stopped in the doorway, overwhelmed by the black expanse of his clerical clothes.

"Dan Kamowski," he said before the young intern could interject an introduction.

"You're Beth Marie's minister," Cecelia said, taking a step toward him and holding out her hand.

He stuck out his own hand awkwardly as he sank onto the sofa again.

She looked around for Mason Dugger's grandson, suddenly afraid. "What's wrong? Have they found Beth

Marie?" But the young man had already taken up his post out on the front porch again.

Kamowski cleared his throat. "No, ma'am." His lowered voice and a gesture indicating she should sit beside him on the sofa seemed to signal his preference for a private conversation.

"You're a friend of hers? A neighbor?" he asked.

"I've known Beth Marie since she was just a little bitty thing," she said, restraining her impulse to embroider that plain fact. "Is there something wrong?"

The priest's eyes wandered the pattern of the carpet in jerky little movements. "It looks like there could be."

"What?" she insisted softly, looking over her shoulder at the door. "What's happened?"

"Would you know anybody named Ignacio?" the priest asked. "Hispanic kid, about eighteen or so. Skinny."

"Ignacio?" She startled him by throwing her hands up in the air as she repeated the name with delight. "Of course. That's it. Bless your heart! I've been trying for over an hour to come up with that name. That's the boy who worked for Beth Marie. He did her flowerbeds this fall."

The priest nodded, looking thoughtful. "You know where he lives?"

"I think he used to work at that horse farm east of here. But they shut down weeks ago. And Beth Marie had run out of work for him too. I thought he'd probably moved on." She paused and frowned. "But isn't that funny? I saw him today. Not long ago, in fact. He was on foot, and I would have stopped and given him a ride, but he crawled through the fence and struck out across the field."

The priest stared at her hard a moment, then shifted his gaze to the front window where they could see the intern pacing nervously on the porch. When he spoke again, he dropped his voice even lower. "Do you think you could show me where you saw him? I don't know this part of the county too well."

"Of course." She looked puzzled. "Just as soon as Norton gets back. You don't think the boy has anything to do with Beth Marie, do you?"

Kamowski leaned closer and put a beefy hand on her arm. "Ma'am. Listen to me carefully. I know something about this boy. You're going to have to trust me. I think Beth Marie may be with him. I don't know if she's in any actual danger. But the longer this goes on, the more likely that becomes. I need to find him. Find them."

Cecelia frowned and moved her arm slightly so that his hand fell away. She wasn't used to preachers in black shirts and backward collars. Maybe they had different ways of thinking about things. All she cared about right now was finding Beth Marie. "How do you know all this?" she asked warily. "How did you find out?"

He started to brush the question aside, but then stopped as if he'd thought better of it. "I came by here earlier today. Just to make a call on Beth Marie. I had a feeling there was something she might want to talk about."

"Oh?" Cecelia sat up straighter and looked at him narrowly. "Do you get those feelings too? *I* had a feeling this morning when I was driving by here. Something just told me to stop and check on her."

Kamowski's eyes widened slightly; then he looked at the floor. "Well, I don't know. I wouldn't want to—" He looked up and, seeing the eagerness on her face begin to dissolve, changed directions. "Of course, anything's possible, I guess," he finished lamely.

The pouches around her eyes that had begun to sag lifted again and her eyes brightened. She reached for his wrist and patted it encouragingly.

"Anyway. I found somebody else here. Some fellow with a ponytail. His car's out back. He was snooping around upstairs."

"But I locked the door when I left."

"You were here too?"

"Yes. Like I said. I got this feeling—it must have been around eight this morning."

The priest shrugged. "I don't know how he got in. He said the back door was open. He told me the bedroom upstairs, well, it looked like she might have been forced to leave."

Cecelia's eyes grew rounder as she lifted her plump fingers from his wrist and put them to her mouth. "Did you look?"

"Yes." He let a moment go by to indicate that he, too, thought the scene looked ominous. "This guy with the ponytail—he said he was a friend of hers, a reporter—"

"Geoff Granger," Cecelia said faintly.

"Yeah. That's what he said his name was. Said they'd been working together on a story. Beth Marie called him this morning, he says. Someone was with her. He wanted this guy Granger to get a story in the newspaper by tomorrow about his mother. Angelina Mascarenas. She was a prisoner at the Bromley Unit, sent up for murdering a sheriff."

"But they haven't had women there for years. He would have been just a child."

"Yes. According to him, she died there. He thinks she was innocent. That there was some kind of plot and the prison doctors killed her." The priest paused and drew in a long breath. "Of course he's whacko. But he was right about his mother. She was innocent."

Cecelia closed her eyes and held up her hand. "Just a minute. Don't go so fast. What name did you say? The mother."

"Angelina Mascarenas."

"And you think—"

"I don't think, Mrs. Ramsey. I know. The woman was innocent." There was a long moment of silence and then he continued. "Anyway, this Granger character saw the kid's name written on Beth Marie's calendar upstairs. Several times—'Ignacio.' Along with payments she'd made to him. He suspected there was some connection. He didn't know it was for the work."

"But you told him—"

"No. Not what I just told you. See, by coincidence, I ran into this kid at the Dairy Queen just this week."

"No," she gasped, covering her mouth again.

Kamowski frowned at the objection. "Yes. I'm sure it was him."

"But it wasn't a coincidence," she said flatly. "You should know that. When people's paths get tangled together at times like this, it's not a coincidence."

Kamowski shifted uneasily on the sofa. "He'd just gotten some groceries from the food bank at the mission. He'd come into that Dairy Queen across from The Walls to get out of the cold and put the stuff in a string bag so he could carry it better. Like he was going to have to walk a long way. Anyway, the voucher from the mission fell out of the bag and I picked it up after he left. It had his name on it—Ignacio Mascarenas. I took the reporter with me and went into town, just to check and see if they had any more information about him at the mission."

"Did they?"

"Nothing except he got food for two people."

She had closed her eyes, trying to concentrate on all these details, but she nodded to indicate she was following the thread of his story.

"Anyway, I didn't tell this Granger character what I knew. I don't trust reporters in general, but this one in particular rubbed me the wrong way. For one thing, why didn't he contact the police after he got the call from Beth Marie? He said he thought at first it might be a hoax and he wanted to check it out. Then he said he called Somerville and found out the sheriff was out of town. Says he was afraid some greenhorn might let things get out of hand. I don't know that I believe either excuse. I think he wanted to check out the story all right, but to get on the scene before the police."

"But Beth Marie's safety was more—"

"Lady, I don't think this guy would let anybody's safety come before his story."

He was silent a few moments while she sorted this out. Then he glanced toward the front window again. "I haven't exactly told the police everything I know about this either," he said. "I didn't even tell the deputy—what's his name?"

"Norton?"

"Norton. He was here when I got back from the mission. Is he the one the girl—" He traced a loop in the air with one hamlike hand, a substitute for words he was uneasy with.

Cecelia looked at him sharply. "You didn't tell him?"

The priest looked suddenly subdued. His hands dropped between his knees. "This kid," he started slowly. "Ignacio. I know how he's feeling. He's scared to death. If some kind of posse shows up, no telling what he might do. Out of nothing but fear. Not because he would want to hurt the girl. You understand?"

Cecelia tried to follow in her imagination the emotions the priest had described.

"I've been in his place before." He took a deep breath. "I did some time myself. I don't usually spread that around, of course."

Cecelia opened her eyes now. The priest had leaned forward, his elbows on his knees, and was rubbing his hands together nervously, the motion making a dry, raspy sound. She nodded.

"So now then, Mrs. Ramsey, if you would just listen carefully to what I'm about to say. If it doesn't sound like a good idea, then just forget it. Forget I ever said anything about it."

She nodded again, though with less certainty.

"I take it you have an idea where this boy might be. At least you're the last one who's seen him, and you know where this horse place is that he'd been working at. Do you think you could take me there? We might be able to find him. And if it was just you and me, no cops, I might be able to talk to him. Get him to give it up, whatever crazy scheme he's got going. Maybe even—"

"Help him get away before the sheriff gets there?"

He glanced quickly at her in surprise and then away again. "Who knows? I'd have to talk to him." He started to add something, then shook his head and shrugged.

Cecelia looked down at her hands in her lap. "What makes you think you can talk to him, get him to do this?"

The priest sat up straight again and rubbed his large hand across his mouth several times. Then he looked at her and said, "I knew his father."

Norton felt his tires slide and saw the gravel spray up in a long arc as he turned onto the road to the campground. He knew he was driving recklessly, not out of any necessity but to give vent to his feelings—frustration, fear, rage. The rage was directed in so many directions that he recognized its danger. Whoever had kidnapped Beth Marie. Beth Marie herself. The priest who had known about the situation before he did. Satterthwaite. Lurline. The sheriff. All the stupid citizens of this county who expected him to make their lives safe.

But most of all, as he caught sight of a thin man in a jeans jacket at the public telephone in front of the cinder block restrooms, reporters. Especially Houston reporters whose whole profession consisted of trying to make law enforcement officers look bad. Norton could feel his wrath narrowing to a cone, like a heat-seeking missile aimed at the man's back.

Get a grip, he told himself. You can't afford to go beating up on this guy just because he's scum. You've got to get every ounce of information out of him you can.

The cruiser skidded to a halt, and Norton was slamming the door before the man, one hand over his ear to block interfering noise, turned and stared, then buried his head inside the phone enclosure again. Norton forced himself to approach with a measured stride, meant to convey both restraint and menace. The man was speaking into the receiver faster, bending over the instrument as if to shield it. Norton reached an arm over the reporter's shoulder and pushed down the cradle.

"What the hell—" The reporter spun around, the dead receiver hanging in his hand.

"Geoffrey Granger?"

"What do you think you're—"

"I'd like you to come with me, Mr. Granger."

"What do you mean? I haven't—"

"Withholding evidence. Right into the car over here, if you don't mind."

"Fine." The man, his head bobbing in ironic agreement, replaced the receiver. "I don't finish the story, it doesn't get into the paper. What happens then, Dick Tracy?"

Norton was careful to keep his grip on the man's arm loose but firm. He opened the passenger door for him, then stood aside as he got in. He said nothing more himself until he had backed the car up and put it in gear again.

"I want to know what you've got to say about the disappearance of Beth Marie Cartwright. And I want to know why you didn't say it sooner."

"You ought to know the answer to that yourself. I called the sheriff's department. You can check with your dispatcher. She told me both the sheriff and the chief deputy were out of town."

"That's beside the point. It was your duty to report

this immediately. Not make decisions about how it should be handled." His voice was carefully low, but he felt a tremor running through it.

The reporter's hands, loose between his legs, twitched in a gesture of ironic resignation. "All right. Maybe so. But that's not getting us anywhere now, is it?"

"Who were you talking to just now?"

"The news desk at the *Chronicle*. Thanks to you, they've only got part of the story."

"Don't worry about your story. I'll see that you get patched through again. Why don't you just start at the beginning again and tell me your story."

The man sighed heavily and stared out the side window. "I met her a little over a week ago—"

"No," Norton broke in abruptly. "Start with this morning. We'll go back to that later."

Geoff Granger looked at him curiously, then shrugged. "I got a phone call very early this morning. Around six, I think. It was Beth Marie."

At the sound of her name in the other man's mouth, Norton shifted his grip on the steering wheel.

"She said I had to get a story in Sunday's paper about Angelina Mascarenas, a woman who'd been an inmate at the Bromley Unit some years back." He paused, forcing Norton to look over at him again.

"And?"

"I take it the woman's dead now. She died in prison about seven years ago. I think she was from the Valley."

"Where was she?"

"I said. The Bromley Unit. The women were moved—"

"No!" Norton shouted. "Beth Marie."

The reporter raised his eyebrows. "I have no idea. He'd hardly let her tell me that, would he? Do you want to hear this or not?"

"Go on."

Geoff leaned back in the seat and stretched his long

legs as far as he could under the dashboard, taking his time. "He wants the world to know his mother was innocent. That seems to be the whole point of this escapade. For some reason he also believes his mother was killed by the prison authorities."

"Killed?"

"He says their story was that she had cancer, but actually they killed her. Martyr was the word he wanted me to use, I believe."

"And you couldn't pick up any clue as to their whereabouts. No noises or anything?"

"Nothing. I think maybe they were outside. It could have been a pay phone. But that's all. I didn't even hear any traffic noise. However, I have reason to believe she's in danger. And naturally I'm concerned about that."

"Reason to believe?" Norton repeated. "What's that supposed to mean? Did she say that—that she was in danger?"

"No. But I could hear another voice in the background. Like he was telling her what to say. What she said was she'd be killed if his story wasn't in the paper tomorrow." He lifted an arm and looked at his watch. "It's two o'clock. I've got maybe an hour to get back to the news desk with this before they go to press."

# CHAPTER · NINETEEN

HOWARD HAD NOT WANTED TO LET them go. "Deputy Norton's in charge of this investigation," he said, his voice high and strained. "I don't think you should leave till he gets back."

"Mrs. Ramsey's not feeling well," the priest told him as the two of them appeared at the front door. "I'm going to take her home."

Howard repeated his objection, looking down the road in the direction his superior had disappeared. Larry Rostow was upstairs, supervising the technicians.

"He knows where he can find her," the priest went on, as though Howard had said nothing. "She's a friend of his. I'll be back as soon as I get her home." The priest's voice sounded determined.

As Howard watched them edge down the front walk and climb in the old lady's little blue station wagon, he had a sinking feeling he might not be cut out for a career in law enforcement.

Cecelia insisted that Father Kamowski drive, though he had a hard time inserting himself between the steering wheel and the seat back. "I'd be too nervous," she said. "And I can concentrate on directions better this way."

Dan tried to make a map in his mind as they drove so that he could find his way through this maze of back country roads again if need be. But in paying attention to the endless strings of barbed wire and fence posts, he lost track of landmarks in the distance. Eventually it occurred to him that, without the old lady beside him, he'd be lost. Her chattering didn't help much though, and her directions were filled with references to names that meant nothing to him.

"See that old shed up there," she said now. "That's what used to be the Gilpin homeplace. Heaven only knows what's become of Troy and Euline. The last I heard they were in a nursing home over in Tyler. I went to school with all their kids. Nine, I think they had. Of course, none of them live around here anymore. For all I know they could be dead by now. In fact, Tyrone, the oldest one, is."

"Are we getting close?" Dan asked, trying to keep the irritation out of his voice. It was obvious the woman was having a hard time focusing.

She shook her head sadly. "I guess we already are, aren't we? I mean there's always a chance. But when you get to be my age, well, it's not a chance any longer. It's certainty then."

"The horse farm," he said severely. "Are we getting close to that? Where you said the boy worked."

She blinked. "Yes. Yes, we are. In fact, it's right over this hill that I saw him. He was crawling through the fence. When we get past this next patch of timber, you'll be able to see the barn. It looks like something out of a picture book."

Kamowski scanned the curving lines of low hills, searching for a figure, imagining Ignacio's bent back as he crawled between the strands of wire. He knew the kind of fear the boy would be feeling. It would sharpen his mind to a single point, making it hard for him to think beyond that point, to consider alternatives, speculate about consequences. His senses would be heightened to an almost unbearable pitch, a primitive response to danger. The priest remembered his own attempt to escape pursuers, how that had felt. He had been only a little older than this kid when the highway patrol caught him on the road to Louisiana.

What he couldn't understand, though, even as his eyes searched the folds in the hills, was what had brought the boy to this place. Why had he undertaken such a desperate act? Kamowski's own crime had been generated by nothing more complicated than greed. Ignacio's, he knew, was of another order altogether. Greed made a certain amount of animal sense. But to project his imagination into the damaged mind of this kid—it was more than he could manage. It meant confronting a darkness that took away reason itself, smothering the mind in a thick, heavy blanket of— What? Was there even a name for it? To name it was to apply reason to a force determined not to be analyzed.

And the girl. Kamowski was afraid to let his mind dwell on the girl. For just as surely as the darkness in Ignacio was determined not to be mastered, it also craved dominance. How that craving might play itself out, he would not allow himself to imagine.

He glanced at the woman beside him. She had grown suddenly quiet. Her white hair, compacted into one of those kinky styles designed to mask disarray, was now straggling around her forehead, and there was a bewildered look in her eyes that unsettled him. He was acutely aware of what an unlikely pair the two of them were. Don Quixote and Sancho Panza looked like a well-trained SWAT team beside them. A doddery old lady whose marbles were rattling around loose and a priest sweating out exposure of his prison record.

He was worried about the past intruding on the present. How what he had been might affect what he had become. She was beset by the present and the future.

What she had left of this world and what she hoped for in the next one. And yet, in these skewed states, they imagined they could talk some sense into a crazy migrant worker gripped by an insane fantasy. Well, at least the two of them had some experience living in irreconcilable realities. That might prove to be an advantage.

They had just entered the section of road hemmed in on either side by tall stands of pine when the old lady laid her hand on his sleeve. "What was that you said?" she asked, frowning up at him.

He shook his head. He hadn't spoken.

"Back at the house. About this boy's mother. It just came to me. You said he was right about her being innocent. How do you know that?"

Dan thought the remark had slipped by her, and he'd been glad. He hadn't wanted to make any explanations. "It's a long story," he said.

She kept her hand on his arm and her eyes on his face, waiting.

"I knew his father," Kamowski said grudgingly. "I heard the story from him."

"Oh?" Evidently that didn't satisfy her curiosity.

Kamowski moved his arm slightly so that she dropped her hand, but she continued to stare at him.

"In prison. She was accused of shooting a sheriff. The guy, her husband, he told me she was innocent. She hadn't even known what was going on. He brought her along with the intention of shooting the man and setting her up as the one who did it."

The old lady gasped. "No! He told you this?"

Kamowski nodded.

"And he let her go to prison in his place?"

"Well, see, he ended up there too eventually."

"But not for murder."

"No."

"But why? Why did he let her—"

"He was afraid. He figured they wouldn't give a

woman a death sentence, but they probably would have sent him to the chair." It was beginning to dawn on him that she assumed he had heard this confession as a priest.

"And you couldn't tell anyone."

"No." And he couldn't have. It could have meant his life. Alberto Mascarenas had been out of his head, awaiting sentencing for a charge of possession, the night they shared a county cell. Kamowski, already sentenced, was waiting for transfer to the prison unit in Rosharon. As a member of the flourishing Nuestra Carnales gang, Mascarenas managed to get just about anything he wanted, even in a jail cell. He hadn't been confessing when he told Dan about his wife; he had been bragging. At that point in Kamowski's life, long before he became a priest, it had never occurred to him to snitch on another prisoner. It was too risky, especially one as well-connected as Mascarenas. Still, he had been repelled by the man's gloating revelation, though he'd also been careful to conceal his reaction.

"That poor boy," Cecelia said.

The priest nodded. His own father had always been a shadowy figure to him back in Brooklyn, one he remembered mostly for the terror his tyrannical, often violent behavior inspired in his wife and children. Dan had last seen him on his deathbed, and then it had been twenty years since they had talked. But whatever anger, fear, even hatred he felt for the brutal old man, he had never had to be ashamed of him. A boy might expect to be afraid of his father. He could endure that. But how could he bear feeling ashamed of him?

Just what did Alberto Mascarenas's son know about his father? If he was calling his mother a martyr, he probably suspected she was innocent, at least of murder. But how well had he known his father? What story had the family concocted? Had the mother acquiesced in her own sacrifice? Had she sustained with her children some fiction about their father? Kamowski didn't know the answer to that question. And he had a feeling it could be crucial if he were to convince the boy to give up his hostage.

"I can see why you're concerned about him," the old lady said, her voice quavering for the first time. "I wouldn't want anything to happen to either of them. We'll have to be very careful, won't we?"

Kamowski nodded curtly. He didn't want her going soft on him now. "Is this it?" he asked, pointing to the barn with the weather vane on top.

"Yes. Turn in up at that gate with the brick pillars."

He maneuvered the station wagon up the gravel drive and pulled alongside the barn, which had a door at one end marked "Office." It appeared to be deserted. Kamowski got out, moving slowly and deliberately, and knocked on the door. Then he walked around to the open barn door and called out.

"Ignacio! Ignacio Mascarenas." No sound.

He turned back to the car. "You stay there," he called to the old lady. Then he entered the shadowy interior of the barn. In the darkness he stumbled over a loose hay bale and, a few feet farther, some discarded tack lying on the ground. But there was no sign of life.

Outside again, it occurred to him to look on the bare ground for tire tracks. The drive ended at the barn, but perhaps something would show up beyond there. He walked several yards past the end of the gravel, then bent down over an open patch of sand. There were faint tread impressions in the dirt. But how old? It had rained one night last week. Hard enough to obliterate any tracks left from before the operation shut down. These must be recent.

He stood up and gestured for the old lady to roll down her window. "What kind of car did Beth Marie drive?" he shouted to her.

"White," she called back.

"No! The kind. The brand. Big? Little?"

"Oh, little. Yes, little. Japanese, I think."

Kamowski squatted down to inspect the tracks more closely. They were made by narrow tires, all right. And not very new. They led back behind the barn. He followed them several yards farther, then lost them in the grass of the pasture. He could see, though, from the double line of compressed grass, where they were leading. Down the far side of the hill toward what looked to him like a big ditch.

He glanced back at the car. The woman was leaning out the window with her hand cocked behind her ear, waiting for him to call out more instructions. He shook his head to indicate she was not to follow. He didn't want to shout again. If Ignacio and the girl were anywhere around, he'd already made too much noise.

He started walking in the direction of the two lines of bent grass.

Cecelia watched him go, shaking her head, then slid across to the driver's seat and moved the gearshift into neutral. She waited a moment, then jerked her body forward against the steering wheel. Gradually the car started to roll down the incline.

Kamowski spotted the trailer before he had gone fifty yards. Its aluminum side caught the afternoon sun, glinting dully. He stopped, scanning the ditch for the car. Then he heard the dry sound of tires rolling over the grass behind him.

He turned, choked off the shout in his throat, and waved his arms frantically, signalling her to stop. The old lady's white head barely showed above the steering wheel. The station wagon came on, rolling faster down the incline. Then, just as it came even with him, she jerked it to a halt with a metallic squeak.

Kamowski stuck his head in the window. "What do you think you're doing?" he demanded in a fierce whisper. "I told you to stay back. It could be dangerous."

"No more for me than for you," she whispered, not as fierce but just as obstinate.

He glanced back at the trailer in the ravine. Any minute they could be spotted. Maybe already had been.

"Stay here," he ordered the woman, not sure that she would obey, but not wanting to waste any time. Then he set off, loping the remaining distance down to the ravine. At least he could beat her there.

It wasn't until he neared the lip of the ravine that he caught sight of the car. It had been edged down a sandy slope of the ditch behind the trailer to hide it from view, but he could see the rear fender. Kamowski froze. This was it. Up to now, finding them had only been a possibility. Now, suddenly, it was real. The kid was probably inside. And the girl.

He heard the station wagon lumbering to a stop behind him and the creak of the emergency brake being pulled up. He had to move.

Stepping sideways down the steep slope, he made his way as quietly as he could into the ravine. Then, holding his breath, he edged along the wall of the tilted trailer, listening for voices inside. He could hear nothing. Maybe he'd been spotted. Maybe the kid was waiting for him. Maybe he had a gun.

Kamowski sidled up to the door, slightly ajar, and hesitated. In the stillness, he heard the door to the station wagon squeak. "*Psia krew,*" he muttered in Polish. Why wouldn't that woman stay put?

Still no sound from within. He must have been spotted. What kind of gun would it be? A pistol might miss him. But a shotgun—Dan swallowed, then called out in a voice that surprised him with its solid force. "Ignacio. Ignacio Mascarenas!"

Some kind of red bird he could see in the underbrush just beyond the ravine whistled carelessly. He heard the old lady sliding and puffing down the slope behind him.

Wiping a damp palm across his black shirt front, he extended his arm and gingerly pushed open the flimsy door. It grated inward, then swung halfway closed again.

Grasping the edge of the door frame, Kamowski swung himself up into the trailer, smacking the door with his shoulder. He'd braced himself to take the impact of a bullet, a knife, a body. But the sound came from behind him. A step and then a woman's cry. He spun around, his arms raised across his chest.

"Are you all right?"

He opened his eyes. Cecelia Ramsey, small twigs caught in her hair as if in tangled fishing line, stared in at him from the doorway.

He dropped his arms slowly, then turned toward the rear of the trailer. His body seemed to fill all the available space in the cramped enclosure. He couldn't even straighten up completely. He took a couple steps toward the kitchenette, reached out to touch a black iron skillet sitting atop the stove, then drew his hand back.

Turning slightly to his right, he pushed open the narrow door to the bathroom and quickly ripped back the brittle shower curtain, the only hiding place left. Even before his brain had registered the blank space inside, he was staring, dumbfounded, at the foil-covered toilet seat and the pictures arranged above it.

"They're not here," Cecelia said weakly behind him.

He withdrew his head from the bathroom doorway and looked at her. Red streaks had crept up the folds of her neck.

They stared at one another mutely. Then she bent and picked up a limp piece of cloth from the floor. When she held it out away from her, he could see that it was an oversized T-shirt with an iris printed on the front.

"Beth Marie's," she said.

# CHAPTER • TWENTY

IT WAS TIME TO ACT. THE LONGER SHE stayed in the trailer, the less her chances were of surviving. She had no idea where Ignacio was. He might reappear at any minute. But if he were gone long enough, she might be able to get free, get away. She was calmer now. She had to do something. She couldn't just wait for whatever he was planning.

For one thing, Ignacio was losing whatever remnant of sanity had made his initial restraint possible. At first he'd been distant and contemptuous toward her. He'd only seemed interested in using her to publicize his mother's plight. But ever since the trip to make the telephone call this morning, his self-control had been slipping away. Some fury was making him mad, crazy, maniacal. And it would use whatever stray, unfocused energy it found within him.

She figured Ignacio must be eighteen, maybe twenty. Had he been, all those years, so obsessively devoted to his mother? If Ignacio had been a child when she was sent to prison, she must have still been quite young. Even younger than I am now, Beth Marie thought. And beautiful, at least to a small son. He might not have understood what was happening, but he would have wanted to defend his mother. Yet he would have been powerless. Powerless and ashamed of his inability to protect her, to save her. Perhaps slowly and without his conscious understanding, his whole life had become focused on her.

When she had died, how old would he have been? Eleven, twelve? Was it then that the notion of consecrating himself to restoring her honor came to him? Or had it grown in him gradually, paralleling his change from boy to man? Perhaps he'd kept himself purposefully distant from other women—even schoolgirls—in order to remain true to her and the great task he had laid upon himself.

Beth Marie remembered now how he had always drawn back his hand quickly after she had counted his pay into it. How he had avoided looking at her directly. What she had taken as an illegal alien's fear of discovery was actually a dread of touching her. A horror of his natural fascination betraying him, betraying his mother. Here in the trailer, lying only a couple of feet away on the floor last night, that might be the closest prolonged contact he had ever had with a woman outside his family. Until, in the car, he had leaned out the window, pressed against her. She shut her eyes, and a whimpering noise came involuntarily from her throat. She could still feel the scrape of the belt buckle across her face when the pillowcase touched it.

All that energy, so tightly bound into a single taut cord for years. Was that why he had called her evil? Because the cord had suddenly frayed, threatened to come undone?

But that wasn't fair. It wasn't *her* fault. Yet even as the protest welled up in her, she knew Ignacio's mind wouldn't be working that way. If he felt himself bending from his course, drawn from the purpose he'd devoted his life to, he would blame her. What would happen then?

She drew her knees closer to her chest, trying to shrink within the stinking, oversized sweatshirt. Think, she told herself. Don't lose control. Not now. Hysteria, any show of fear, might provoke an attack. Pull yourself together. Do something before he comes back.

If he came back. Maybe he'd scared himself so badly he had simply abandoned his plan and her. Maybe when he'd run off he hadn't stopped running. Maybe he was trying to put as much distance as possible between himself and the figure he felt was luring him from the purity of his purpose. She drew a deep breath, allowing herself to hope for a moment.

But say he didn't come back—how long would it take the police to find her? Did anyone even know she was missing? Norton wouldn't be looking for her till tomorrow—was it still only Saturday? And even if they were looking for her right now, would there be any clue to lead them to her? Would anyone think of Ignacio? Would they know anything about him? Had he left any traces behind?

The first thing she needed to do was get this pillowcase off so she could see. Leaning down, she rubbed her head along the bench seat, trying to push the cloth up. It was more difficult than she expected. Each time she had the cloth scrunched up above her ears, she would raise her head and it would slip down again. Finally, she slid to the floor and, kneeling there, scraped her head along the edge of the bench seat. At last she managed to push the hood up past her forehead. Slowly she rolled her head sideways, sliding away from the bench. Then, struggling to her feet while keeping her head dropped forward, she shook the pillowcase loose.

She took a deep breath and looked around. Having her head free felt like a major victory. At least she could see her surroundings now.

Shuffling her bare bound feet, she made her way to the kitchenette at the end of the trailer. Water. Water first. She hadn't had anything to drink since the night before.

On the counter she found a plastic milk jug filled with murky water. Using her teeth, she worked the cap loose, then tipped the jug toward her. Water sloshed out onto the sweatshirt and her bare feet, but she managed to fill her mouth and then jerk the jug upright again. She stood there a moment, letting the wetness soak into her parched tongue and searching for something she might use to loosen the nylon cord around her wrists.

There was a skillet on top of the stove but she didn't see how it could help. She managed to pull open the single drawer in the counter. It was empty except for a couple of plastic spoons and some dried-up packets of ketchup.

Maybe the bathroom, she thought. Maybe a discarded razor, a hook, anything. She shuffled the few feet to the bathroom and bumped the door with her shoulder. As it swung open, she peered into the shadowy interior, uncertain at first what she was looking at. Crumpled foil, smoothed across the toilet tank. A candle stub stuck on the seat. Pictures attached to the foil. One a magazine photograph of a well-dressed woman in dark glasses, her black hair in a chignon, the other a card with a pastel picture of Mary. She shook her head, dazed by the bizarre display. It was as if she were looking into the deep interior of Ignacio's heart.

If he hadn't told her about his mother and his plan to vindicate her, she wouldn't have been able to make sense of the pathetic little shrine. The picture from the magazine could not possibly be of his mother, of course. But it must represent the way he had come to picture her in his imagination—a figure of martyred innocence.

And now some other force had broken loose inside him, threatening to overwhelm his original plan. If Beth Marie had had any doubts about his growing hostility to her, the smoothed-out foil, the candle stub, the pictures on the toilet tank made it all clear. It was the rage of the zealot fearful of his own apostasy. This mother-goddess would be a jealous divinity. And at her shrine Beth Marie might easily become the sacrifice to atone for his weakness.

Just then she heard the trailer door creak. Her heart lurched against her rib cage. She felt the floor tilt slightly as he stepped inside, and she stiffened her knees to keep from collapsing as she heard his angry shout.

Before she could turn from the bathroom door, his arm had struck across her shoulders, knocking her facedown onto the floor of the tiny bathroom. She twisted to the side as she fell and her head hit the side of the shower stall. Stunned by the blow, she couldn't draw up her bound feet in time to kick him as he came at her. All she could do was wrench away and bite as he bent over her, tearing at the filthy sweatshirt.

Her teeth sank into his ear, and he cried out, jerking upright. Then he drew back his hand and slapped her. Her head struck against the shower again. Again, she raised it, amazed at her own tenacity and how everything seemed to be happening in slow motion.

Her resistance surprised him. He didn't hit her again, but scrabbled backwards on his knees. She saw him cast one agonized look at the shrine. Then he grasped her feet—she was kicking and trying to roll away, but there was no room—and dragged her out into the middle of the trailer. The nylon cord caught on the metal doorplate and she felt a loop slip past her heels.

He stood over her for a moment, panting and staring as though he didn't recognize her, his eyes dull, almost blank. She tried to sit up, rolling to the side and pushing herself up with one elbow, but he placed one foot on her shoulder—she recognized once more her father's shoe—and steadily pressed her back again. She tried to lift her head again, struggling against his weight. He lifted his foot, and, with almost leisurely deliberation, drove it, heel first, against her jaw. She felt something crack in her mouth. Her head dropped back, rolled to the side.

When she could focus again, she saw that the blank stare was gone. His eyes, narrowed now, had been ignited by her resistance, their shared physical exertion, and the novel savor of his own dominance. As she watched, his thin chest began to swell until a guttural snarl exploded from him.

"No, Ignacio!" she cried.

He fell forward on her then, slamming one grimy hand across her mouth and nose. She tried to twist her head loose, but he leaned his forehead hard against hers, lifting his weight while pouring a stream of vituperation, half English, half Spanish, directly against her face. His warm saliva spattered her cheeks. His eyes were clenched shut; his other arm was tugging at her oversized jeans. Abruptly he opened his eyes, staring blindly, unfocused, like two holes into darkness.

The cord around her feet had loosened, and, scraping one heel against the instep of the other foot, she managed to kick free of the coil. His hand was still across her mouth and nose, and she was struggling for air. Maneuvering her feet beneath her, she arched her back upward and to the side, trying to heave him off her. He slipped sideways, then recovered and braced himself against the trailer wall with his knee. Lifting his head, he shifted both hands to her shoulders, pinning her flat again.

"No, Ignacio!" she screamed. "Let me go!"

With the scream, his eyes snapped into focus again. He jerked himself upright, slid his knees to either side of her waist, and took his hands from her shoulders. She struggled to raise her shoulders, but he shifted his knees to pin her upper arms. She could feel her burst of terrified energy beginning to drain away. Again she tried to heave him off, then to pound him in the back with her raised knees.

But he continued staring at her, hardly heeding either her bucking or blows, not angry now, but as if in the grip of fascination. With one hand he grasped her hair and tried to pull her head backward, but the short strands slipped through his fingers.

She was laboring for breath. Maybe, she thought suddenly, if I'm still. Maybe if I'm very quiet. Maybe he'll come to his senses. And for a moment she did stop struggling and stared up at him straddling her. She could see the vinyl peeling from the ceiling over his head. She could hear the outer door squeaking as it swung back and forth in the wind. She could see his chest swelling and contracting as he panted with exertion and exhilaration. She tried not to breathe as she watched him.

Then something began to spread across his face. Not a smile, but a manifestation of the force rising within him, distending his face, filling out the lean concavities, making it taut and turgid. Then, slowly, almost somnambulistically he began to unbuckle his belt.

She knew then she should never have stopped fighting. Gathering her strength, she tried again to heave him from her. His knees rocked forward onto her upper arms, almost forcing the bones out of their sockets. She screamed and flailed her feet helplessly. Slowly, with the same dreamy, detached expression on his face, he drew back his hand and struck her across the mouth.

The pain itself seemed strangely detached from her now, as if it were merely incidental, though she could taste the blood. When she lifted her head, he hit her again, deliberately, methodically. Then, as she struggled against the buzzing in her head, he hit her again. And once more, after she could no longer raise her head.

She heard him laugh, a hard, mocking explosion that jerked his whole body and crushed her hands under her. She raised one leg and gave a feeble kick. Then she swallowed and lay still a moment, took one shuddering breath, and said, not screaming this time, but trying to control the terror in her voice, aiming for the exact, necessary pitch. "Your mother, Ignacio. Your mother! You're doing this for your mother. Remember? Who will believe you? Are you going to throw it all away?"

The dark eyes flickered for a moment. Then as he frowned down at her, the anger came back. "Whore!" he hissed through his teeth. "You have no right!"

He would have struck her again—she was waiting for him to shift his weight for the blow so she could get her knees up under her—but they both heard at the same moment the sound of an automobile engine. Ignacio froze.

She screamed. It sounded even in her own ears like a paltry wail, and she knew it would never carry beyond the trailer walls.

He clapped his hand across her mouth again and leaned forward, pulling the knife from his hip pocket and holding it to her throat. Then he scuttled sideways off her, slid his other hand to her arm, and wrenched her upright against him.

"Get up," he whispered hoarsely, keeping the knife at her throat. "Keep quiet."

Staggering himself, he dragged her to her feet and pushed her toward the door, one arm around her shoulder to hold the knife.

"I can't—"

"Shut up!" he hissed, and she felt the knife scrape her throat as his shoes grated against her bare heels. "Down the steps!"

Even so, she would have cried out again once they were outside, except that he, sensing her desperation, muffled her mouth with his hand once more. She saw that the trailer sat in a ravine, and he was pushing her up the far side. Stumbling clumsily, their legs tangling together, he forced her toward a thicket of wild plum and myrtle just beyond the reach of the eroded bank. Once they were hidden inside the thicket, he forced her face down into the debris of dead leaves, one knee jammed into her back.

She listened to his rough breathing for a long

moment, then felt his grip on her tighten suddenly. Had he seen someone? Was someone coming? *Please, God, please.*

For several minutes he didn't move, hardly even breathed. Someone is coming, she thought. Someone's there. And she would have called out then if she could have lifted her face from the dirt and dead leaves.

Then at last, as though he'd been waiting for the moment, he jerked her head up. Before she could spit the pungent earth from her mouth, he covered it again, the knife pricking her back this time as he dragged her to her feet and pushed her out the far side of the thicket toward a line of pines fifty yards away.

She felt nettles and thorns cutting her feet, this pain clearer and sharper than when he had hit her. She was already limping from his shoes kicking against her bare feet. His hand across her mouth was slimy with her blood mixed with the muddy mucus around her nose.

He was panting hard in her right ear. She tried to move as slowly as possible, but he jabbed her back with the knife and kicked at her ankles whenever she paused. She swallowed the mess of dirt and blood in her mouth so that she could breathe and tried to keep to the pine needles that covered what seemed to be a game trail through the timber.

It wasn't long before she lost all sense of direction. They crossed a couple of narrow washes—or maybe they crossed the same one twice. Once they came close enough to the edge of the woods so that she could see a plowed field, dark and studded with pale stubble, through the trees. She didn't recognize it. She wondered if he knew where they were.

Finally they broke out into a small clearing where a single sweet gum had shaded out the undergrowth. They stood trembling there in the sudden space, stopping as if by common consent. He didn't prod her to go on. This was it, this was going to be the place.

He didn't force her to the ground, as she was expecting. Instead he pushed her against the tree, using it as a brace while he twisted to look around. After a moment she felt his breathing slow gradually. Then she could feel his muscles slacken. He took a deep breath, held it an instant, then blew it out noisily, as though realizing there was no threat of discovery here.

Her knees suddenly went weak beneath her, and, if he hadn't caught her and jammed her against the tree, she would have fallen. It was over.

She tried to breathe evenly, husbanding what strength she had left for his final assault. Around them, small birds skittered in the branches, making curious, chipping sounds. Otherwise everything was very still. Even the wind had stopped blowing. Then she heard the slight metal chink of Ignacio's unbuckled belt.

Immediately, her body was rigid again. She didn't know at what point she had decided, but she knew that she would force him to kill her before she would submit to him. She felt her mind adjusting itself to concentrate on that single point, that one goal, as if focusing light down a long, dark tunnel.

She heard the belt being pulled awkwardly with one hand through the belt loops, keeping alert to twist away as soon as he released any of his weight from her.

Then she felt it on her neck. Not the knife, but the brittle thickness of the belt. So intent had her mind been on fighting that, before she could take in what he was doing, he had circled both her neck and the tree with the belt and was turning her around, facing outward, ramming her bound hands against the rough bark and tightening the belt simultaneously, jerking it clumsily and painfully against her throat so as to have length enough to buckle it on the other side of the trunk.

When the hasp of the belt had caught and he had threaded the end through the loop by the buckle, he turned loose of her for the first time since he had found her invading the trailer's shrine and stepped back, panting wearily. He looked at her with scarcely any emotion now. Not anger, not lust, not even contempt. It was almost as though he didn't see her at all, didn't consider her any more than he would have attended to an animal he had staked to a tree.

He walked around the tree to look at the belt, jerked on the buckle to test it, then dropped his hands to his sides. She was afraid to breathe. Was he only going to kill her now? Quickly. Mercifully.

Ignacio looked up slantwise at the top of the clearing as if he were trying to judge the time by gradation in the light's intensity. Then, without a word, and without even looking at her again, he turned and began walking away through the woods.

# CHAPTER TWENTY-ONE

AFTER THE OLD LADY HANDED HIM the girl's nightshirt, Kamowski had searched the trailer without finding anything that might indicate when or where the pair had gone. Mrs. Ramsey had begun to fold the quilts she identified as belonging to the Cartwrights, but he told her she should leave them alone. They might yield some important evidence that could be destroyed if they were handled. He did not tell her what he found in the bathroom. He merely stared at it mutely, carefully noting the contents, and closed the door.

What should he do now? He didn't know the country well enough to strike out searching for the pair on his own. And the old lady wasn't looking too good. She had dropped the quilt she had been folding back onto the bench and stood over it, visibly grieving.

He went outside and stomped up and down the ravine for a while, examining the Toyota but finding nothing of consequence inside it. In the end there was nothing more to do but go for help.

In fact, making it back to the station wagon was almost more than Cecelia Ramsey could manage, even with him practically hauling her up the crumbling sides of the ravine. All the way back to Point Blank, she looked like a rag doll, collapsed against the door on the passenger side. She propped one elbow on the window and leaned her forehead in her hand. It was only when he saw her lips moving that he realized she was praying. Dan looked away quickly and frowned. It made him nervous when a layperson did something, naturally and without effort, that he as a clergyman should have thought of first.

He tried to picture the girl's face so he could pray for her protection. But she came to his mind in only a hazy way, as though he were seeing her in his peripheral vision. His meeting with her had been brief and primarily motivated by his own fear of what she might be up to with that reporter. The only prayers that came to him now were snatches from the ferocious Imprecatory Psalms—*Pour out your indignation upon them, and let the fierceness of your anger overtake them.* Kamowski would have been glad to knock either the boy or the reporter around himself; calling on God to do it was the next best thing.

He asked the old lady if she wanted him to take her home—they would pass her place on the way back—but she insisted on going back to the Cartwright house. "Norton will want to talk to me," she said. "And if anything I can tell him will help at all—well, who knows?" she ended lamely.

The deputy was, in fact, anxious to see them. He charged through the front gate as soon as the station wagon pulled up. "I told you to wait here," he said before they were even out of the car, directing this accusation to the priest.

Dan kept his face expressionless. "Mrs. Ramsey," he began, and saw the deputy's mouth harden, as though anticipating that he was shifting the blame to the old lady.

But Cecelia, still hobbling around the front of the car, interrupted, raising a shaky arm and waving it at them both. "No, no, Norton. Forget all that. We found her! Beth Marie. No, not her. But where she'd been."

Norton turned back to the priest. Dan nodded, then stood meekly by as Cecelia recounted disjointedly the details about Ignacio, the trailer, and what the two of them had found there. The deputy's arms dropped limply to his sides and his fingers twitched while the old lady's tale wound down. When Norton turned toward him again, mutely looking for confirmation or elaboration, Dan kept his own gaze stubbornly fixed on the ground.

"Her car was still there?" Norton directed the question to the priest.

Kamowski nodded.

"Did it look like . . . was there any sign . . ."

Finally Kamowski spoke. "Hard to tell much, the place was in such a mess anyway. We didn't see any blood," he added. "Nothing like that."

Beneath his fair moustache, the deputy's lips flattened to a thin line.

"They can't be far though. Not if they're on foot," Kamowski added.

The deputy gave a weak snort. "He could have another vehicle, one we couldn't identify so easily."

"No," Kamowski said. "There was only the Toyota tracks going down to the trailer. Nothing else."

Norton looked at him with what might have been disdain if his face hadn't been so set once again in immobility. "They could have walked to the road, had another car waiting there."

Kamowski shook his head. "I don't think so."

"Why not? Seems like you know an awful lot about this. You didn't know before, did you, who it was?"

Cecelia caught hold of the deputy's sleeve. "Brother Kamowski's been trying to help, Norton. He knows the boy, don't you see?"

Norton stared down at her blankly for a moment.

She reached over and grabbed his other sleeve, planting herself between the two men. "If it's anybody's fault, it's mine," she said. "I just saw the boy on the road a couple of hours ago. I told Brother Kamowski that when I got here. We thought we ought to go looking right away. It seemed like the right thing to do. Instead of waiting."

Gradually, almost grudgingly, Norton lifted his gaze to the priest's face. "Okay," he said, "we'll work all that out later. So what do you know about this guy?"

"I don't think he would've had a car," Kamowski said stiffly. "I don't think he has much of anything. That's what makes the situation dangerous. He's got nothing to lose."

Norton put one hand flat on the station wagon's hood, then gave it a decisive tap with his knuckles. "All right," he said, looking at the priest. "Let's go. Think you can find your way out there again?

They left Cecelia standing there beside the station wagon.


Geoff had tried to get more of the story in to the *Chronicle* on the way back to Point Blank in the sheriff's cruiser, the dispatcher in Somerville patching him through to the news desk after the deputy had given her orders to put out a bulletin for a young Hispanic male in a white Toyota. But the dips the meandering road took kept interfering with the connection. The deputy only glanced at him scornfully once. "It's not going to help her anyway, you know. Give it up."

Geoff shrugged and dropped the speaker back in its rack. There was no point trying to reason with the guy. He would have liked to know where the sheriff was, but he refused to ask, sensing that Norton would also refuse to answer.

When they pulled up at the Cartwright house, the deputy had jerked open the door and jumped out, ignoring Geoff, as though he were now too trivial to waste any more time on.

"Fine," Geoff muttered to himself, mentally composing headlines. *Manhunt for Mother's Avenger. Deputy Kills Lover's Kidnapper.* "See you in the funny papers, sucker."

He was still sitting in the patrol car, scribbling notes, when he saw a blue compact station wagon pull up along the front fence and his nemesis, the big priest, pry himself out of the driver's seat. Geoff slipped out of the cruiser to listen to the exchange between the deputy and the priest. Had he been out looking for the girl? Just then an old lady made her way around the station wagon and inserted herself between the two men. He could hear her high-pitched voice explaining to the deputy that they'd found the place where the girl had been taken. He couldn't catch the lower tones of the priest's voice, but it was evident no body had been found. Not yet.

Geoff checked his watch. Almost five. Maybe they could squeeze in that new information to the story if he called now.

Just then the deputy shouted instructions to a gangly assistant and headed for his patrol unit, waving an arm at the priest, who was making his way more slowly to his van. The cruiser took off in a spray of gravel, followed by the priest's van. Two technicians climbed into a department van and followed more slowly, keeping well back from the dust cloud raised by the other two vehicles.

Great, Geoff thought. There went the details for the story.

Then he noticed the old lady, still standing staring after the dust roiling up on the road.

Geoff sauntered to her, the tips of his fingers stuck in his jeans pockets. "Ma'am?"

She turned and blinked at him mutely.

"Are you a friend of Miss Cartwright?"

She nodded, still looking blank.

Geoff took her arm. Maybe the excitement had been too much for her. "Let's go inside." he said.

They passed Satterthwaite, standing uncertainly on the porch. Geoff didn't even look at him as he ushered the old lady through the door.

"I'm a friend of hers, too," he said, once he had her parked on the sofa. He sat down beside her, turning toward her with one hand protectively on the sofa back. "You found where he'd taken her? You and the priest?"

She still had that stunned, disoriented look. He wasn't sure how much he was going to be able to get out of her, and the minutes were ticking away. He repeated the question.

She nodded, but her eyes had slid away to the side.

"Where was that, ma'am? And can you tell me what you found there?"

Slowly her eyes slid back to his face, and for the first time she seemed to be concentrating. "You're the one, aren't you?"

"The one?"

"The one Beth Marie was working on a story with." She frowned as her eyes focused inward as if searching her memory. "The reporter. Jim? George? No. Something Granger."

He sat back, startled.

"You're the one she called. The one who's supposed to get the story about the boy's mother in the paper."

He raised one eyebrow in brief, grudging acknowledgment. "Yeah. I'm the one. Now then, what I need from you are some facts. I managed to get the bare essentials in for tomorrow's edition. But if I could have a few more details—like where he took her. What you found there."

She shook her head wearily. "Not much. One of those T-shirt things girls wear for nightgowns these days."

Geoff slipped his notebook from his jacket pocket. "Really?" So she must have been kidnapped sometime during the night. *Dragged from her bed in her nightclothes*— he needed to get that line in. "And this was where now?"

"Out at the old MacGruder place. In a little old tin trailer." Her voice had begun to quaver.

Geoff reined in his impatience. "The MacGruder place?"

She blinked hard several times.

"Why didn't you call the police?" she demanded suddenly. "The police. You should have done that. Just think what could have happened to her by now."

He looked down at the pad in his hand, smiling wryly and shaking his head. "Well, I did try, you see, but—"

"Not hard enough." She was holding herself erect now, energized by her anger.

He took a full thirty seconds to reply, and when he looked up again his face had hardened and he had given up all pretense of solicitude. "Look, lady. The best thing I can do for your friend right now is make sure this story is on tomorrow morning's front page, like the Mascarenas kid wanted. I have an editor waiting for some details. He's got to have more information or it's going to end up somewhere inside. For all I know the girl could already be dead. But on the off chance she's not, this story could save her life."

The old lady slumped back against the sofa's arm, and he knew he'd finally won. "I'll have to show you the way," she said.

By the time Kamowski and Norton got back to the trailer, the sun was already dipping near the horizon. Norton parked the cruiser at the barn, wanting to check for himself if any more tracks might tell them if a car— other than Beth Marie's and Mrs. Ramsey's—had been driven down to the ravine.

"Where's her car?" he asked Kamowski as they followed the indentions in the grass toward the red slash of erosion behind the barn.

"He drove it down an easier slope on beyond the trailer—see the metal top there?—and parked it on the far side. Hiding it as much as possible from the road, I guess."

The deputy was already leaping down the side of the ravine, sliding in the red clay and bumping against the flimsy aluminum siding at the bottom. He disappeared on the far side of the trailer. Kamowski stood at the lip of the arroyo, contemplating the descent.

The deputy reappeared at the other end of the trailer, not saying anything. Without a word, he pushed open the door, still half ajar, and swung himself up into it without touching the facing. He recognized the iris-embroidered knit shirt lying on the bench immediately. He bent down and moved it slightly with one finger, enough to stir a slight scent from it. Then he straightened and began scanning every open surface in the trailer—the floor, walls, counters. He noted the skillet, the quilts, the puddle under the plastic jug of water.

Finally he stuck his head into the bathroom cubicle, again taking care not to touch the door frame. He stared, frozen for a moment, then dropped to his knees, shouting for Kamowski.

When he felt the big man's weight rock the trailer as he climbed in, he yelled over his shoulder, "You didn't tell me about this."

"Sure I did." He edged down the narrow space to stand behind Norton. "What do you mean?" He stuck his head in over the deputy's kneeling figure. "What? What happened?"

The little shrine had been destroyed, the foil ripped from the back of the toilet tank and the magazine photographs torn down. They lay crumpled on the floor.

The old lady drove at a maddeningly slow pace over the graveled back roads. By the time they reached the white fence of what she had called "the MacGruder place," the sun was just sinking below the horizon. Not much longer and the winter evening would turn black.

They had already established that, after she led him to the deserted horse farm, she should go home. The woman was obviously exhausted and would only be in the way. She pulled her station wagon to the side at the gate, waiting for him to turn in, but he pulled up in front of her and cut his lights. He opened the door of the Mustang, waved an acknowledgment, and watched while the little station wagon backed up, then turned around and headed in the direction they'd come from.

Though he hadn't told her, he had no intention of letting his presence there be known. That was a sure way not to find anything out. After the station wagon's taillights disappeared behind him, he drove on past the gate and pulled off into a rutted track just beyond where the gentrified fence ended. He reached in the backseat for his camera and got out, slinging it over his neck and patting his jacket pocket to make sure he had his notebook.

Following the fence line, he kept an eye on the tall barn through the trees. He could see the sheriff's department vehicles drawn up beside it. Then he caught sight of figures moving down the hill behind the barn. A thicket of wild plum blocked his view, so he climbed through the fence, which had turned to barbed wire a few yards back from the road. Careful to keep himself screened by the thicket, he saw that the figures were headed toward a ravine at the bottom of the hill. Had he dumped the body there maybe?

Crawling back through the wire, he followed it down to a spot he estimated was approximately parallel to the ravine. On his side of the fence, the red gash in the earth flattened out and became a mere wrinkle. From there he could hear the voices of the technicians coming down the gully, muffled by the eroded clay walls. Then Norton barked commands at them. But nothing more. No shots. No exclamations or calls for an ambulance.

Geoff leaned against a fencepost in the dusk and waited. After a while he heard Norton call one last order, then caught sight of the deputy making his way back up the hill.

The reporter bent through the fence once more, cursing the wire as it caught his camera strap, then made his way, crouching, up the ravine. The first thing he caught sight of was the white Toyota. If the car was still here, they must be on foot. Beyond the car was the trailer, the shine of the aluminum dulled by the descending night. He could hear voices inside.

"You notice if the electricity's on up at the barn?" one of the technicians asked. "We could run a cable down here."

"No. But we're gonna have to get some light. If the power's not on up there, he'll have to send for a generator. These batteries ain't gonna hack it for long. Either that or we wait till morning. Suit me fine."

"Forget it. He'll have the whole department out within the hour."

"Well. You can't blame him. I mean—"

"Shine that over this way would you? I think I got some hair here on the floor of the shower. No telling what that guy done to her."

There was a grunt and a pause. Then a light moved across the small square of screen in the side of the trailer. Geoff moved toward it.

"See?"

"Yeah. I got it."

"No blood though. Not that I've found yet. Maybe that's a good sign. I mean these greasers, don't they usually use a knife? I thought he might have carved her up by now."

"It ain't over yet," the other one grunted.

Geoff moved back a step, then edged over to the

Toyota and glanced inside. Nothing there. But why had they left it behind? And how far could they have gone without it?

They could be out in the woods somewhere. He shuddered, thinking of being inside that dense tangle of contorted vegetation. Strange noises. Animals. Snakes. Cobwebs catching across your face. He began to back away from the trailer, down the ravine the way he had come.

# CHAPTER • TWENTY-TWO

CECELIA DROVE EVEN SLOWER than usual on her way back home; she felt as if she had scarcely enough energy to depress the accelerator. Her praying had become nothing more than a kind of internal wail which served to block out scenes she imagined of Beth Marie. She pulled into her carport, went in through the kitchen door, and dropped her purse onto the counter, taking care to avoid the red eye of the machine beside the telephone.

Without bothering to turn on a light, she went into her bedroom, switched on the electric blanket, and sank onto the bed to untie her orthopedic shoes. She sat there, staring at nothing, as the dusk absorbed the shapes around her into shadows, then crawled beneath the blanket without taking off her clothes.

I'll just rest a minute, she thought, so I'll be ready if they need me. She tried to shape the internal moaning into words, but *the shadow of his wings* was all that came to her, and more in a picture than words—deep concavities of warm hovering darkness.

In her dreams, Cecelia saw them all—Catherine, her own daughter Lois, Mama and Aunt Min—climbing in an open car, like the first one her daddy had ever owned.

They were driving away, waving at her. "Good-bye," they called back. "We're going to see Beth Marie."

"No! No, you can't!" she cried, running after them. "She's not ready yet! She won't want you to see her like this!"

But they drove on, waving and laughing at her. She stood still and started to cry. Why had they left her behind? Why was she always left behind?

Then she looked up and saw Cody, the girl from the honky-tonk. She knew it was Cody because her freckled bosom came right to Cecelia's own eye level, though she was dressed in a buckskin outfit and a flat-brimmed hat.

"Hello, Cody," she said.

"I may be wild," the girl said, "but I'm not Wild Bill. I'm Annie Oakley, and I can shoot the pants off any man, living or dead." And she gave Cecelia a knowing wink before she climbed atop some kind of mechanical contraption with a saddle thrown across it. "Come on with me," Cody-Annie said genially, her eyes crinkling at the corners as she smiled down at her. "Bring your rifle. We'll have us a manhunt!"

Then she rode away, the saddle pitching and bucking while she hung on with one hand and blew kisses to Cecelia with the other. Just then the saddle dipped and lunged, tossing her high into the air, spinning. Cecelia lost sight of her high overhead, though she knew somewhere outside the illuminated stage of the dream she was falling.

Outside, a southwest wind picked up as the darkness thickened, pushing clouds heavy with warm Gulf water lifted off the coast of Tamaulipas. A wedge of cold air, sliding down like a glacier from the Rockies, had just encountered the left edge of this damp mass as it cut diagonally across Watson County. The waning moon, already intermittently obscured by scudding clouds, was now lost as the wind-borne moisture piled up and thickened against the implacable wall of frigid air. It would not be long before the vapor began to condense and slide earthward down the cold wall.

Midway between Cecelia's drive and the strip of sidewalk leading from her front door to the vague margin of the road was a bright yellow tube on a post. "Houston Chronicle" was printed on the side in inch-high black letters. It would be hours before the rattling '78 Buick that brought the weekend papers to scattered houses along this back road deposited its large Sunday roll, sacked in plastic, in the yellow tube.

A shutter on the north side of the house strained against a rusty nail anchoring it to the brick. With the next gust of wind, the nail gave way and the shutter swung out, then banged back against the side of the house. Cecelia woke from her dream with a start. She lay still for several minutes, trying to separate the noise from her dream. It had sounded like a shot. She slid her legs over the side of the bed and sat there a moment, still pondering the dream. Had it been sent to tell her something? Already the details were fading from her memory. What was its message? Try as she might, she could sense nothing she could have named as the prompting of the Spirit.

The wind was whining through the crack under the window over the sink, the one she never managed to get shut all the way. Dreading the pain that would shoot through her feet as soon as she stood, she had just pushed herself up and taken one limping step toward the kitchen when she felt the carport door blow open and a cold gust sweep through the house.

"Mercy, mercy," she muttered, shuffling into the kitchen. She started to slam the door hard against the wind when she paused, thinking she heard another sound. For a long moment she stood there in the dark doorway, waiting. Then she pulled the door carefully closed and turned the lock. The wind stilled suddenly around her, though a current continued to whistle under the window over the sink.


After Norton had set the technicians to work inside the trailer, he made his way back up to the barn and crawled into the cruiser where Kamowski had waited for him. They sat there in silence for several minutes. He didn't feel frantic nor even impatient now, only tired and numb.

"I've called for the dogs from the Bromley Unit," he finally said. "I figure it's the quickest way. They can't have gotten far, not if they're on foot, but I can't leave the scene until another officer shows up, and I don't have enough people here to start a ground search yet anyway."

Kamowski nodded. He knew the guy was only speaking aloud in order to check out his own reasoning. Neither of them had mentioned what had been obvious from the wrecked shrine—that Ignacio must have returned to the trailer after Dan and the old lady had been there. What the shrine's destruction might mean neither of them wanted to speculate about, at least not aloud.

The shrine had been a powerful symbol to the boy, and its devastation was thus equally symbolic. If he had made the shrine to honor his mother, as a place to renew the pledge that was driving him, what must its destruction mean? Privately, Kamowski knew the implications didn't look good. And he figured they must look equally bleak to the deputy.

"How long should it take for them to get here with the dogs?" Dan finally asked, just to give the other man a chance to speak again.

"Not long. Maybe thirty minutes." Norton checked his watch.

Kamowski looked at the sky from which the color of

the brief winter sunset had rapidly drained. Clouds were moving in. Rain was forecast before morning. "You wanna—" he said, flicking a thick finger toward the windshield to indicate the woods rising on the hill beyond the ravine.

Norton shook his head. "I'll do better staying here, waiting for the dogs. I want to be with them when they start off." He looked away out the side window again, then said, clearing his throat, "I guess you've been praying?"

"Yes."

"And Mrs. Ramsey. She would be too." There was another pause, and then he added, "I would. Except—"

"Except you want to kill him."

Norton jerked his head back from the window and looked at the priest. "Yes. And I will. If I see him, I'll kill him. I'm telling you this."

"You want me to stop you?"

Norton shifted, leaned over and picked up the radio transmitter. "Just pray," he said.

Geoff wasn't sure why he'd gone to such extremes to keep from being discovered leaving the arroyo. Probably because he'd taken such pains to get to the trailer without being seen. The deputy would never have let him past the line of vehicles parked by the barn at the top of the hill until the forensic team had finished going over the trailer with a fine-tooth comb, a process that could take hours. Now, since he'd pulled it off—slipping in the back way—he didn't want to spoil his triumph by getting caught.

He'd been about to slip away down the arroyo the way he had come, when the trailer started to rock and one of the technicians clambered out. Geoff dodged behind the Toyota and crouched there, holding his breath as the guy scrambled up the side of the gully, the beam from the flashlight he'd switched on in the dusk swinging erratically as he stumbled and grabbed for a handhold.

The man left inside the trailer began to whistle an old Beatles tune. The glow from the flashlight disappeared beyond the rim of the ravine. Carefully, Geoff crept from behind the car and made his way up the far side of the gully. He'd just reached the lip when he noticed the whistling below had stopped. The trailer rocked again and a voice called out, "Hey! Who's there?"

Geoff crouched behind an overhanging bush, his heart pounding. Another flashlight snapped on and played up and down the bottom of the ravine. The man made a rumbling growl and swore under his breath, then made his way to the end of the trailer and shined the flashlight in the direction from which Geoff had approached the trailer. The high sides of the arroyo must distort sounds below.

When the man made his way back to the trailer door again, the reporter scuttled farther back into the darkness, then crept within the cover of a nearby thicket. A circle of light bobbed along the hillside as the first man returned. He watched the technician slide down the soft incline into the ravine again.

"What's a matter, Mike? Getting the willies out here by yourself?"

The other man snorted and the trailer rocked again as they both hoisted themselves back inside.

Geoff hunkered within the thicket, considering his options. He couldn't get back to his car by following the ravine bed now. He'd have to keep as close as he could to its edge till he came to where it flattened to no more than a dip in the field. From there he could find the fence again and simply follow it back to the car.

Just then a spotlight erupted from the barn on the top of the hill, pushing a dim lake of illumination to the edge of the thicket. Either they'd gotten the electricity turned on there or a generator had arrived. He'd have to move farther back into the trees to keep from being spotted, away from the ravine. And he'd have to hurry. His hunch was that the deputy was only waiting for more personnel to arrive before they started searching the woods. The wind was picking up. If they were going to start a search at all tonight, it would have to be soon.

He needed to get out of here as fast as possible. If he turned directly to his left and kept the glow of the lights on his right, he'd surely come to the fence eventually. But for now, he'd have to keep well within the trees and underbrush.

With a shudder, Geoff bent beneath the only opening in the low branches of the thicket and felt his way farther into the dark undergrowth.

After the truck with the cages of tracking dogs chained to the flatbed arrived, Kamowski decided it was time to leave. He remembered the dogs. Their yelping still sent waves of panic through him.

The deputy had been radioing orders for equipment back to the dispatcher in Somerville when the truck's lights angled up the drive to the barn. He dropped the transmitter and jumped from the cruiser. As soon as the truck pulled up beside the barn, he was gesturing toward the ravine, explaining the situation to the head dog handler.

The dogs came boiling out of their cages. There must have been half a dozen, all in a frenzy of hyper-active olfactories. Dan shuddered. They'd give the dogs the girl's T-shirt to sniff at the trailer, then give them their head. Who knew what they'd find. Or when. If it started to rain, even the dogs wouldn't be much use.

He didn't want to think about it. It was out of his hands. The law and its ways had always been out of his hands. Even after he'd been yanked back from beyond its borders, he still felt a strange sense of disorientation within its precincts. Not in all the intervening years of prison, seminary, priesthood, had he learned to be comfortable there. The law protected other people who had grown up inside its sheltering wall. People who took an earnest interest in their lawns or the PTA. Nice people like Dell. He'd never been tempted to slip outside its boundaries again—not as long as he had something precious to preserve—but he never imagined he was like those other people. Once you experienced the retribution of the law, you felt forever alien to it. That's why he didn't want to listen to the dogs. It was him they were yelping for.

He got out of the car and wandered away from the truck toward the road. That's what he was always trying to explain to people he worked with in the prison ministry, how outlaws were really that—outside the law. The inmates understood what he meant. Only a few of the others did. He had hoped maybe this Cartwright girl would be one of them.

He stopped and zipped up his windbreaker, remembering the ripped tinfoil and the wadded pictures in the trailer. The first time he saw it, the shrine had made Dan think of some kind of a knightly quest. Did its destruction mean the boy had decided to abandon his quest? Probably not. That kind of rage wasn't a decision; it went beyond reason. The whole plan had never been rational to begin with. This wasn't a change of mind but a change of heart. And not for the better.


She had already made up her mind to die when she decided to fight back in the trailer. And while he was beating her, she had believed he was going to kill her. Then, when he dragged her from the trailer into the woods, she was certain he planned to murder her there, where it would be harder to find the body. She even thought in terms of "the body," so thoroughly had she managed to divorce herself from what was happening.

Now, at the moment of returning consciousness, she was having to adjust to the fact that she was still alive. She knew because she hurt so badly. Her bare feet were cut and bruised. Her hands and wrists, bound for so long by the nylon cord, were raw and inflamed. Her head throbbed, radiating pain from vague spots on her skull. She wasn't sure if her jaw was actually broken, but swallowing was painful. The belt cut into her swollen neck, tightening every time she slumped toward the ground. But worst was the cold. She was so cold there was nothing left to feel the cold—only the cold itself. And now it had started to rain.

He wasn't coming back. She would die here. Not quickly, but slowly. They would never find her. Not in time. She wondered if she had the courage simply to let her knees sag and speed up the inevitable.

# CHAPTER • TWENTY-THREE

CECELIA DIDN'T TURN ON THE light. Instead, she stared out the kitchen window into the space of cleared ground behind the house where her mother used to raise tomatoes and cucumbers. The rows had melted almost flat again over the years; she could barely make out their undulations under the green glow of the mercury vapor light above the well house. She had seen clearly, though, the back of the plaid flannel shirt before the door to the outbuilding shut.

She made her way in the dark back into her bedroom, still muttering "Mercy" in muted periodic ejaculations. Groaning and huffing, she dragged the ottoman she used to elevate her gouty feet to the closet and climbed up on it, steadying herself on the closet door with one hand and stretching to the back of the shelf with the other.

She had always been terrified that some child might discover the rifle. However, because it had belonged to her father, a man of few possessions, she could never bring herself to part with it. None of her younger male relatives would she have trusted with it.

She had to move two hatboxes and a quilt wrapped in plastic before she could drag the .22 from the back of the top shelf. Groping along the left side, she found the box of ammunition. She had never loaded a rifle before. However, she figured if she told him it was loaded it ought to be.

Taking the rifle into the bathroom, she closed the door before turning on the light. Her fingers were stiff, and she dropped several cartridges before she was finally able to tug open the bolt and insert one into the chamber. After she had snapped the bolt back, she turned off the light, opened the door, and shuffled back into the kitchen with the .22. The window over the sink still whistled with a subdued but shrill complaint. She kept her eyes on its lighted square as she made her way toward the red eye on the counter.

From long habit, she could dial the number almost without looking, but it took eight rings before Mason Dugger's grandson picked up the phone.

"Deputy Satterthwaite."

"Howard?"

"Who is this?"

"Cecelia Ramsey. Remember—"

"Yes. Yes, ma'am. What can I do for you?"

"Is Norton and that Brother Kamowski still out at the old MacGruder place?"

There was an uneasy pause; Cecelia hurried to fill it. "Have they come back yet?"

"No. No, they haven't."

"Do you think you could reach them on your car radio? The telephone thing, I mean."

"Well, I *could*. But—"

"Good. I have an important message for them. Really for Brother Kamowski. His wife wants him to call her, see, and—uh, there's an emergency. The son of an old friend of his. A matter of life and death. Tell him he should come here. To my place. He can call his wife from here. Tell him I'll give him the details when he gets here." She had worked out the wording ahead of time. It wasn't an outright lie.

The boy breathed noisily into the phone. She pictured the Dugger chin. Best not to give him too much time to think. She hung up the receiver.

All he could hear were slight skitterings in the brush around him. Birds, probably. But did birds perch so low to the ground for the night? He tried to estimate the location of the noise, but it seemed to have moved. Did snakes make noise when they crawled over dead leaves? He reached in his jacket pocket and pulled out the miniature flashlight, feeling pleased with himself, both that he'd come so well prepared and that he'd avoided using it till he was sure it couldn't be seen. As soon as the light came on, the skittering stopped. Everything was still.

He shone the beam all around his feet. Then directly in front of him. This was silly. It was time to get out of here. He tried to estimate how much off his original course he'd gone, knowing he needed to go back to the right some to strike the fence. But a tangle of vines had looped themselves into the branches of the trees in that direction, making a curtain of thorns and leaves. So he had to detour around that. Then he hit a boggy place full of Spanish sword where water had collected from the recent rains. He didn't remember crossing a bog before. This wasn't making sense. Maybe he should just turn around and go back.

He closed his eyes, trying to find the way by mentally rolling a film backwards. When he felt briars raking across his hands, he thought it was working. He'd made it back to the curtain of vines. But the flashlight revealed not the draped vines but a barrier of some kind of bush, chest high, and covered with barbs. He had no idea where he was now.

He swore softly. "This is stupid," he said aloud. This wasn't the jungle, for crying out loud, just the East Texas woods. He couldn't be far from the pasture. He hadn't been walking that long. Probably if he shouted he could still be heard by one of those sheriff's department yahoos. But no. He'd rather sit out here all night, with the ticks and spiders and snakes, than endure that humiliation.

To save the battery, he turned off the flashlight. After a while, as his eyes adjusted once more to the darkness that seemed palpably thick now, he could make out minute noises.

"Okay," he told himself, speaking out loud, "just use your head. You're a human being. You've got superior intelligence. What makes sense here?" He remembered reading that, if lost in the woods, you were supposed to sit and wait in one spot till someone found you. But that was just it. He didn't want anyone to find him. What he wanted was to find himself. Or rather find his way out.

Then he thought of the dogs. Hadn't he heard one of the men in the trailer say Norton had sent for the dogs? What if they struck his scent? Shit! He pictured the beasts, howling their hopeless, frenzied ululations, coming at his throat. His grip tightened on the flashlight. He had to get out of here somehow.


The rain was going to make a mess of the trail. They had brought four dogs from the Bromley Unit, more than enough under ordinary circumstances. But by the time they'd taken the dogs down to the trailer and shown them Beth Marie's nightshirt, rain was already threatening. The dogs had caught the scent with no trouble, but a steady rain would disperse it and confuse the animals.

Kamowski had wandered away from the cruiser, both to escape the dogs and to stretch his legs. He supposed Norton was either still down at the trailer or had gone off with one of the tracking teams.

It was one of the technicians who delivered the garbled

message from Satterthwaite. The guy got the intern at the Cartwright house on the radio for him again, but Dan could make no clear sense of the message.

"I could get the dispatcher for you. Maybe she could patch you through to your wife," the technician said doubtfully. "But she's got a lot of lines tied up with this search already. It could take a while."

Kamowski nodded. "Maybe I'll just go on to Mrs. Ramsey's then."

He headed to the van, pulling the hood of his windbreaker up against the rain that was just beginning to spit. Actually, it was a relief to have this excuse to leave. He hadn't realized just how desperate he was to escape—and not just the dogs.

He climbed in the van and eased it back down the drive to the road. He didn't want to think about what the trackers might find at the end of the trail. It was out of his hands anyway.

At times like this—when Kamowski felt helpless, when he couldn't explain circumstances in a way that would make sense to anyone, certainly not to anyone who wanted the consequences divided up between guilt and innocence—his brain retreated to dealing only with the natural processes. Adrenalin, shortness of breath, chemically heightened sensations induced by fear. The sheer physics of force and the resistance of bone, tissue, blood. The way a doctor would react in an emergency room to the aftermath of a wreck. Not trying to determine responsibility. Leaving that alone while he worked on the bodies.

If they found the girl, Kamowski figured he might be able to think of something to say to her later. Supposing they found her alive. And if they found the kid—well, he'd probably never get a chance to talk to him. Either way, he felt useless. *You ain't the Messiah, remember,* Berkowitz had told him. *Ninety percent of the time, being a priest is just going through the motions.* Right now he'd be grateful to have something as simple as motions to do. Something merely routine. Well. He'd call Nell from the old lady's house and find out what was going on. It sounded like somebody in the congregation had had a death in the family. He could handle that.

At the next crossroad he turned left, a little uncertain of his direction in the dark. He switched to his bright lights as he topped the next hill, but it had started to rain and the angle of the beam reflected back in a shimmering glare so that he had to lower them again. On the far side of the hill he could make out a small brick house he thought he recognized as Cecelia Ramsey's. It looked pathetic, its isolation in the ocean of rural darkness emphasized by the green glow of the light on the pole out back. No interior light showed through the windows though, and he slowed to a crawl as he came up even with it, reluctant to stop. It must be her house; he could see the station wagon in the carport now. Maybe the old lady had already gone to bed.

Just then he saw a small point of yellow light—probably a flashlight—blink on and off. It appeared to come from the front picture window. He stopped the van and the light winked at him again, moving up and down. Why didn't she turn the lights on? Had the storm knocked out the power?

He edged the van up to the short strip of sidewalk and got out warily. He was about halfway to the front door, the rain pelting him, when it suddenly opened and the flashlight shone on the steps.

"Hurry," she called in a high, breathy whisper. "Get on in here. I can't turn on the lights yet. You have to do the rest."

The rain was in fact making a mess of the trail. What Norton had hoped would only be a brief shower had turned into a slow, steady drizzle, the kind that would go on all night. By the time they had gotten the dogs down to the trailer and set them on the trail, the ground was damp. At the outset, one of the handlers had told him that dampness actually released the scent and helped the dogs, but Norton could see now he had said that just to placate him because later, when it began to rain in earnest, the same handler told him that the runoff, spreading into puddles and sliding downhill, was dispersing the scent and throwing the dogs off. They had been tracking over an hour now, having returned a couple of times to the trailer to start again. The handlers were still following their dogs but with no real conviction any longer.

Already there had been at least three false alarms taking them in various directions. The first time, convinced by a shepherd's insistent yap, Norton had gone out with the head handler, leaving the command post to the technicians. The dog had gone to ground where a creek had cut away the earth from the roots of a sycamore, scratching at what turned out to be an animal burrow.

Later, back at the trailer, Norton had told the technician to call Larry Rostow in to cover the command post for him. He suspected Sheriff Dooley had gotten a ride back from Houston by now. Then he had left again with another handler. They had followed a dry streambed for a while until the dog had circled an oak motte obstinately. But when they shined their lights into the branches, they found the eyes of a raccoon staring back at them wrathfully.

Now he was out with the main handler again. The man kept trying to explain to Norton how well his dogs ordinarily worked and why they were having a hard time tonight, but Norton wasn't listening. He plunged ahead through the wet leaves and mud, just for the sheer sake of keeping moving. His arms were sore from fending off the branches. He no longer took any pains to keep them from springing back and lashing the fellow following him.

Once they broke out into what appeared to be an old

logging road. Rain was standing in the ruts already. The handler, pulling in the dog, commanded him to sit.

"Hey," he shouted to Norton. "This ain't working. We can't just go on wallering around in this mess all night."

Norton stopped but didn't turn toward him.

"It's not working," the man repeated stubbornly. "This ain't helping her none."

Norton knew the man was right, but he didn't intend to stop. If nothing else, there was always random chance. It was conceivable, given the laws of probability, that they might stumble across something. A random chance was better than nothing. It was better than giving up. They had to keep going.

But he didn't say this to the other man. He stood there, his flashlight illuminating the droplets forming at the tip of each leaf on the yaupon growing across the logging trail. Then he turned and aimed his light back at the handler, taking in the man's eyes trying to squint the water off his lashes. Water from his saturated hat brim was slowly dripping down his neck.

Norton opened his mouth, then shut it again, clamping his lips together. It would be impossible anyway, an insurmountable task, making this man see that the rain and the cold and the dark didn't matter. How strong would words have to be to compel him to believe how much it didn't matter?

His silence stretched on, too long. The other man was lifting his arm in a gesture of appeal and opening his mouth to speak again himself when the sound of another dog trailing came faintly through the trees. Their eyes locked.

"Sounds like about a quarter mile," the handler said wearily, yanking at his dog's leash. "But don't get your hopes up none."

She tried to tilt her head up to catch the falling drops

on her swollen tongue, but the constriction of the belt against her neck wouldn't allow even that much movement. As the rain splattered against her face, slowly wetting it and collecting in runnels, she was able to lick moisture from her lips. What she tasted though was her own dried blood, slightly moistened.

It was only a matter to time. How long had she been telling herself that now? Hours? She had fallen into a half-conscious stupor, sagging against the tree. Gradually the ringing in her ears from the blood constricted in her head roused her sufficiently to lift her weight again. And she found herself still alive.

She could feel her mind losing its sense of time. Not thinking straight anymore. Only holding images that swam and dissolved and reformed into other images. Though she had a sense of herself located in space, it was a space constricted to the rough bark and the cold. Inside the space was buried a small, pulsating core of will, powerless to do anything but keep her weight braced against the tree. Other than the tree, she was only aware of the images that floated in and out of her attention with no coherence.

Her mother, rigid between the plain white sheets, closed her eyes when the pain became so bad she could no longer disguise it. And her father hacked out his lungs into the handkerchiefs her mother washed and bleached by hand. It was just a matter of time for them too. A long time. So long it had been hard to keep on loving them. Because they had been on the inside of the pain, a place she couldn't go, couldn't reach through. Not then. But now she was inside it, and they were here with her.

Norton though was still on the outside. He could only stare at her from a distance. From inside the pain she could see him even better now, almost the way he had appeared to her that first time, when she had taken the impress of every sharp, piercing line of his strangeness as if his image were being scored on the damp clay of her heart with a stylus. There had been a sweetness in that pain, one that made her long for more. Accurate, fine, precise. Not the wide, blunt tedium of this misery whose end she could not even imagine.

He should have killed her. She should have made him kill her. Then there would have been an end.

# CHAPTER TWENTY-FOUR

H E HAD TO MAKE HIMSELF STOP moving. And once he had stopped, he had to keep himself from moving again. The part of his mind that operated logically kept repeating this over and over: Just stop. Keep still. Someone will find you. That's what the books say.

But what the books didn't say was just how hard standing still might be when it was dark and raining and you were ringed by crowding growth and alien breath. When you were not just afraid, but so disoriented you hardly had a sense of your own arms and legs, as if the very boundaries of your body were melting away into the engulfing blackness. He no longer noticed the lashings and scrapes because another part of his brain was blocking out those sensations and driving him, propelling him through any barrier as if its very resistance obliged him to thrash his way through it.

As he'd feared, the flashlight battery hadn't lasted more than ten minutes once he switched it on. How long had it been since then? His sense of time as well as place had skewed so that he could not have said how long he'd been sliding down creekbeds and staggering through branches and brambles.

He started uphill again, the only direction he could still discern, instinctively feeling for footing that was ever higher. The trunk of a sapling caught him across the shoulder. Staggering forward, he caught the toe of his boot against a rotting stump and went sprawling head-long into invisible, wet muck matted with dead leaves.

He lay there a moment before he raised himself on his knees and forced his lungs to inflate slowly. Then he blew out again steadily for almost a full minute. The pounding in his ears slowed. He put his hands to his face and rubbed them over his forehead and down his cheeks, marveling at how much touch could be like see-ing, as if his fingers were transferring information about form and texture directly to his eyes. After a couple of minutes he could discern the boundaries of his own body reasserting themselves. Gradually, gratefully, he felt his grated skin start to burn and bruises on his head and arms begin to smart.

"Okay now. Stay where you are," he whispered to himself. "Just stay where you are. Don't move." Cautious of rising to his feet again, lest they begin to move, betraying the small share of control his reason had regained, he put out his arms carefully, feeling first along the base of a serpentine vine as thick as his wrist. It twisted away upward on his right. To his left, his arm brushed against some bush that showered down its weight of rain as his touch rocked it. Distinctions were coming back to him. Vine, bush. Left, right. In the dark, alone, distinctions were what he had to hold onto.

He moved a foot or so forward and to his right, thrusting his arms ahead of him and sweeping them slowly back in a double arc. Nothing. A space. He allowed himself to rise to a crouch, expecting a low branch to check him. He swept his arms forward and back again. Again, he touched nothing. No brambles, no springy switches or branches raked his hands. Slowly he straightened and took another step forward, then stopped, sensing some change. The rain. For a moment there it had been falling directly on him, steady, from overhead. He took another step, arms extended, and the back of his left hand struck a rough surface. He felt along it with his palm. A tree, one standing alone. The rain rattled above him on what remained of its leaves. Not much shelter. Not as much as the underbrush provided. But at least he could breathe here.

He flattened both hands against the trunk and began to feel around it, unaccountably hopeful at the rough reassurance of its deep bark after his long disorientation. Then, with no warning, he heard his own voice coming to him in a kind of gargled wail of dismay. His senses had betrayed him once more. It wasn't bark or bristles or moss or even scales he'd touched, but the unexpectedly soft sogginess of fabric and slick, waxy skin.

Kamowski looked at the .22 lying on the kitchen counter. Through the window over the sink he could see the outbuilding she was pointing to, under the pole light.

"What's the gun for?"

"In case he started to leave. I couldn't let him get away. I would have had to stop him somehow."

"And you think you could shoot him?" He looked down at her deflated face catching the green glow from the pole light. Would Dell ever get so old she would look like that?

"I don't know. I would have told him to stop first. Then I could have tried." She stared toward the well house as though she had considered all the possibilities thoroughly.

"Why didn't you just send for the cops? Why me?"

She tilted her head at him and raised her eyebrows high so that the wrinkles around her eyes were stretched almost flat. "Because you know him. Or his father.

Remember? You were going to talk to him. That was the plan."

Dan rubbed his large hand over his mouth. Had he said that? He lowered his head to the window's level and peered out, surveying the lay of the land around the outbuilding. Had the kid seen his van pull up out front?

"Go call the sheriff's department," he said. "Not that turkey they left at the house. Call the dispatcher in town. Tell her to get hold of Norton or whoever's out there. Tell them the kid's here."

She started to make a small, objecting noise, then broke it off and pulled open a drawer by the telephone. "I have to look up the number," she said, aiming the flashlight into the drawer and switching it on.

"Tell them to hurry," he said, picking up the rifle and heading for the front door. As he stepped outside into the rain, he wished he'd asked her where the breaker was for the pole light. Then he decided it didn't matter. The light would only be a disadvantage until he could get the door open.

The rain was slow, more drizzle than rain now. He made his way around the west end of the house to the corner he had reckoned would take him closest to the door of the well house. Did the boy know he was there? Was he waiting for him? Either way, whether he took him by surprise or not, the boy's nerves had to be on the verge of giving way altogether. If he didn't have a gun, he'd have a knife for sure.

He paused and threw open the bolt to make certain the rifle was loaded as she had said, then in five quick strides covered the distance and pushed open the well house door.

There was a scuttling movement in the corner back behind the water tank. The kid must not have seen him coming.

"Come on out," Kamowski said. "It's over. I don't want to shoot."

There was another movement and the sound of something metal falling over.

"It's me. The priest. Not the cops. Come on out. I don't want to hurt you."

Something shifted. Then he heard the water tank reverberate with a dull thunk as something struck against it. His left hand holding the stock under the barrel tightened. Realizing he was making a large black silhouette in the doorway, he stepped to the side, straining to see into the corner where the noise had come from. He should have brought another cartridge. If he used this one for a warning, he'd have nothing left.

Just then he saw a hand grip the pipe to the tank.

"All right," he said, speaking low and steady. "All right. Come on. Just step on out from behind there."

There was another pause, then the hand loosened and the boy's torso appeared, outlined by a green rim of light. The next second he had propelled himself from behind the water tank toward the open door. Kamowski lunged almost simultaneously and swung the rifle barrel down and back so that the kid caught it across his lower belly and pitched forward, jerking the weight against Dan's trigger finger.

The noise inside the shed stunned them both. But in the one dazed moment before the boy could gather his feet beneath him again, Kamowski fell on him, pinning him against the dirt and the door frame. The boy cried out and then lay still, though his eyes glinted in the eerie light.

One hand still grasping the rifle, Kamowski pushed himself upright, gripped the boy's shoulder with the other hand, and half dragged him to his feet. He wasn't sure if the kid was hurt or not.

"Did I hit you?"

The boy snorted weakly.

"With the gun, I mean. Are you shot?"

He didn't answer, but from the little Kamowski could make out, there didn't appear to be any blood.

Kamowski gripped his upper arm. "All right, friend. Let's go inside out of the rain."

The boy tried to jerk away, but Kamowski's grasp tightened.

"We got some talking to do," the priest went on in a low, even voice. "The sheriff's hunting you. You better come on with me before he gets here."

Ignacio's body stiffened, but when Kamowski jerked his arm, he stumbled along before him. Inside the house the lights came on, but Kamowski skirted it and headed them toward the van parked out front. He yanked the side door open and shoved the boy inside, then climbed in after him and turned to slam the door shut. When he turned back he could see the knife blade.

"Put that away," Kamowski said.

All he could hear in response was the kid's thick, shallow breath.

"You use that on the girl?" the priest said, lowering himself awkwardly onto the backward-facing seat. "You kill her?"

There was a long silence. When Ignacio spoke, his voice was cold with contempt. "It would make no difference. She is a whore."

"Where is she now?"

His shoulders gave a spasmodic jerk. "Out of the way."

"Not dead then?"

Ignacio snorted and twisted his head sideways. "Her life is not worth mine."

"The sheriff's on his way now," Kamowski said evenly. "You're gonna get caught, whatever."

Ignacio laughed, a single, sharp bark.

"If you try to run, they'll shoot you."

"You think I care if they do? You think I am afraid?"

Kamowski sighed. "Probably not. You probably ain't

got enough sense to be scared right now. But I'm just telling you that. I'm not here to save your life. I'm here to tell you something you might oughta know."

"You know nothing—"

"I knew your father."

There was silence in the van. Even Ignacio's ragged breathing stopped for a while. The front porch light came on.

"We were together once, a short time."

"Where?"

"Houston. Harris County jail."

"You were a prison priest? You visited him?"

"I wasn't a priest then." There was a pause. Finally Kamowski added, "I was in jail there myself."

Ignacio frowned. Then his face hardened again. "So?"

"So he told me about your mother."

The knife came up suddenly at an acute angle. "Bastard!"

"Yeah, well. You're right about your mother too, you know. She did it for him. She didn't shoot that sheriff. He set her up."

Ignacio jerked his head away and made a strangled noise, but Kamowski, watching for this moment, shot a hand out and clutched the boy's wrist, forcing his arm backward till the fingers loosened. Grabbing the knife with his other hand, he felt the boy's wrist suddenly go limp in his grasp.

Kamowski sat back and went on in the same even voice. "He was a bastard, son. But then I was too. That's why I was there in the same cell with him."

Ignacio was bent forward over his knees, sucking in sharp breaths. "She was a saint," he said finally, "a martyr."

"Maybe," the priest said. "Maybe not. Maybe she was just stupid."

The boy's head jerked up.

"Leaving her two kids like that to go to prison. He wasn't worth it. Besides, it didn't do him any good. At least not then. He may be dead now for all I know."

"We heard he went to Mexico," Ignacio muttered.

"Whatever. Anyway, it sure didn't do you any good, did it? She shouldn't have done it, kid. You're right about that. She shouldn't have left you. Not for him. Not for that. It was wrong."

Ignacio's face tilted upward so that the priest could see it clearly for the first time, contorted between grief and anger. "She left me. Me and Rosa. It was wrong." His lips stretched back over his teeth, his mouth opened slightly, as though he were screaming soundlessly into the darkness.

"You gotta be plenty mad about that. First your father takes off. Then your mother."

Ignacio's dark eyes locked ferociously on the priest's face.

"She had no right. Just like you been thinking. All these years. She was wrong."

The boy's face had frozen, even his eyes not moving. Kamowski took a deep breath and went on. "And now look at you. You're going to prison, amigo. Just like him."

"No!" The boy half sprang up, but Kamowski shoved him back into the seat again.

"I'm afraid so. Not much way out now."

"I am not like him!" Ignacio started up again, but the priest pushed him down once more.

"Maybe you're like her then. Stupid. Sacrificing yourself—for what?"

"Because she—"

"Was stupid? Was wrong? So you're going to do it all over again? Is that it? Stupidity runs in the family?"

Ignacio collapsed over his knees again, holding his hands over his ears, rocking back and forth.

Kamowski glanced out the rear window. He could see no sign of lights coming along the road yet.

"Look," he said, "it's over now. You hear me? The sheriff will be here in a few minutes. You let me handle it. I'll go along with you. See that you get a lawyer. I don't know how much time you'll get for this, but you need some time anyway." He shook his head. "It's gonna take a while." He sighed, then muttered to himself, "It looks like I'm gonna be around myself for a while."

He waited then, listening to the boy's breathing grow steadier. Finally Ignacio lowered his hands and raised his head. "I am not like him. I will not run away," he said in a stony voice. "I am not like my father."

"Maybe not, son," Kamowski said. "Maybe you're not."

They had to struggle across the creek again, this time through a couple of inches of water, and find a way up the sandy cut on the far side. Norton wasn't certain, but it seemed that the dog's ululating howls were coming from the top of a hill. He was sure it was no false alarm this time.

A quarter of a mile through heavy undergrowth was a long way, and the rain made it even longer. Before they reached the clearing, they met one of the handlers headed back down the hill.

"I think the ambulance can get closer if they come around on the Big Notch cutoff," he shouted to them. "A damn reporter found her, can you beat that? No flashlight even. He set off some flashbulbs—that's what we caught sight of first. Woulda been tomorrow before we found her ourselves."

Ahead, just up the rise, they could hear human voices shouting amid the cries of the dogs, and at last they could see lights coming through the trees.

"They've found her!" Norton called back to the man behind him. Then suddenly his stomach lurched. Till then he'd only thought of finding her. Now, imagining, he was abruptly afraid. He stopped momentarily, his hand holding back a dripping branch, as if gathering himself. Then he thrust forward up the hill and into the weak circle of lights concentrated on a form several men were huddled beside on the ground.

Before he could see anything but the bent slickers, he was shoving them away and choking on his own voice as he dropped to his knees beside the figure he could hardly recognize as Beth Marie.

# CHAPTER • TWENTY-FIVE

**N**ORTON ROUTINELY USED THE emergency entrance at the Watson County hospital and thus had gotten to know most of the people on the ER staff there. He didn't want to see any of them today. Instead, he pulled into the visitors parking lot in front, turned off the ignition, and sat staring into the tangle of brush below the pines that crowded against the edge of the concrete. Last night's rain had stopped, but the sky was still overcast and the wind had picked up. Today he could understand why animals hibernated. He wished he could disappear into some dark tunnel, sleep, forget it all.

He had gotten very little sleep. After he'd finally made it home around two in the morning, he kept going over and over the long day, following hypothetical trails like the dogs last night. *What if, what if*—the words started him in various directions that took him nowhere. What if he hadn't gone to Houston? What if he'd managed some way to take her with him? What if he'd been at the house with her?

All the standard reassurances he'd offered to the families of victims for years—*you can't be everywhere, ma'am . . . these things just happen . . . you can't blame your-*

*self*—they all mocked him now. He continued to feel responsible for this disaster.

Beth Marie hadn't wanted to be alone; she'd made that clear. And when she needed him, he hadn't been there. It didn't matter that neither of them expected something like this to happen. In fact, that was the point. No one ever expected it. That's why he should have been there. In case. He had failed her. In the worst possible way.

He lowered his forehead to the steering wheel and closed his eyes. What could he say when he walked in that hospital room now?

A tap at his window made him jerk his head up. An expanse of blue nylon windbreaker, then the priest's face leaning down filled the car window. "Gotta minute?" Kamowski shouted against the wind.

Norton nodded and gestured for him to get into the car. He had heard that the priest was with the Mascarenas kid when they picked up him up at Cecelia Ramsey's place. How the three of them had all turned up there hadn't been the riddle first on Norton's list to solve. All he had cared about last night was that the guy had been caught.

Sheriff Dooley had told him that the priest stayed at the station till the kid was booked and then called some lawyer from his congregation to represent him. According to the sheriff, this lawyer ordinarily didn't take on public-defender cases and hadn't been too happy with the assignment. The sheriff himself had been surprised. Wasn't Beth Marie a member of St. Barnabas? So why would the priest want another member defending her attacker?

Maybe Kamowski wanted to explain that now, Norton thought as the big man crawled into the car. He hoped not. He hadn't even wanted to see Mascarenas last night. If he had his way, the guy would simply be obliterated, wiped off the face of the earth. He didn't want to hear any more about him. No details. Nothing.

He wanted it to be as if Ignacio Mascarenas had never existed.

"You seen her yet?" the priest asked, slamming the door so hard the car rocked.

"Not since last night. I was just on my way in."

"What she's been through—it's terrible." Kamowski blew on his hands but kept his eyes averted, contemplating the same dark tangle under the trees as Norton. "It's gonna take a while, you know, to get back to normal."

Norton only nodded and turned his head to look out his side window.

"I talked to him. Before the sheriff got there."

Norton cleared his throat and finally turned toward the other man. "Okay. So let's have it. What happened?"

The priest shook his head and pulled his protruding lips down at the corners. "You know as much as I do. More. You saw her. I didn't."

"Yeah, I saw her." Norton's voice, rising, was a retort. "And it wasn't a pretty sight. She wasn't even able to speak."

Kamowski waited before he spoke again, letting the silence cool the heat of Norton's tone. Then he said, lowering his voice deliberately, "If I knew any more, I'd tell you, son."

"You said you talked to him. You must have gotten something out of the son of a bitch."

"That's not what we talked about. I left that to the lawyer."

"So what did you talk about—the weather? Just tell me. I have a right to know."

The priest looked at him dolefully, nodding his head slightly several times before he finally spoke. "I guess that's the question, isn't it? Do you? Have a right. Anyway, I'm telling you the truth. I don't know. You'll have to find out from the doctor. Or from her."

There was a pause while Norton stared at him until his gaze broke and wavered uncertainly.

Then the priest went on, turning to contemplate the darkened brambles again. "I think you ought to know this guy's story. Not because I want you to feel sorry for him. But, well, just because you need to know."

The telling took no more than five minutes, though Norton kept glancing at his watch conspicuously and turning away to glare out the side window.

"Probably some part of him hated his mother for leaving him like that—for choosing his father over him," Kamowski finished. "He couldn't admit that, of course. He just took it out on another woman. But his hatred was geared to his love. One as strong as the other. To him, his mother represented something almost—no, not almost—something absolutely sacred. It was a pointless sacrifice she made, of course. But sanctity's a funny thing. I mean you wouldn't expect it to make sense, would you? And the boy's devotion to her, turning her into a martyr, you can call that senseless too. Even sick. And when it got mixed up with the anger, it only got sicker. But it wasn't that way at the beginning. He was just a little boy then, devoted to his mother. I know that kind of feeling's supposed to change—get transferred or something when you're a teenager. But that didn't happen for him."

Norton pulled the key from the ignition and unsnapped his seat belt.

"You know how it is when you're a teenager," Kamowski went on, ignoring his impatience. "Girls are a whole other kind of creature."

"Okay," Norton said, "so he had some kind of noble ideal about his mother that got screwed up. You say his mother was innocent, and you can verify his story because you knew the father. But that doesn't change anything for me. All I know is what he did to Beth Marie. The guy's sick. How he got that way's not my concern."

The priest appeared to study the dashboard before replying. The wind made a whistling noise through one of the back windows that wasn't rolled up all the way. Norton reached one arm awkwardly over the seat back and yanked at the handle.

"This town lives on people's sickness, doesn't it?" Kamowski said finally. "Somerville would dry up and blow away if it weren't for the prisons. You and me both would be out of a job if nobody was sick anymore."

Norton turned to stare at him. "So? I should be glad there's creeps like this guy out to hurt women? Or maybe you think I should feel bad because I make a living protecting people from them? Just because you've been on the inside—" His voice was rising, and he stopped short and faced forward again. "Protecting," he repeated bitterly and thumped the steering wheel with his fist.

Kamowski sighed. Norton waited for him to say the inevitable—the galling assurances he didn't want to hear.

But the man only reached over and put a heavy hand on his shoulder. "You're going to be thinking about that for a long time, son," he said. "You and Beth Marie had been, uh—seeing each other?" he finished awkwardly.

"About a year."

The priest nodded. "Made any plans?"

"I had, ah, just about decided—" Norton broke off awkwardly and rubbed his hands together between his knees.

"Really?" The priest took his hand away. "She knew?" The inflection was halfway between a statement and a question.

Norton inhaled deeply. "Not yet."

The priest made some inarticulate sound, and Norton felt his chest burn with constriction. The silence went on a long time, but he couldn't bring himself to say anything else.

Finally Kamowski, pausing with his hand on the door handle, said, "I have a couple more people to see here. I may do communion for one of them. Anyway, you go ahead. It'll be a while before I get up there." With that, the door opened and he was gone, making his deliberate way across the parking lot, leaning into the wind.

Norton stared after him, suddenly feeling abandoned.


Upstairs at the nurses' station he discovered they were planning to release her in the afternoon; they'd stabilized her after the exposure and checked for concussion. A doctor hurried up to the counter, asking for charts, and Norton was relieved to see that he was an older man with thin, slightly rumpled hair and stolid folds of flesh sagging around his mouth.

The doctor glanced up coolly at the deputy's uniform. "Girl you brought in last night," he said, "she's all right. He beat her up some. Wasn't raped though." He put the chart down, shoved it across the counter to the nurse, and picked up another one. "Can't understand why not. He certainly abused her enough in every other way. Maybe he was impotent. Anyway, you won't be able to charge him with that. More's the pity."

He scribbled away for a moment, then glanced up as though surprised to find Norton still standing there. "Don't worry. We were thorough. I took two different series of swabs, just to be certain. We couldn't get anything out of the girl herself. Residual shock, I imagine. I don't know if she knew the guy, though I heard he was in her bedroom. Of course, they always claim—" He stopped and glanced across the counter. "I expect you'll know more about that than we do. I understand he was Hispanic."

Norton nodded, looking down.

"Well." The doctor handed the last chart to the nurse. "I'll be glad to testify. I made a copy of my notes. Want me to send a copy over?"

Norton nodded again and turned away.

As he made his way down the corridor, trying to keep his boot heels from echoing on the hard floor, he remembered the way she'd looked last year after her fall from the fire lookout tower. Bruised, a little swollen.

He'd been intrigued with her from the beginning though, when he first saw her at the big house across from Cecelia Ramsey's. Like Kamowski said, she was a whole other kind of creature, her distinctness still a constant surprise to him. But as the months went by, even the difference had become familiar. *Make yourself at home*, she'd say when he went out to Point Blank. And he had.

But last night in the woods her eyes had flickered open for a moment as he bent over her and panic had glinted flatly from them, the way animal eyes reflect in the dark. She hadn't even recognized him before she lost consciousness again. The guy with the scraggly ponytail and a camera slung across his chest had stood back, staring at her. Norton hadn't trusted himself to talk to him, other than to tell him to report to the sheriff directly. Granger had a lot to answer for, but Dooley would take care of him. The reporter had left with the EMTs who carried Beth Marie away on a field stretcher through the dripping trees.

Norton stayed behind to collect evidence and inspect the site. He had been excessively careful; he wanted nothing to botch this investigation. By the time he made it back to the command post at the horse barn, they told him the ambulance had already left. He hurried in to the hospital in Somerville, but they'd already sedated her. He hadn't insisted on seeing her. Instead, he'd returned to the station, made his report, and gone home, full of frustration and obscure anger. She hadn't recognized him.

He put his palm on the wide hospital room door now, hesitating a moment before pushing it open. Her head was turned toward the window. She didn't move when he called softly from the doorway.

"Hey. You awake?" He tiptoed across the floor to her bedside.

There was a dark bruise on the left side of her forehead and another along the opposite jaw. Her lower lip was swollen around a cut, and the raw abrasions on her neck were covered with oily gauze. Her left upper arm was bandaged.

But she wasn't asleep. Her eyes, dark and sunken, were staring blankly at the tilted blinds.

"Beth Marie," he said, and her eyes closed, clenching shut. "It's me. Norton."

She moved her head very slightly, side to side.

He reached back and pulled the institutional chair up close to the bed. He sat leaning forward, rubbing his hands together with a rasping sound, wondering at how impossible it was for him to divine what she was feeling, what she had meant by that minuscule negation. The small shake of the head had put her a million miles away, on another planet, some place he didn't know the way to.

For a long time she lay there, not turning toward him or opening her eyes. His hatred for the man he still knew only as a name began to expand inside his chest. He tried to swallow it down before he spoke.

"The doctor says you're going to be okay," he finally said.

Her eyes flew open and she stared at the ceiling, her swollen lips tightening against her teeth.

Norton felt his bloated hatred suddenly recede, shrunken by the cold of fear. He lowered his head into one hand.

"He said—"

Startled at her voice, he looked up as she paused, swallowing to overcome the croaking hoarseness of her voice. Tears leaked from the reddened edges of her eyes, soaking instantly into the pillow. He rose, leaning over her and stroking the tears backward, dampening her hair.

"He called me a whore," she finished.

Norton's hand jerked slightly, and he leaned against the metal frame of the bed to steady it.

"He said—"

"Hush. Hush. It doesn't matter."

"Yes." She had to stop and swallow again. "It matters. Listen to me."

She turned her eyes toward him now, finally, and he gripped the bed frame harder.

"I was a fool. Geoff. Ignacio. You." She closed her eyes again and turned away. "Why are women such fools?"

"What do you mean? What—" He took a deep breath and stopped himself.

"None of this would have happened if he hadn't—"

"What? Hadn't what?"

"Seen your car there. And Geoff Granger's." She twisted away again and spoke into the pillow. He could only understand her because the pitch of her voice rose to a wail. "'Go ahead, experience life,' he said. Well, I've experienced it all right, and look at me!"

"But this is just—"

"This isn't *just* anything, Norton."

"That's not what I meant, sweetheart. I mean, if it hadn't been you, he would have found some other woman to—"

"But I'm not 'some other woman,' am I? I'm me. Beth Marie Cartwright. Or I was. What am I now, Norton? Experienced? Or is that just another name for what Ignacio called me? What are the options? I don't know, Norton." Her voice was beginning to break. "I don't know who I am, what I am anymore."

She rolled to her side, drawing up her knees, her head curved downward on the pillow. He could see her shoulders shuddering, but he was afraid to touch her. What did she mean? The guy was just a foul-mouthed bastard, that's all. Crazy. So maybe he had seen his car at her house. And this other guy, the reporter. Norton had no idea what had been going on with him. But how could she possibly lump him, someone who loved her, in the same category with those two?

He dropped back into the chair, staring at the curve of her neck, the gentle declivity right behind her ear. It was a part of her body that always undid him, it looked so vulnerable, so exposed. If she only knew. If she had only known.

"Hush, Beth Marie," he said gently. "Sweetheart. Stop it." He was still afraid to touch her.

After a time her shoulders stilled. Then there was only the movement of her unsteady breathing. He watched, aware after a while that he had matched his own breathing to hers, striving, with all the intensity of his will, to compel her belief.

"He said—" she began again, still turned away from him.

But he broke in, his tone preemptory now. "He's wrong."

She did stop then, surprised into silence at the flat contradiction.

"*I* know who you are," he said, gaining courage. "The most precious thing in my life. Everything I need. Like air and water. And there is another option. Because I can't live without what you are. Not any longer." He held his breath then, waiting.

After a moment, the fingers she had knotted into the sheet under her chin loosened. She lay there another moment, motionless, as though playing his words over again in her head. Then she turned her head, not to look at him but to stare up at the ceiling.

"You're just—"

"No!" he stopped her again. He couldn't stand to hear what he knew she was going to say. "You're right. What happened to you wasn't 'just' anything. But neither is this, Beth Marie." He touched the fingertips of his right hand to his chest. His breath came shallowly. "This isn't pity or guilt or even consolation. And I won't let what happened take you from me."

She did look at him then, and it hurt to see desire battling distrust, instead of coming effortlessly as it once had. He knew how empty his boast was without her belief added to his own. She started to speak again, then stopped, her lips still slightly parted, and lifted one hand, reaching for his. And all he knew was thankfulness.

Cody tugged at her leather skirt as she sat down on a folding chair beside Cecelia, trying to stretch the hem closer to her knees. It wasn't exactly right for a church wedding, but it was the best she'd been able to do on short notice after the old lady called her up last night and invited her. Anyway, she thought, it's not a real church. Just the old hardware store, still smelling like oil and sawdust. The priest didn't seem like a real priest either. He was too big and talked more like a gangster than a preacher. His wife, though, sitting on the front row, she looked like she ought to. Even her red dye job looked almost natural. Cody noticed the priest glancing at his wife from time to time, as if he were steadying himself against her.

Well, good for them. Cody didn't see how anybody stayed married as long as they obviously had. She wondered if the guy standing down in front of the priest, his hands crossed just below his belt buckle, would last that long. She liked his moustache, even though ordinarily she wasn't attracted to the law-abiding type.

Just then the little electric keyboard started up, accompanied by a guitar and a rasping fiddle. Cecelia put her hand on Cody's arm, indicating that they were to stand up. The door opened to the room that had probably once been the manager's office, and out came the girl she'd seen with Geoff at the marina. She'd looked excited then, like she was waiting for something to happen that would change her life. She looked even more like that today.

Towering over Cecelia in her spike heels, Cody gazed around at the congregation speculatively. She'd like to look like that someday herself.